P9-EGC-558

THE GOOD GIRL'S GUIDE TO GETTING KIDNAPPED

THE GOOD GIRL'S GUIDE TO GETTING KIDNAPPED

YXTA MAYA MURRAY

razOr
bill

An Imprint of Penguin Group (USA) Inc.

The Good Girl's Guide to Getting Kidnapped

RAZORBILL

Published by the Penguin Group
Penguin Young Readers Group
345 Hudson Street, New York, New York 10014, U.S.A.
Penguin Group (USA) Inc., 375 Hudson Street, New York, New York 10014, U.S.A.
Penguin Group (Canada), 90 Eglinton Avenue East, Suite 700, Toronto, Ontario,
Canada M4P 2Y3 (a division of Pearson Penguin Canada Inc.)
Penguin Books Ltd, 80 Strand, London WC2R 0RL, England
Penguin Ireland, 25 St Stephen's Green, Dublin 2, Ireland (a division of Penguin Books Ltd)
Penguin Group (Australia), 250 Camberwell Road, Camberwell, Victoria 3124, Australia
(a division of Pearson Australia Group Pty Ltd)
Penguin Books India Pvt Ltd, 11 Community Centre, Panchsheel Park, New Delhi – 110 017, India
Penguin Group (NZ), 67 Apollo Drive, Rosedale, North Shore 0632, New Zealand
(a division of Pearson New Zealand Ltd.)

Penguin Books (South Africa) (Pty) Ltd, 24 Sturdee Avenue, Rosebank,
Johannesburg 2196, South Africa

Penguin Books Ltd, Registered Offices: 80 Strand, London WC2R 0RL, England

10 9 8 7 6 5 4 3 2 1

Library of Congress Cataloging-in-Publication Data

Murray, Yxta Maya.
p. cm.
Summary: Fifteen-year-old Michelle Pena, born into a powerful Mexican American gang family,
tries to reconcile her gangster legacy with the girl she has become--a nationally ranked runner and
academic superstar.
ISBN: 978-1-59514-272-6
[1. Gangs—Fiction. 2. Identity—Fiction. 3. Kidnapping—Fiction. 4. Foster home care—Fiction. 5.
Mexican Americans—Fiction. California, Southern—Fiction.] I. Title.
PZ7.M9664 Go 2010
[Fic] 22

                    2009021091

Printed in the United States of America

To Elizabeth Baldwin and Ryan Botev,
of Pickle Design

Boom chaka chaka, boom chaka chaka, fast girl, oh you fast girl, fast girl. You gonna take it fast girl, yeah you fast bad girl...

That was the song playing in my head the afternoon of Friday, January 4, 2009, when I went out to Pasadena City College to *kill* in the All-American track and field championship regional qualifiers. My name's Michelle Peña, and maybe I'm just a fifteen-year-old ninth grader, but I was feeling some adult-sized freakishness as I pumped up my gumption for the 800m, the 400, and the 200 dashes.

Coach, Kiki, and I had just walked from the parking lot to the racing track, moving out from under the bone-white bleachers to the stadium. Hundreds of parents and racing geeks crowded like rock-concert fans into the stands, waving homemade signs that spelled out *GO CHERRY!!!* and *LOVE U LISA!!!* in shiny silver glitter and scarlet sticker hearts. Just before we moved onto the grass that stretched beyond the bleachers, I slung my red Nike duffel bag over my shoulder, and squinted out at a crew of high-anxiety females stretching their protein-packed hams on the racetrack.

And then I caught the pink, punk-rock hair of my biggest rival, murder-on-legs, state champion dasher Lisa "Money" Smithson.

My eyes zeroed in on her like a laser gun in those Will Smith action death flicks Kiki loves so much. Money had already lined up on the blocks for the 800m, stretching her neck as easy as one of those sharp-fanged human-hunting tigers I read about in Frank's bio books. I checked out her blue-and-silver Yale-Westview Cougars jersey, and her professionally trained thighs that were model-skinny but so strong they could probably squeeze a World Wide Wrestler dead. She wasn't even smiling, sweating, or barfing, even though this regional would be the last cut before the All-Americans in two weeks. As for me, though, I was freak-*ing*.

"You are looking so awesomely *Psycho* right now, Mish," Kiki said right next to me, holding her silver Sony video camera, as usual, and filming my face. "Seriously, put a bad wig on you, and you are so Norman Bates. I am loving it."

"Aw, I should have trained more." I kept staring at Money, which is what we call Lisa because she's got bags of it. "I spent too much time studying for the decathlon tryouts!"

"If anything, you trained *too* hard for this race," said Coach Gregory. Coach was a tall, paper-pale dude with thick glasses that gave him a dazed look. "Just relax; do some deep breathing. I've got to go make sure you're registered."

As Coach skedaddled off, Kiki zoomed in on me with her video camera. "Don't deep breathe; you are *perfect* just the way you are. . . . You're Lawrence of Arabia, and I am zooming in on you right before you ride into a flaming desert battle. Okay?"

I pressed my thumbs on my eyebrows. "Kiki, either I'm tweaking worse from nerves than I thought, or you're doing that weird movie Mad Libs thing again. Either way, I don't understand a syllable you're squealing."

"Just turn three-quarters so I can get a good CU of your crazy." Ki's last name is Markson, and I did know that *CU* was film-talk for *close up*. She'd been my best friend ever since two years ago when I showed up to Rosa Parks K–12 in my baggy chola clothes and my no-makeup. Kiki has little spiky dreads, hazel eyes, and on her long, almost too-skinny bod she wore a plaid minidress and white lace-up boots. She was going to be a film director after she transferred with me to Yale-Westview in their new "gifted disadvantaged" scholarship program. After Y-Dub, she'd go to UCLA undergrad and then NYU film school. At least, that's how we had it all planned. "Peel the onion!" she hollered out at me.

"Okay, ugh . . . Grrrr, girl, *grrrrrr*!!!" I scowled for her, making big biceps. I'm about five foot six already, with straight ebony hair and a valentine face, black staring Mexican eyes. When I'm goofing around with Kiki, I feel all jazzy and pretty, even though I'm pure muscle under my red singlet. When I'm studying or racing, though, I get so serious-headed I can feel my eyes bugging, so I know I look like a mad dog or a shark. "How's that?"

She smiled with a huge open mouth. "*So* Method that for a second I thought you were totally going to kill me!"

"Hey, P! Princess Peña! *Michelle, over here!* We got our eyes on you, muchacha!"

That yelling came from behind me, all at once, explosive. "Who *is* that?"

Kiki swung her head around. "Huh? I don't know."

"Did you just hear someone call me . . . 'P'?"

I peered back at the bleachers, barely making out two gangy-looking boyz. They were at the far edge of a row, in the middle of the section. All I could see were their shiny shaved heads, dark blue baggies, and pepper-red bandanas. And I would have bet a million dollars that their arms were stained blue with some nasty Snake Brothers tats, too.

"Woo-woo," they yelled. "Hey, P! Want to talk to you, sister."

"Do you know them?" Kiki asked. "What are they calling you?"

"Nothing, they're not calling me," I said, turning away from them fast.

"That's right, don't worry about the fans," Coach said, as he came jogging back up to us. "And stop distracting her, Kiki."

"She doesn't distract me, Coach," I said. "Kiki loosens me up."

He looked at his watch. "Eight hundred's in ten minutes." Bending down, he rubbed my shoulders, taking my duffel bag from me.

"Mish, we'd better do our thing if we're going to do it," Kiki said.

"Aw, yeah, hit me."

Kiki and I got ready to sing this tune we warble for good luck before every race. She began puffing out one side of her mouth, and making the same beatbox sound I'd been playing in my head ever since I woke up that morning:

Shhhh, tat-at-tat, uh-huh girl

Boom chaka, boom boom chaka, uh-huh, oh you fast girl, you fast girl, you fast, you fast, you fasssst girl

And then we were laughing and rapping it:

Ki and Mish gonna dom-i-nate

Those li'l girls gone beat your butt

You push them down; they don't hes-i-tate

Cuz they never, never, NEVER GIVE UP!

"All right, then," she said, knocking her head against mine. "Go get 'em, Mish."

I gave her a hug. "Thanks for always being here, Ki."

"That's what best friends do: be supportive of each other." She slapped my butt and pushed me toward the track. "Now just get out there! And win!"

2

"**H**ey-hey!"

"Hey, Michelle."

"'Sup."

"Luck to you."

"Ride it hard, girl."

Hustling out to the track, I got into my lunge right next to Money Smithson in row number ten. The eight other girls knew the compete was between her and me, and the best they could hope for was a third. Still, we all nodded at each other, sisterly. We were all more or less the same cinnamon-sugar public-school color. That is, except for Money.

"Hi, Michelle," she said, her pastel hair sticking up on her skull like Easter basket grass, and her bluebird eyes glittering as bright as the diamond stud in her nose.

"Hey, Money."

Her perfect face tweaked. "Could you not call me that? It's so, like, putting us at different levels."

"Oh, sorry. Lisa, man, how you doing?"

She glanced at the sparkle-signs in the stands and cussed. "I'm so stressing. My dad is beyond pressuring me to win this. You know how parents try to deal with their own feeby middle-class childhoods by *so* ruining yours? Or, um. Uh . . ." Her eyes widened. "Okay, that was *totally* insensitive. You're all sort of orphaned, and, like, a 'person of poverty.' I'm super sorry."

"Hey, steroid-butt, you can cut that yapping!" yelled out Martha Jones from Compton, over in track number one. Martha's tall, chocolate, freckled, and an assassin on high jump.

"I am *not* on steroids; that is gross," Money said. "I'm on spirulina and protein." She rolled her eyes, and mouthed *Ghetto!*

"Money, just shut up and listen to my news, girl!" I cackled, because a little ribbing from a Privileged can't twist my undies. "I'm going to be applying for a transfer to your school. At Y-Dub, you know? Me and my friend Ki are hitting that scholarship. We could be on the same team, girl. Go Y-Dub!"

She goggled at me like I'd just broken her brain. "You mean, Yale-*Westview*? That program for disadvantaged kids? Because the school got sued?"

"Ooooooooh," Cherry Villa from Pico Union said over in track number six. "Girl, I think she is calling you *affirmative action*, Michelle!"

Money popped her mouth open. "No, I'm not! I just heard that the kids who were going to transfer on that program were all, like, toothpaste heirs from Bolivia and chess champions from Uganda with State Department connections. I mean, the scholarship's for 'disadvantaged' kids, but you still have to be either, like, *royalty*, or get in the 98th percentile on the ISEE. And if you're entering the high school, you've got to either know Kanji, college freshman Spanish, or beginning ancient French." She sighed, weary-sounding with the unfairness of the world. "I think that maybe you're, like, *too* underprivileged, you know? You hang out with a way different crowd than us."

"Money, you don't know what you're talking about," I said, in a scratchy, high voice, as *now* my undies were good and twisted. I knew suddenly that one of two things was gonna happen on that track: either I would cry so hard I'd probably croak . . . or, more like, I was gonna bust somebody's head.

Elizabeth Carlton, running number five and from Agoura said: "Yeah, Powerful, don't listen to this KKK."

Money started yapping in that skittish voice white folks use when they're called on their racialness. "I'm not saying it's right; it's totally unjust that she is beyond not qualifying for prep school! But, the only thing is, she *did* bring two total Mexican Sopranos here today. *So* mobster! Didn't you hear them yelling for her from the stands? And calling her some weird name. Like, 'pee' or something." She pointed at the Snake Brothers–looking dudes.

"I did hear it," Martha said. "And I knew you'd be crying on about it sooner or later, which is why I told you to keep your butt shut."

"I don't want to be rude. It's just that those kinds of people don't show up at Y-Dub. *Ever*. They would get arrested. Um . . ." Money blinked at me, flaring her nostrils so her diamond stud glimmered. "Michelle? Why are you looking at me like that?"

"Ladies?"

The starter had just come walking up to us. He was a dude in a green baseball cap, with a little pistol that had blanks in it.

"Okay, girls, talk's out, heels in," he called out.

"Oh, oh," said Elizabeth. "Look at Powerful. Michelle's not saying nothing. Check her out. Ain't she just get all quiet and spooky looking?"

I smiled at Money then, really wide.

"Oh, no," said Cherry. "I saw Powerful smile like that last February at the Whole Foods Dash at Santa Monica College."

"When she chopped your head off and ate it in the 400?" Martha asked.

"Ye-es."

I stretched my neck easy. "Mmmmm! I feel *good*. Man, but is it a pretty day."

"Oh, *oh*," said Elizabeth. "Girl only grins like that before she draws *blood*—"

"Oh, she gonna *kill* you, dummy!" Cherry squealed.

Money shook her head. "I have the state record in the 8. *I'm* winning this."

"And I have a magic bikini at home, and when I put it on, I turn into Beyoncé."

I winked at Money. "You just hurt my feelings, Lisa."

"Oh," she said. "You look kind of crazy right now."

"Well, maybe I am, because, just so you know, I am going to *break* you today, Money. Not that we still can't be buddies when I go to Y-Dub, but all day today, I'm going to burn your ass like you're wearing some firecracker panties." I put my hands together on her shoulders. "But I'm sorry about your dad. Serious, I am. I hope he can get over your loserdom."

Money saw I meant it. She must have seen the victory roaring inside of me. The poor poopie started crying: a big, crystal tear welled up quivery in her left bluebird eye.

"Ho!" the starter yelled out. We all crouched down.

And then I wasn't so much of a girl anymore, but a supernatural animal with mercury in my blood and rockets under my armpits.

The gun went *BANG!*

I leapt, and was in the air.

3

Race you, race you. Last one there's a rotten egg, baby.

Bam went my feet like the devil's dogs, and I could set the track on fire. *Slam slam* went my legs, burning with flames and the wind lifting up my wings.

Bap bap bap bap thudded the racers behind me. But I was made of voodoo magic, and nothing could stop me from scorching to the finish.

Fast girl, uh uh *you a* fast *girl*

You *fast, bad* girl!

"Ugh." I heard Money grunting. Then: *Whup! Whack!*

From that butt-crunching sound, I knew Money had just taken a skid because she was running so pell-mell trying to keep up. Racing isn't safe, see, especially against a contender like me. A girl can fall hard enough to turn herself into asphalt pudding, like when Gail Devers crunched her muffin in the '92 Athens Olympics and it was a humiliation. Or when Perdita Felicien splattered her tuckus all over the track in the '04 O's and got slaughtered. Or like Money, here, munching her meathead at the All-American regionals and making my day.

But I didn't look behind me to see ol' Money eat dirt. I concentrated on my triumph, flying on my swift wings. And, *oh*, but does two minutes go by in a blink when you are winning. I always wish that sweet floating feeling could last longer.

I flamed over the finish line. The board read 2:02.70, a monster score that kicked me into the front of "under sixteen" girl-racing history in the western U.S., and almost the whole country, except for New York and Minnesota.

Elizabeth came in second, with 2:03.60.

Money had picked herself up, raging hard enough to come in third, at 2:03.65. 2:03.65 basically means that I crushed her into itty-bitty pieces until she was just a blob of jelly on the ground with a bloody knee and two big eyes and a little mouth blubbering *Oh my God*.

So, that's who was going to the nationals in two weeks. The rest didn't matter.

The crowd roared. People stood in the bleachers, called my name. *Mi-chelle! Mi-chelle, Ma Belle! Mi-chelle! Peña the Powerful!* Kiki and Coach hopped like drunk rabbits, Kiki trying to film everything at the same time, swinging her camera around.

Working to get my breathing steadier, I motored around the track, looking up, looking back. "Yeah!" I yelled, laughing hard. "Yeah, man, yeah, *watch out!*"

But then, my laughter died in my throat when I saw them again.

Those boyz.

They'd clambered up through the crowd, as if to get a better look at me. Baggy pants, shaved heads, tats, gold pirate earrings. This time, I recognized them. One was Lalo Gutierrez, and the other was called Tha Force. Lalo was my age, and he had a chubby belly from his apple pie habit, and his skull buzzed except for jellybean-purple bangs. Tha Force was fifteen too, wearing a wifebeater on his tall and muscled li'l bod. Force stared at me and then spat, way more disrespectful than he *ever* would have dared to be back when my bro Samson was King of the Snake Brothers. Long time ago, before my mom, Reina, got put in jail, we were even friendly: Back in Eastside

Montebello, all the soldiers and me watched TV together, sugared the engines of our enemeez, played soccer. Ancient history, now. I'd heard that Dragon Mendoza became the Snakes' leader after Samson got penned in Chino. So there were no family ties any longer between me and these boyz. A bad chill went through my bones: I *knew* there was no good reason for them to be here.

"Go, killa!" Elizabeth and Cherry called out, high-fiving me. And Martha: "Way to bust the clock, Power."

I high-fived Martha casual, like my pulse wasn't jangling from sighting those thugs. "Thank you, girl."

"Yeah, congratulations, Michelle." Money came sweating up to me with a bubbly bloody knee, the word *congratulations* wriggling like a hamster doing the mambo in her gullet. Tears trickled down her face, but we both pretended like she wasn't crying.

I gave her a hug. "Thanks, Lise, and you made good time, even with your fall. You're tough, baby. And I also really hope we don't have any hards."

" 'Hards'?"

"Hard feelings, *ésa.*"

"Yeah, right, 'hards.' " Money grinned at me like somebody'd just snapped her spine. "There are no 'hards.' But let's see what happens at the nationals. *Michelle!*"

When she hollered my name like that, I wasn't looking at her. I wasn't even looking at Kiki and Coach, who were galloping toward me, calling out my time: "Two-oh-two-seventyyyyyyyy!"

I'd peered over at Lalo and Tha Force again. *Dang it! Go away!* They'd stopped halfway between the bleachers and the track. Tha Force closed one eye and pointed his right hand at me like it was a cocked gun, pulling the thumb-trigger. Then him and Lalo turned away, disappearing into the crowd.

"*Michelle!*" Money yelped again.

"What?"

"Your face!"

On my mouth, I felt something slick and wet.

I touched it. My hand dripped red.

"You're bleeding!"

4

No, no, you just calm down, now. I didn't get shot in the eyeball or anything. Don't let your imagination run away with you just because I got gang connections!

It was only my nose.

"Okay, even though it was amazing footage—I think that the whole hosing nose-blood was a little OTT," Kiki was saying, about three hours later. We had finally gotten out of the stadium and were piling into the backseat of Coach's Dodge Dart.

I shook my head, peering out the car's rear window—but there were no more signs of rascals hunting me. Thankfully, I hadn't seen those boyz again after that last little episode, though I didn't know where they'd gone off to. "My nose wasn't that big of a deal, and you know I ran *better* than fine."

"Takes a spaz to know one, Mish," she said, cocking an eyebrow at me as she put her video camera next to her on the seat.

"That reminds me," I said. "Have you eaten anything?"

She laughed. "Yes, dysmorphia is as over as pleather. But stop changing the subject from how much you maxed out." She started digging through her skirt pocket. "Actually, I had a feeling that you were totally going to *destroy* today—"

I hooted. "I do have to admit, people, I was a record-breaking *machine* out there! What'd you think, Coach? Got the golds in the 800, the 400, and the 200. Come on, you know I was hot!"

His baseball hat waggled back and forth as he clutched the driver's wheel. "I'm still trying to figure out how we're going to afford tickets to the Kentucky finals on the school budget."

"Well, right now, you'd better just hit the gas, jack," I said. We were headed back to Rosa Parks, which was in Inglewood, only like twenty minutes in good traffic. Except it would take us more like ninety on account Coach drives as slow as an eight-thousand-year-old blind lady who's died behind the wheel. "I'm going to be late for my Ac Dec tryout. It's in half an hour."

Grinning, Kiki pulled a little box out of her pocket. It was wrapped with pink paper and tied with a gold bow. "In honor of your amazing ability to cut the competition off at the knees."

"Oh, you did not!"

I tore the present open and peered down at a weird-looking little thing: a baby-pink leather heart, glittering with silver metal studs, and with these little silver wings on it, and a hook. The middle of the heart was stamped: *Prada*.

I frowned at it. "What is this, some kind of a key chain with a heart-goob thingy on it?"

"It's a key *fob*," Ki corrected me. "Chains are totally déclassé; fobs are awesome. Look at it! Isn't it cute? Way better than jangling your keys around on that twisty-tie like you always do. And it's Prada, Prada, Prada!"

"How'd you afford it?"

"Annihilating some Shanghai heiress in a high-stakes movie trivia challenge on Facebook."

I kissed her on the cheek. "I love it; thank you."

"You're welcome." She smiled.

Bending down, I tucked the box into my duffel bag, which was already stuffed with a mish-mash of gold medals, my paperback

Academic Decathlon Super Quiz study guide, my keys knotted together on the grotty supermarket twisty-tie, and also a wad of papers left over from a transfer application to Y-Dub.

"Oh my God, can you imagine if we actually got in?" Just as I grabbed my study guide, Ki snatched the app. It was printed out in fancy script and decorated with the Y-Dub shamrock insignia. The first part of it looked like this:

Application for the Yale-Westview Martin Luther King Awards

Dear Candidate for Special Admission to Yale-Westview Preparatory Academy,

After enjoying an energetic dialogue with members of the civil rights community, the Dean of Yale-Westview, the oldest and finest private preparatory school in the United States, has decided to award full three-year scholarships to five incoming tenth graders from around the globe. The winners of the Martin Luther King Awards, who will join our grades 10–12 high school as freshmen, will have academic records reflecting the *highest* degree of scholastic excellence *despite* their suffering from disadvantages arising from their racial, ethnic, cultural, gender, or sexual identities; their poor grasp of the English language; their physical disabilities; or poverty. Please be advised that only students scoring in the 97–100th percentile in the Independent School Entrance Examination (ISEE), earning above a 3.8 grade point average, and otherwise demonstrating artistic or athletic gifts of the highest caliber will be considered for this program. A two-page essay and an interview with staff will also be required. In initiating the Awards, Yale-Westview admits no liability, yet is happy to satisfy any legal doubts that it abides by a non-discrimination policy, opening its doors to *all* students, regardless of color, creed, religious affiliation, linguistic or class shortcomings, homosexuality, physical handicap . . .

"Gawd, I want us to get in here, girl!" I said, reading it over her shoulder, and pawing at the attached color glossy brochure. "They got *everything.* Y-Dub has a library with thirty thousand books, a film lab, wheatgrass bar, and a racetrack as big as the one in the Staples Center—"

Kiki nodded, her dreads dancing on her head. "And their teachers are so smart they practically have psychic powers—"

"—And they've graduated Nobel Prize winners, and they've got students so rich that they wear panties made out of hundred-dollar bills—"

"—And so brainy, they were probably grown in test tubes, and so *white* that you get, like, blinded, if you look at them." Kiki bit her lip, crumpling the paper a little in her hands. "But, not joking—I think you have a shot, Michelle. You've got the racing, the poetry award, the essay award, the dean's list; you're probably going to get the decathlon—"

"What about you?" I swallowed. "You got dean's list and Math Champ two years running. But, you know, I wouldn't go if you didn't get in—um . . . *oh.*"

Just that second, I'd jerked my head to stare out the back window, where I saw a banged-up, gray-primer-painted Chevy following us.

Tha Force sat behind the wheel of that damned car, and I could make out his superintense brown eyes burning at me. Next to him rode Lalo, with the purple jellybean bangs and the Emeril belly.

Oh my freakin' gawd, I thought, a sick feeling suddenly twisting in my stomach.

"Come on, let's be real," Ki was saying. "You're all *Good Will Hunting*;

you're totally what they're looking for. But I'm so *not* prep school. I mean, I'll admit it: I've had a *tiny* problem with being socially acceptable, which is why people kept trying to flush my head down the toilet until you started body-guarding me. . . . But someday, it's going to be like, wow, Kiki, she is a total visionary; let's put her on the cover of *Vanity Fair*. And then at our ten-year high school reunion I will come back and completely *dominate* and crush them to death." She grimaced. "Oh, God, it would be *so* grossly horrible if we went to different schools."

"Yeah, it's harder to leave people behind than you'd think, Ki." I snatched another glance at Force and Lalo out the back window.

Kiki tucked her chin into her chest and stared at me. "Okay, that was you talking again about your life *before*. Wasn't it?"

"Ugh."

"I mean, I think that at this point you can finally tell me about the deep dark terrible secret you have in your past. So, come on: What were you, a fat girl with a lisp? Had a little Winona shoplifting mania? Whoa, wait a minute." She followed my gaze. "Check out those guys. Very *The Wire*."

She picked up her videocam and started filming Lalo and Tha Force.

Lalo's eyes got really wide when he saw Kiki's camera. Force said something, and Lalo ducked down, coming back up with these furry black things in his hands.

Both boyz slipped the furry black things over their heads. Ski masks. Lalo and Force bobbled their masked-up faces at us for a second, and threw us a Snake Brothers sign, which is the pinkie outstretched, and the thumb and forefinger, too, with the other two fingers down. Then they scooted out of the lane, fast.

Ki and me went totally quiet, mouths open.

"That was weird," Kiki said.

I slid back down in my seat, clutching my study guide so hard my fingers went white.

"They were looking at you." Her eyes widened. "They were the guys in the bleachers. Do you know them?"

"N-no."

"They were *following* you. Totally gang members—did you see what they were doing with their hands? What is that called? Hurling signals or something?" Kiki was still filming so loonily that she kept ramming the nose of her videocam up against the rear windshield so it went *smack. Smack. Smack.*

Coach looked back at us. "What are you girls talking about?"

I hunkered lower. "Nothing, just please keep going; we're going to be late."

Kiki shivered. "Woo, those guys are like obsessed with you. That was actually kind of exciting."

"Yeah, it was."

She wagged her head around. "I mean, where are *my* stalkers?"

"You can have them."

"Put your safeties on," said Coach.

"I wish they'd come back, so I could get some more footage of them staring at you." Kiki sat back down, holding her videocam in her lap. She looked thoughtful for a second. "Mish, am I always making a movie of your life, or mine?"

"What?"

She hunched her shoulders. "Nothing."

I stared out the window, hanging onto my book as we drove, and drove. Slow as a three-legged dog.

"Oh, well. Move your chin a little to your right, Mish, and I'll make you a star," Kiki said, turning around to get another shot of me as we finally pulled up to school.

5

Coach got me back at about four twenty, which was only ten minutes before the decathlon tryouts would start in the auditorium. Rosa Parks is a year-round K–12 in South L.A. Inglewood, and it's all crammed up in two crappy, vanilla-colored stucco buildings with asbestos and stinkage problems. It has a dinner-salad-sized field in the back where we're supposed to do the sports. Out in front, there's a big sign with the words *Excellence* and *Distinction* painted in red on either side. It has a wood door and little concrete steps leading down to the street, which is where Coach dropped me off.

I slung my duffel onto my shoulder, still peering out for Lalo and Force.

Kiki waved at me from the backseat. "You going to be okay here by yourself?"

I squinted at the street. "Yeah. Just go home now, Ki. I'll talk to you later."

"Okay. Coach, you going to drive me?"

"Sure."

They waved again, and off they went. I stood out there for maybe five more minutes, slapping through my study guide and trying to concentrate on geography or geology, not gangster-ology. A space had opened up on the Ac Dec team earlier in the year, and ever since I'd heard, I'd started studying up on Latin America (this year's quiz theme) so hard that it was a miracle I hadn't grown an extra head to fit in the factoids I'd learned. I was having trouble reading, though, as I was feeling *mighty* shook up from two sightings of villains in one day. I blinked hard at the pages. If I let myself get all discombobulated just because I'd crossed paths with some cut-price soldiers I used to know in Montebello, then there was *no* way that I'd be able to liquidate my Ac Dec competition.

But it was just as I was prepping to bring them nerds some hurt that I heard the sound of another car.

I peered over the top of my guide as the Chevy pulled up. Tha Force lounged behind the wheel and Lalo sprawled next to him. The boyz still wore those stupid masks, too.

A hot shot of adrenaline zapped my chest. *Dang it! Dang, dang!*

Hiking up my bag, I pounded up the stairs and into the school.

"Hey, P!" Tha Force called out.

The fools tumbled out of their Chevy, Lalo like a marshmallow man and Tha Force with his little muscles rippling under his wifebeater.

"Go away, and what you doing with those masks, *freaks*?" I snarled.

"Just want to have a word, girl," Lalo said. "About ya brother, King!"

"Get her, man—use a choke hold," Force said.

Their hands reached out, swiping at me. A sparkling, spazzy fear filled my whole body, and I broke into a real run, pumping through the after-hours-empty hallway that leads to the RP auditorium.

Thuggies coming for me—thuggies gonna hurt me—HELP!

But right before I started hollering, my mom's harsh voice echoed in my mind, telling me that I was bringing shame on the Peña name:

You got to make them fear, ya, Michelle. It's the first rule for a Queen.

Yes, Mama.

And they won't till ya make them. See? Ya gotta earn your place.

Earn my place?

Through sweat and blood, girl. That's the only way you gonna make it in this life. And if anyone—I mean anyone—*tries to knock you down, you rise up and crush them. You hear me, Michelle?*

Y-yes. I do, Mama. I'll rise up and crush them, like you say.

I skidded to a stop, maybe fifty feet away from the auditorium. Whipping around, I crouched down in a fighter's position and swung my duffel at them. "What do you two chickenheads think—*whoa*!" I yelled, just as Tha Force whapped his hand on my mouth.

Lalo bent down and grabbed my feet in his chubby mitts. Force hauled me up from under the armpit with his left hand, while keeping his other hand smashed over my face.

"Aagggggh!" I kicked at both their heads in one big thrust, knocking them both between the eyes. Just as they let go of me, I spun in the air, landed on my feet, and kicked Force's nuts.

"*Aiiii, no, mami!*" Force yelped.

Lunging him off balance, I grabbed his shirt before control-falling with him and walloping him onto his back. I jumped back on my feet and slammed my knuckles one-two in his mouth till blood stained his lips. Then I worked my murder on Lalo by sweeping him with my left leg. He toppled headfirst into the ground like he'd fainted.

"Ughghg!"

"You bring the hot?" Force gasped at him.

"Nah, man," Lalo gargled. "What we need Dragon's hot for when we're just picking up a girl?"

"We do, dummy! Check out my balls!"

"Why you laying hands on me, ya dirty scoundrels?!" I hissed at them, and when neither of them answered, I picked up my duffel from the ground and smacked Lalo on the skull.

"Waaaaaaaa! We supposed to get ya, P!" Lalo slipped the ski mask off his dented head, as did Force.

"It's like you're in hock, and we're coming to claim ya," Force grunted. "King never paid Dragon for his wad—after that deal went down with Patssi—"

"Samson didn't pay Dragon for his what?" I spat.

"You know, herbal," Force jabbered. "*Marijuana?* King *owes*! And the Burner's gonna smoke us if we don't get him his bank! So we got to hold you like a hostage until King coughs up the dough!"

"You get out of here, Force, and bring your puppy with you before I take you to the *pound*, son," I said in a voice that nobody here, not Coach, not Frank, not even Kiki had ever heard me use before. Heck, *I* never even heard me talk like that before, but I know how I learned it: It was the *dire* voice the King of the Snakes and the Queen of the 99s used to monologue with their enemies. Then I growled even meaner: "Because you're acting like you don't know who I am."

"It's our orders, P—"

"I'm *royal*, Force. My brother's your King, and my madre's Reina Peña. You mess with the Princess, you *know* you lose your head."

"Dragon's King these days. And both King and Queen's in jail, anyway."

Lalo was scared now. "But she is royal, man. That's why we call her P."

"You think I don't know that?" Force snapped.

"Samson might get a way to mess us," Lalo breathed. "And Reina'll get one of the 99s to cut us."

"Reina ain't seen her in two years. She's over and out, anyway."

Clip, clop, clip, clop, clip. "Michelle?"

The clopping sound was Mrs. Hunnigan's high heels. She was seventh-to-tenth grade math. Brown hair blown into a flip, no glasses, pink lipstick, purple suit.

My whole body jittering, I turned around. "I need help, Mrs. Hunnigan."

She walked closer, frowning, while Force and Lalo got even more freaked. They took a couple of steps back, shifty-eyeing me. "Who are these boys?"

One of the classroom doors in the hallway opened, and another teacher poked her head out. This was Mrs. Leonard, who taught the K through third graders. Also, down the hall, the auditorium door opened up, and two sophomores peered around at me with big fish-eyes behind Harry Potter glasses.

Mrs. Leonard said, "I thought I heard something—what's going on here?"

"These are some gang-related troubled teens, ma'ams," I panted. "They're grabbing at me. They have ski masks like bank robbers."

"*Shit*, we're gone!" Force yelled. He and Lalo raced like madballs down the hall, toward the back door that led out to the teachers' parking lot.

"Go into the auditorium, Michelle," Mrs. Hunnigan jabbered. To the kids peering around the auditorium door, she said, "Get back inside. I'm going to go call the principal."

"Get the security guard down here." Mrs. Leonard looked school-shooting wiggified while she slammed the door shut.

Mrs. Hunnigan banged into the wall as she scrambled around the corner.

I hulked there, with the sophomores still peeping me from behind the auditorium door. "Um, um, well. Okay, that was . . . interesting. . . ."

Boy, did I just feel weird! The truth is, I was *bugging*. Who knew I could talk like that? After two years away from Montebello, did I just call myself a gang Princess? That was nasty!

I skittered around like this for a minute or so, muttering to myself all tense and crazy. The crowd of kids watching me grew. First I peered hard at them; then I looked away. Then I looked again.

"What you lookyloos staring at?!" I finally belted.

"Peña's cracking under the pressure," one of the sophomores said to another. "The legend is no more. Her sweeping the prelims was a fluke."

"Monroe Park is going to win it," the other soph said.

And then this is when Miss Gang Princess here remembered that she had a tryout to dominate, and yet another title to conquer.

"Oh, no! Oh, my . . . eessh . . ."

I picked up my duffel and ran into the auditorium. Up on the stage sat ten of the geekiest juniors and seniors that ever scuttled across Rosa Parks's little campus. In front of them stood Mr. Rye, an English teacher and supervisor for the RP Ac Dec Society. Down in the seats were a sprinkling of kids who hadn't made it past the preliminary rounds.

When the nimrods on the stage saw me, they sighed in disappointment, wiping their glasses on their shirts.

"Michelle, we're just getting started on the team tryouts," Mr. Rye said in a peevy voice. "We thought you were forfeiting. I told you it would be difficult to juggle a tryout and a race in the same day. We had to proceed without biding our time for one student."

"No, I'm here!"

"And did I hear some sort of racket out in the hall?"

"Sorry!" I pounded up to the stage, where I sat next to Monroe Park, a junior who weighed about seventy-nine pounds and had a chin like a bran muffin, but was *monster* on history.

"Damn, damn, dang." Monroe shook his head.

"Hey, Monroe, man, good luck," I said, barely getting my brains together enough to shake his hand good-sportishly.

He smiled sheepish. "Good luck to you too, Michelle."

We got started right up, answering a batch of Q's.

"Evo Morales is the president of Bolivia!" Monroe said.

"Charles Darwin conducted experiments on rye finches in the Galapagos Islands!" I said, my voice crackling hoarse from my stress.

"Argentina fought the Falklands War with the U.K. in 1986 over the Falkland Islands!" That was Babette Cheever, out. (The real year is 1982.) She walked off the stage with her head hanging low.

"The Cuban Missile Crisis ended on October 28, 1962!" Monroe said.

"Ecuador's biggest city is Guayaquil!" I rasped out.

Just then, Mrs. Hunnigan, Mr. Wells—our eighty-five-year-old security guy with liver-colored spots on his head—and blonde-headed, green-suited Principal Victoria Fisher came rabbling into the auditorium. Everybody stopped.

"Principal Fisher?" Mr. Rye asked.

"Mrs. Hunnigan tells me I have to talk with Michelle." The principal had a pencil in her hand, and she thrashed it in the air like a baton. "Come on, Michelle, let's go to my office."

I kept copping my squat and shook my head.

"*Michelle.*" Principal Fisher and Mrs. Hunnigan waved me to come on down.

"No, ma'ams. I studied *really* hard for this, Principal Fisher." My eyes started welling up, the way a normal girl would have cried in the hall when two thugs tried to whack her.

"Told you," I heard a voice hiss from the audience. "Cracking!"

Mr. Rye, Mrs. Hunnigan, the security guy, and Principal Fisher all exasperated at each other while I kooked out. I sobbed. "I'm gonna make this team!"

Finally, Principal Fisher buckled. "Okay, Michelle. We'll have a mindful and open dialogue after the tryouts. I'll be in my office."

All the other kids were staring at me, like, *You're screwing with my concentration, Peña!*

"Thanks, Principal Fisher." I wiped my nose as the grown-ups took their leave.

We got started again.

"Montezuma was the head of the Inca Empire!"

"No, that's the Aztec Empire. Zac Harris, out. Thanks, Zac."

"The Mexican War of Independence went on from 1810 to 1821!" Monroe said.

"The national flower of Peru is the Cantuta!" I said.

It came down to Monroe and me. He blinked out of his thick plastic glasses, wiggling his muffin chin. I was super sweaty and freakish.

"Ricardo Lagos was elected the president of Chile in 2006!"

That was Monroe. And in case you don't know, that's really, really wrong.

Mr. Rye said, "No, sorry. If Michelle gets this, Monroe, you're out."

I got up to the mic and took a deep breath and smiled at everybody, trying to appear all ordinary. "Hi, um. Okay. Yeah, I got this one."

"Michelle, you all right?" Mr. Rye asked.

I pressed my hands to my eyes. *What did them gangsters want with me? What were they going to* do *with me? Damn, don't think about it! I've got to focus!*

"Michelle?" Mr. Rye asked again.

"Yes, sir, I'm all right," I said, after about twenty seconds. I looked back at the audience, who were all staring at me excited like I was going to physically blow up from the pressure. But I stood up super straight. "Michelle Bachelet was elected the president of Chile in 2006," I said, clear and strong. "She's a lady, by the way, which makes that mama pretty superfly, if you don't mind me saying."

So I won.

For a minute, after I gave Monroe a consolation hug, I clutched onto my new team sweatshirt, feeling pretty happy about having made the team. I also felt *fiendish* exhausted. I sure did not want to have a mindful and open dialogue with Principal Fisher. For one thing, she'd probably try to mental counselor me because of me bawling like an abnormal. And second, Principal Fisher was a civilian, and so couldn't do jack-nothing about Lalo, Tha Force, and the Snakes. The only person to chatter to about my dilemma was my bro Samson. He'd tell me what was going down with Force and Lalo.

But right now, all I wanted to do was get back to Westchester, eat three Gelson's Gourmet chicken potpies, ambush Frank with a hug, and go to bed.

So I tucked my Ac Dec sweatshirt next to my medals in my duffel bag. Skedaddling out of the auditorium, I ran to the bus stop. The sky was a darker golden, with sunset coming on. I hopped on my bus, and went on home.

That is, to my foster home, I mean.

6

The next morning, for about a minute, I was in heaven.

Frank was holding my face in his big dad-hands and looking up my nose.

"And you said it bled for how long, Michelle?"

"Twenty minutes," I sighed as he cradled my head like it was a precious jewel.

Actually, to be more precise, I was in Frank's kitchen. Frank was loaded with cash and he lived in swanky Westchester, a Westside hangout that happened to be on the knife's edge of Inglewood's school zone. His house was worth five million bucks, with this kitchen that had warm, pumpkin-colored wood floors and a white old-fashioned stove. Watercolor paintings of oranges and apples glowed on the walls alongside a bookshelf, which was stuffed with cookbooks, and also medical doctors' first-aid manuals with scary instructions on how to give CPR and stitch up busted arteries. The refrigerator was the size of a polar bear, and when you opened it, out tumbled meatloaf, sunburn-pink Kool-Aid, and tons of veggies. Our white spotted pound dog, Squiggy, liked to park right under it, panting with his pink tongue flapping and his little nads showing.

So it was pretty and all, but the real reason that kitchen was heaven was because Frank was there, holding onto my face with those daddy hands of his.

"Mmm," he muttered, eyeballing my nose. "Boogers is all I see."

"Shut up!" I gag-laughed, while Squiggy barked for treats.

Frank Redman was my foster dad and had agreed to take me into Westchester even though two sets of Montebello foster parents had already kicked me out for gang relatedness. I couldn't hope for a better pop. He's tallish, has lots of soft brown hair, and a whittled-looking face with green eyes. He's also gay, and he's stressed out. Like, it was Saturday, but he was going to work anyway, on account of a patient having an emergency. He was a bone cancer doctor. Right now, Frank tried to drink coffee, tuck in his shirt, and give me a mini-medical exam all at the same time.

"Still," he said, "you gasped at me for a whole hour about your race and your decathlon tryout, but didn't see fit to tell me that you had an epistaxis last night?"

"Epistaxis?"

"It's doctor-speak for 'nosebleed.'"

"Sorry, Frank, too tired. And then when I told you about Lalo and Tha Force you started fussing over that."

"This morning I had three messages from Principal Fisher and two from Coach Gregory. They think you're either about to be assassinated by Latino hoodlums or have another breakdown like last year." Frank patted my cheek all awkward, and I could tell that the warmy-fuzziness was starting to make him stiff up. As a general rule, he wasn't much of a toucher. "Okay, um, examination over." I kept my head stuck forward anyways so he'd have to keep holding onto me with his freezy mitts.

"I did not have a nervous breakdown back then," I said. "I was just upset. And yesterday, I busted those boyz' ass—uh, *butts*."

He nodded. "Lovely! Yes, you're *so* tough, Miss Ass-Butt Buster. Still, though I'm new to this single-father business, thanks to Stephen, I think that most parents in my situation would call the police. I mean, those boys are criminals, right? If only of the juvenile variety."

"I love the way you talk, Frank. 'Juvenile variety.' When I go to Y-Dub, I'm going to talk like that."

He lifted his hands away from my face, then took a step away, like I was an emotion-bomb he was worried would go off if he disrupted me with too much cuddling. "So! Your nose is fine." He tugged on his shirt and smoothed down some invisible wrinkles. "But—since we're speaking of Yale-Westview—*again*, I've got to say that I'm starting to worry about your fixation with this scholarship. You know, I do 'get it.' It's not like I don't understand overcompensation myself—"

"What do you mean, 'overcompensation'?"

"Trying too hard to make up for something you think you lack. You think I didn't do *plenty* of that as a gay boy growing up in Fresno? Nearly killed myself in football. Complete stupidity! And, sorry to tell you, getting into prep school won't fix the fact that you have idiots in your family. Like your brother, who attracts such *wonderful* friends. What were their names again?"

"Lalo and Tha Force."

He made a face like he'd bitten a lemon. "Those aren't human names; I'll never remember them. You have to write them down so that I can . . . I don't know . . . tell the police, and they can do squat about it. Ack, it's at times like these that having Stephen around would be a real help. . . ." He squinted. "Erm, that's twice he's come up in two minutes isn't it? I think I'm going to stop talking about my ex now. Because I am *really* over him now. Almost. No, I am."

I'd wandered over to the *New Yorker* notepad stuck up on the fridge, and wrote down *LALO, last name's Villar, I think, and the other guy was THA FORCE—don't know his real name*. "I don't mind you, Frank. Stephen was the bonehead not wanting you to foster pop me, after all."

Frank said, "No, no. That wasn't why he, you know, divorced me.

But we are going to *really* quickly change this subject. What I'm saying is, don't fret about me. It's my job to suffer insomnia over you. For example, about these mashers with the unfortunate nicknames." He cleared his throat, stumbled on his words for a second. "Because, well, y-you must *never* let anyone like that touch you, Michelle. It's very important that you stay safe. For God's sake—um, well—what would your social worker say if I let anything happen to you?"

I nudged his shoe with my toe. "Aw, I'm okay, don't stress, Frank. But, I don't think you're going to be able to get any intel on the Snakes. The Westchester police don't have much to do with Montebello. That's why I'm going to go down to Chino this morning and ask King about it. He'll know what's going on."

Frank raised his eyebrows so far back it looked like they tickled his neck. "Are you telling me that you think you'll see your brother today? Because you will not. Remember all the horrible crying that happened after the last time? Even after the antidepressants kicked in?"

"Um . . . yeah, okay, Frank! I won't be disorderly. You're the boss."

Frank pressed his fingers to his temples. "Ugh, I don't speak Urban Mexican Child, and I don't know when you're lying to me."

I threw myself on him, hugging him around the waist while he fended me off with his elbows. "Man, you worry about me too much, Mr. March of Dimes!"

"For all the good it does me!" he said. "I'm racing around completely childproofing my life, but you're still constantly giving me panic attacks. I mean, I'm going to have to start going to a psychiatrist! Not that I should be telling you that!"

"Panic attacks? Shrinks? Aw, buck up, Snoopy, I'm not giving you so much trouble these days—"

"What about the time the marijuana fell out of your drawer, and I almost spent twenty thousand dollars on tween-to-teen rehab—"

"You already tested me, bro. I wasn't smoking it; it was just mistaken leftover weed from before—"

Frank squared his shoulders and used a fake manly voice. "Listen: *I am the foster parent.* You just have to listen to me!" He scrunched together his eyebrows. "Actually, you really do. I mean, I know I'm not your mother. But she's in jail and doesn't even want to see you. Which—maybe . . . I shouldn't bring up. I wouldn't want to make you get overly affective. Which is to say, um, sad."

I put my chin on his chest and looked up at him babbling doc-talk. I started laughing. This little tiny pain shot through me, though, like a love-pain.

Stop that crying, baby. You know nobody loves you like I do, don't you?

I do, Mama.

And nobody'll ever look out for you as good as I do.

Yeah, you look out for me, Mama.

But that don't mean I'm gonna give you my kingdom just cuz ya my daughter. The ruling hand is got to be made of iron if you wanna survive. And you soft. So when I school that weakness outta ya, I do it out of love, see. I do it out of love.

I know you're hard on me because you love me, Mama.

"I love you, Frank," I said.

Stiffening up again, he laughed with a discomfortable crackle. "Huh! Wow. Yes. Good. Because, on the issue, um, of the other thing we were talking about, before—which is to say, right! You are not seeing your brother. It's bad for your health. And mine!"

I watched him careful. He was fiddling with his cuffs, which were already buttoned. *Oh, well, no big deal. He loves me back, sure. But saying the big ol' L word and talking about emotional business just ain't his style. I hope so, anyway.* "Okay, Frank."

He patted my head again with his thumpy fingers before running around the house, getting papers and things.

"We'll talk about all of this tonight—I'm going to be home, what—at seven. Maybe eight. I have this major operation today; it'll probably take nine hours. Lost cause, probably! But, I want you to relax. You need to recuperate from your race. So read a book! Try *The Odyssey.* Don't watch TV. Have Kiki over. Order in pizza. Not with sausage, because of the nitrates. Also, Helena is going to be by around five o'clock and make you some dinner. And then we've got meetings with your principal, Monday. Put it on your calendar—five thirty? I think? Okay? Oh, look at the time. Agh, I have to run."

"Bye, Frankie!"

I waited about five minutes after I heard his Lexus pull out of the garage before I scooted into my bedroom, which he'd decorated for me in Popsicle pink and dusky lilac. Squiggy came scrambling after me, so I had to pet him at the same time I clawed through my wardrobe, looking for the right clothes to wear.

Slapping through my stacks of pants in my bureau, I uncovered a fat bundle of letters buried there—two of them opened, sixteen not. All of them had the same return address, belonging to a raven-haired, ebony-eyed boy named Silver Mendoza, the most beautiful dude I'd ever laid eyes on in my life. Several of the envelopes had writing all over them, too, saying, *Please open this,* and, *Baby, didn't you hear what happened to my brothers?!* and, *I miss you so much I could die. Don't you know that?*

Flipping the top letter up by the corner, I lightly ripped the seal, which already was dented and crumpled up from me crying and heavy-breathing over it so often. But no, *no*—I wouldn't read it.

Hasty, I got a sweater, and covered up that heartburning evidence of an old, long-time-ago life.

After yanking on stovepipe Target jeans and a cherry-red sweater with a picture of Che Guevara on it, I laced up my Nike Monster Shox. Those incriminating letters were stored safe again in a closed drawer, buried deep under brand-new clothes.

I bent down to give Squiggy some kisses—*Smack, smack, smack! Smack, smack, smack!*—which tickled him so his back legs thumped.

I grabbed hold of my phone, money, a couple apples from the kitchen, and my keys, which were still on their grotty twisty-tie. All these got dumped in my backpack.

Two minutes later, I flew down the street on my bike toward the bus stop.

*

I passed by Westchester's fancy houses, with their weird designer cactus gardens and tiny expensive dogs with crazy eyes and eighty-dollar haircuts. *Yap, yap.*

Almost got hit, too, by a black car. At the end of my street, which is Tamara Road, there was a shiny midnight Humvee with a couple of Latino guys in it. An Anglo might have taken them for gardeners or construction. Mexicans on my block are going to be carrying hammers because they still got that white-supremacy thing going in our section of Westchester. But these guys weren't labor. The driver, I couldn't really see at all, except he had some fluffy, licorice-shiny, Elvis-proud pompadour. The boy on the driver's side wore a fresh denim shirt, and long, satiny black hair hid his face. Boy was *big*, too. Bowling-ball biceps gleamed under his cutoff denim shirt, and they were all tackified with Aztec tats. He turned his head and seemed to stare right at me. Mirrored sunglasses and car shadows hid most of his face, but I spied the outlines of a big mouth and square jaw that confused me with some more memories. Suddenly, it felt like my heart burst in my chest.

"*Silver*?" I yelped. I slammed the brakes while still in the middle of the road, just at the same moment a black-and-white cop car started rumbling down the street, the cop waving at me like they do when they think you're good.

The Humvee scooted quick away.

I called again, my voice gone thick with feeling: "S!? S! Baby! Is that you?!"

The cop drove up and idled next to me. "Everything okay?"

"Huh—uh, yes, sir." My heart was slamming like a bird had got trapped behind my ribs. "Thought I saw someone."

I pedaled off, shaking just from the *idea* of seeing Silver as I hot-rodded through the hood, over to the Blue Line stop on Orange Street. Jumping off my bike, I chained it up and skedaddled onto the bus when it putted up.

Sorry, Frank, I said in my head, settling into my seat. *I want to abide you, but today I just can't. Damn, getting jumped by Force and Lalo is messing with my head, see. I'm even hallucinating my old boyfriend like a loony!* In the back row of the bus, I looked out the window as the Westchester mansions slowly shrank down into littler peel-paint houses, strip malls, office buildings, and vacant lots.

I munched an apple; two hours ticked off the clock.

Finally, the bus passed by some bird-squawking garbage dumps, closing in on a gray-cinder-block-looking house of the law.

"Chino!" the driver yelled over his shoulder.

The sun-glittering concrete building looked flung out in the desert territory. A guard stood outside, eyeless behind mirrored sunglasses. On account that Samson had got himself transferred into minimum security about six months previous, the dude didn't even have any big ol' Springfield rifle that I could see. Just probably some .25 or even a taser or a blackjack in his back pocket. It was quiet, real quiet—way too silent for a building full of glistening-eyed, tat-tooed boys with bad histories. My throat tightened up melancholy as I approached the entrance, sidestepping the guard.

This despairing joint wasn't no place for a girl like me to be seen. And *no* place for a King. But this was my stop: the Herman Baldwin Brown Youth Correctional Facility, all the way out in the MF-in', no-hope, break-your-spirit badlands.

I went in.

7

It was even gloomier inside the boys' prison. In the waiting room, there were a couple more guards who were so gray-facedly bored of minding thuggies that they looked like stiffs. The linoleum was scuffed and the sofa was so depressingly smashed down it seemed like it'd died. Miserable-looking juvie dudes with zombie stares and nicotine patches on their arms thumped up to the reception desk to sign out and go do the scut laundry and garden work the county says a body's got to do to therapize itself out of drugs and stealing. And no offense to her, but the reception lady with the frizzy blonde hair and tired eyes looked like she maybe could have used a little therapeuting her own self, too.

"You're Samson Peña's sister?" she sighed, checking her clipboard.

"Yeah, that's me."

"I don't know if you can see him," she said. "He's completely booked with art class and meditation and then his resocialization group."

"I've got to talk to him. I really do, ma'am!"

She shook her head again, but said to go sit down on the dead sofa. About forty minutes went by. I was feeling tasty as an aardvark's armpit by the time a short Asian counselor-looking dude came out. He was big-muscled, had cheeks as rough as sandpaper, and kind sparkle-eyes.

"You're the sister?"

I smiled at him. "Yeah, I'm King's."

He gave me a studying look before pulling out a cell phone from his pants pocket. Yapping on it for a minute, he hung up. "It's too bad you didn't come tomorrow, because he's really scheduled today and we keep to our timetables here. But I had him put in Visiting anyway, and I'll give you a couple minutes with him, doll. Just long enough for you to say hi and tell him you love him."

"I'll take what I can get," I said.

"Going to have to put away your backpack, though." I handed it to him, and he gave it to the blonde lady reception person. He patted me on the shoulder. "Okay, you ready to see him? My name's Kenny, by the way."

"Hi, Kenny."

"You got your game face on? Samson's going through kind of a rough patch."

"I'm ready, sir."

Kenny turned around, walked past the blonde lady. He buzzed open a door, and another guard allowed us into a gray hall. It was lined with little iron-barred cells where strong-looking man-boyz lay on their cots, staring up helpless at the ceiling like they'd been kryptonited. Further on, we passed by a series of rooms where dudes sat in circles, making papier-mâché blobs or talking about their "feelings" with some creepily sincere-looking prison headshrinkers. I started to get queasy, wondering what hanging out in a craptacular house full of shrinked-out cons had done to my once hard-core brother.

King had been in Herman Baldwin Brown for over six months by now, and a year and a half in maximum security before that. He'd been in the pen ever since he got messed up in that deal where he and Patssi Alba sold a big package of Diego weed to this Yakuza who was double-agenting for Uncle Sam. King used to do all the major selling when he was head of the Snakes, and Patssi was like his high sheriff—the only girl in the club, a real, peroxided chola with a crackly laugh. It's really too bad. On the night of the deal, he traded the Yakuza the drugs for money. Like ten seconds later, he saw three police coming at him from behind the corner. A setup. He'd whupped the Yakuza pretty good, grabbed Patssi, and run away. The police I guess thought King was holding Patssi hostage, and so they shot at him—but they killed *her*. He'd escaped for a couple days, but they caught him. So then he went to jail and also kind of crackers.

I hadn't seen Samson in thirteen months. The last time I went to visit him, he'd been in a cage in max, and getting cooped and chained had made him schizy. He'd said some things that made me feel kind of . . . *bad*. That's when Frank said I'd suffered a mini-psycho break-down, and had to dose me with some baby-mg Prozac to help me get my miserable craw out of bed.

I followed Kenny through that palace until we made it to a visit-ing room. We got buzzed in again, and let into a space full of long tables and metal chairs. Boys sat there crossing their arms and lean-ing back in their seats, sticking out their chins at their mothers, who looked bulldog-dismal.

At the back of the room, King sat up so straight it was as if his butt was just gonna rocket out of the chair.

"Aw, baby sister!" His chocolate-cream eyes glowed at me. His black, home-cut hair zoomed all over his head, and, peeking out from an Adidas short-sleeved T-shirt, his Snake and Colt tats glis-tened against his skin. Also, he was so doubly pumped up from his gym time that the boy just looked inflated.

"King!"

He hugged me, with Kenny watching close by. "How you doing, girl?"

"How'd you snag mini-sec?" I laughed up into his face, tears already starting to poke out my eyes. "Man, they just buzzed me in here. You could break this place easy! Don't they know who you are?"

"Aw, Chelle, they put me in here cuz they know I'm over my adversity. Didn't they, Kenny?"

"That's right, Sam," Kenny said. "You've been doing real good. You earned your spot here."

"What, you gone soft, Sam-man?" I asked.

"Aw, Chelle, I've been keeping it *peaceful*, cuz I've been so busy thinking. And *reading*. Like, about Jesus? And Mohammed? And that Gandhi? And it's all been teaching me that I been living the *wrong*, Chelle. The *wrong*." Samson talked super fast, like he knew our time was short and wanted to get all the words in. "It was hard, at first, though, to stay steady. You know, with our temper—"

"*Your* temper."

"But I know I've got to do it. I *swear* I'm gonna be rehabilitating." He squeezed his eyes shut. "No more knife fighting, no more defrauding, no more drug deals. Really, I am gonna to be 100 percent rehabbed just as soon—"

"You rehabilitating, my bright red ass!" yallered one of the boys who'd been talking to a bulldog mama.

Samson tilted his head toward the sound, scowled. "Just as *soon*—"

"King Kong's converting to Islam, homies!" the boy cackled out.

"Yeah, I'm gonna rehab just as soon as *I whup you butt, motherfucka*!" Samson growled at the ding-dong, so Kenny yelled: "Hey, cut it, Sam!"

Samson's eyes were black stars. "Okay, sorry, Ken! I'm just telling her that I've been reading, yeah, about that Gandhi. Chelle! That Indian motha was living *the right*. Like, he was all in the face of some weaponry, but he didn't raise a finger to nobody, even though them—what—English people, were messing with him fierce—"

I grabbed his hand. "I've got to talk to you, Samson."

Samson smiled at me, his teeth super white and Christmas-dazzling, like I hadn't seen him smile since before our dad, Lincoln, died. He had tears in his eyes, too.

"I know I'm chattering, Chelle, I'm sorry. I'm just so *beautiful* in my heart to see you, girl. Though you look different, don't you? Where's your Pendleton?"

"I don't wear that no more, King. But I dressed up for you."

"Chelle, the last time I saw you, I said things I shouldn't. When I said you were bad like Mama, and like me, that was *wrong*."

"It did; it hurt me, King." Now I was also crying.

"Because you're not like her. All that was just *my* hurt talking. Right, Kenny?"

"Something like, yeah," Kenny said.

"Guess what, I won the decathlon tryout, King," I blubbered. "And I won an 800 meters, too. And a 400, and I'm going to the All-Americans—and my foster daddy, Frank, oh, he *loves* me. He's all, you know, shy and kind of funky about it? But I know it—he taught me how to stitch peoples up, and, do you know the doctor word for bloody nose is *epistaxis*?"

He was practically sobbing: "Cuz there's no badness in you, sister; that's all me, and it's Reina. Because you're *good*, Chelle. I know you wanted out of tha Life. And that's how I'm going to be too."

"Time's running, Sam," Kenny said. "Don't forget this is just a five-minute stop before art."

We both cried some more and sniffled.

"Sister, sister, sister, baby sister." Samson whispered the words like a prayer.

I blurted out: "Samson, I'm here because Dragon says you owe."

He wiped his face. "What's that?"

"Lalo and Tha Force came to my school, all with some ski masks. And they were talking about some weed, and money?"

Samson's mug quick turned from brown-red to nearly green. "Whoa, they try and take you someplace?"

"Yeah, they tussled me a little, but then a teach came around and they scrammed."

"Was Silver with them?"

"I thought I saw him this morning. I was hollering after some car like a nut. . . ." I frowned. "But I'm not talking about him—Silver wouldn't lay hands on me—"

"Oh, girl, haven't you heard?" King's voice got louder. "That boy's turned into a Stone-Cold. He's worse than Dad ever was and nearly as bad as Reina."

I shook my head all around. "Did they let you in here cuz ya bumped ya skull? I'm talking about Dragon, and Force and Lalo. Silver used to be my boy, man. But those other punks, they are *creeping* me—"

"Don't make no mistake, Chelle. Silver's gone off the rez now."

"What are you talking about?" I rapped out. "He ain't even really a gangster! S is different than all you villains."

"Um, girl, you need an update, okay?" King said. "Because Silver *is* different, but ooh, like Godzilla ain't no normal lizard and the Wolf Man ain't no normal dawg. After you scrammed, and the Burner whacked T-Rock and Louie, he forgot all them fussy morals of his. Like, he forgot a lot. He went after Diegos who mowed down his brothers, but the man didn't do it with no temperance. Dude was Stone-Cold outta the *gate*."

"What do you mean?"

King grimaced. "When he made his move on the Diegos, he took his time and made them feel it, then just left them for dead. He got comfortable crossing the line and you ain't exactly his favorite person no more. So you don't talk to him, you don't look at him, you don't even breathe the same *air* as that bastard—he's got a hell heart now, and if you see him, you *run*!"

Kenny was looking down his nose at us. "Um, Samson, I think this might be stimming you a little bit too much. I'm going to wrap this up."

"Kenny, she's got a *problem*."

"I heard: some boys bothered her," Kenny said. "But she's got parents, right? She'll take it up with them. Boys messing with her, call the police or the principal. Plenty of adults who aren't in the box, boy. She's their job. There's nothing for *you* to do in here. Because Samson, remember, you're in jail. That's the cost of your conduct."

My brother barked, "Chelle, listen, just go to the tree and—"

I said, "What do you mean? Tree?"

"You know what I'm talking about, Princess!"

Kenny lightly touched my arm. "That's it, we have to go. He's revving up."

"Um. Okay." I did *not* like the look on my brother's face. "Samson?"

"No, Kenny," he started hollering. "Kenny!"

"Don't screw up today, Sam. Just remember that you have kin who *love* you! You've got something to fight for! Okay?"

"What I'm trying to *do*!"

"Like I said, it's time to mosey." Putting his hand on my shoulder, Kenny led me out of the visiting room, telling the other boys to button it when they started whistling at me. *Hi, pretty pretty.*

Passing by the tables, the mamas, the flirty dudes, my sneakers squeaked against the floor. I met eyes with a redheaded rogue and a Mexican one, with a big spider tattoo and a growing-out buzz-cut hairdo that looked like a dead badger on his head.

"*Chelle!*" Samson yelled out, really loud and frightening.

"*Chelle, Chelle!*" The vandals laughed.

"Samson?" I called over my shoulder.

"He's all right, honey," Kenny said, as he hustled me forward. This was the first time I noticed a little scar by his eye, like a tear-tat that had gotten lasered off in rehab. "I *know* that Samson can turn himself around. I've got faith."

"Michelle!" Samson hollered. *"You hear what I say!"*

"I need to know what he's trying to—" I jabbered, but Kenny wouldn't budge.

"Hurry back, child. I'll bet you have people who miss your pretty face back home. And you make sure to keep out of trouble. Learn a lesson from King."

He shut the door with a loud, hollow bang. I gave a jump, feeling like I'd been hit by lightning. But no matter how hard I tried, I couldn't hear my brother anymore.

8

Back out at reception, the white lady with the frizz-wig gave me back my backpack, then led me back out to the front of the building.

"Shoot." I gripped my fists to stop their trembling. "Samson, *man*. You as mental as the last time as I saw you, and here you go rattling me again! And this place sucks." The wall clock read two thirty already. "I'm out of here."

I busted out of the exit and hightailed back to the bus.

Outside, it was late sunshine, Chino smog. The prison parking lot was packed with gangy-looking cars: Studebakers with suicide doors, Humvees, hydraulic-poppin' Impalas. The bus stop was about two blocks away, and I sprinted over there, crossing the street so a car honked at me. *Beep beep! Beep! Hey!* I didn't want to look at anybody, because I was blubbing, so I didn't peep at the car. I rushed toward the Blue Line stop, where a bus was pulling up. I hopped on, snuffling my nose into my sleeve.

"Where you going, sir?" I asked the driver.

"San Fernando Valley, miss."

When he said that, I stopped crying almost right away. See, because Yale-Westview's out there in glamorous San Fernando Valley. Ever since I heard about the MLK scholarship, I liked to get a hold of Kiki and bus it down to that preptopia, especially if I was feeling a little psychological. We'd only done it about four or five times in the last year. Six, whatever. We'd jam around the chemistry lab and the library, and talk like in an English accent so the students would think we went there. And heck! Right then, I was *so* fuddled in my head, and it felt like you couldn't get any farther from all my problems than Y-Dub.

"You pass Ventura and Carpenter?" I asked the driver.

"Go right by it. Hit it in about an hour and a half."

"I'll take a ticket, please, sir."

*

The huge brown-and-blue world ran past the bus window. I sat with my backpack crumpled between my knees and my phone bulging in my pocket. On it were three messages—two from Kiki, one from Frank. The one from Frank said:

Where are U? Helena can't find you. Im in surgery for the next 4 hrs. Call her.

I answered: *Im okay but weve got to talk cuz I guess Im in some kind of trouble.*

I didn't call ol' Helena. Instead, I checked my messages from Kiki, which said:

U still flipping bout those boys messing with U last nite? U doing K?

and then, an hour later, around one o'clock:

Hello there. Wat is up? Mish call me, IM BORED.

It was nearly three now. I gave her a ring.

"Hey, Ki, why don't you meet me at Y-Dub?"

"Where *are* you? I've been trying to get a hold of you—and Helena called here."

"I'm on a bus. Just come on and meet me. We'll go to Y-Dub and walk around."

"Oh, no, not again," she said. "The weekend's not for going to school. And why do you always want to hang out at Y-Dub when we're not even in yet?"

"I like to go so I can get—what's the word—*acclimated* to it. Acclimated. A-c-c-l-i-m-a-t-e-d. That's the word for when you get used to something, Ki."

"I know what *acclimated* means. I had to study enough reading comprehension for those entrance exams you made me take—"

I said, "Listen, girl, when we show up for our first day of Y-Dub, it wouldn't do if on our first day we were all green and confused-looking, cuz then we'd be Unpopulars and they'd pounce us, you know, stick us in a locker and kick us."

"No, I want to go to the movies today," she huffed. "There's a really good French flick playing at three fifteen. And I wanted to go to that Hungarian trilogy *last* weekend, remember?"

"Nah, forget movies. It'll be better if we case the joint—Y-Dub, I mean—and get ready to rule the roost next year. Remember, what's our song, Ki? Got to get in the spirit!"

"I know that Y-Dub is awesome, Mish. But we need a backup plan; that's what my mom says—"

I sputtered, "Backup plan, *shoot*. Backup plan is staying at Rosa Parks with our busted-up used books and our no-uniforms and they don't have a single senior graduating off to Harvard."

"You are nuts," she finally chuckled. "Pop a Ritalin, picklebrain!"

"Come on, pep my *song*, baby. You recall our ditty?"

"Yeah." She laughed again. "I think I might have heard that tune before."

I started to rap: "*Ssss tat-a-tat uh-huh, oh you* fast *girl, you* fast *girl, you* fast, *you* fasssst *girl.*"

Then Ki gave in, and we both started to sing it:
Ki and Mish gonna dom-i-nate
Those li'l girls gone beat your butt
You push them down; they don't hes-i-tate
Cuz they never, never, NEVER GIVE UP!

At the end of it, we were hee-hawing.

"Someday, Mish, you and I are going to have a deep and hairy discussion about how bossy you are—"

"Yeah, sure, just get off the phone and onto a bus—"

"All right, Y-Dub, here I come. Again. At least I'm bringing my camera."

"I'll be there in like an hour and fifteen minutes. Meet at the track?"

"I'll see you there, weirdo."

Click.

Outside the bus window, Chino rolled away. The truth is, I *needed* to go to Y-Dub right then. I had to see myself walking those halls, in a uniform. I needed to see the girl I was going to become.

Who was I, anyway? The girl I was making up in my head? Track star, Ivy League–bound? Golden child?

Or . . . the girl I was born?

While the burned hills turned greener out that window, and the dumpy houses got fancier, I brooded on that question by pondering the history of where I'd come from.

Dad: Lincoln Peña, the first King of the 99s, a big, muscly dude I would have liked to know better, except he'd got assassinated by enemeez when I was eleven. Mom: The 99s' new gang leader, she was a black-haired beauty, and the most dangerous viper woman ever seen on the Eastside. But now she was caged in the pen.

After my daddy got himself (and me, too, nearly) executed by some Limas over turf borders, Mama did a genocide on the ten top Dukes of that Northern Cal gang. Having proved herself as a natural assassin, she got herself crowned the 99s' ruler quicker than them San Fran–based boyz could say "oops." Mama built up our *big* white house in Monty to announce her magnificence, and our palace had this nice, flower-dripping magnolia tree in the yard. She would sit in the living room, in her leather La-Z-Boy chair, receiving her gangsters like gun-toting Cleopatra. Dressed up in her Pendletons, with blue eye shadow glittering up her beautiful face, she'd preside on that throne, listening to the hoods yappering about their bizness probs. Once they'd got finished with their cussing, she'd say stuff like, *Oye, pendejos, you all gonna take ten P from the herbal and split it 'tween yas and baby Samson's club. The Snakes is like our youth group, understand. So if I hear one more queja outta either yas, I'll get Bam-Bam to cutya. Comprende?*

The woman was a force, you know.

There was this one day, Mama had crossed the line into some *felonious* territory by organizing her 99s with guns, masks, tasers, and in less than two months they'd done five home invasions and robbed three banks. To celebrate, she put on a fiesta at our house, with torches and hip-hop mariachis. Samson got so excited he lifted me high in the air, sitting me on a branch of that magnolia tree in our yard, yelling, *Chelle, you a royal girl now and we gonna buy you anything you want, sugar!* I still can see the magnolia flowers, the tree's dark branches reaching to the sky. While I sat up there, giggle-screaming, my best boy, Silver, sprayed me with champagne, kissing me on my cheeks. *Michelle, you're angel,* he said. And, *Princess M,* the rest of them all yallered up at me. Later, they'd call me just *P.* Mama came to me after, wearing a canary-diamond pendant that was like a summer moon, and lipstick dark as a human heart. Plucking me from the branch, she hugged me, whispering in my ear:

Hija, ya are royal. If ya work for it, ya gonna be Queen of the 9s when I gone. Samson's a good boy, but even though you just a tadpole, I see that fire in your sangre. But you got to hear this now, chica. Ya listening, girl?

I'm listening, Mama.

Princess M, when the day comes, you demand a Queen's respect, and they will give it to you. And what that means is, ya never let anyone of these punks touch you.

Touch me?

Like that Silver boy. I see him with my eyes. See, men ain't controllable once they think they got a woman's heart. Your daddy Lincoln learned me that one good. God rest his soul, and I loved him, but I set this club up with that bastard, and when the time came, he would not crown me as his Queen. It's on account of his shortsightedness I had to walk the red road to get where I am now. So you keep yourself in ya own command; that's the price a power. You my daughter. And if you want to stay alive long enough to take my seat, don't you ever let these boyz forget that you rule them, not the other way around.

But—

That's the law!

Okay, Mama, I'd said.

So much for being her royal heir. Today, Mom was serving a fifteen-year jail sentence for those robberies. And after I got ditched by my second foster family when they found out I was Snakes-related, she'd called me from prison, and told me on the phone, in a flat, dead voice: *I don't want to see your skinny butt visiting me in this prison no more, Michelle. You gonna be fine without me, okay? Forget all about the club, stepping in after me. You forget me and put your money on somebody else.*

That day hurt the worst in the world, even if part of me was relieved I'd fallen from grace. Truth is, I hadn't really wanted to be no untouchable Queen like her. And then things got even better for me when I met Frank. I forgot about Mama, and soldiering, and made myself into a brand-new person.

Right?

I was still studying that question by the time the bus slid through downtown and hit Burbank.

And that's also, as it happens, about the time that I spotted a big black car on the road next to the bus, and then a ways behind it a gray-primer-painted car.

I snatched my eyes out the window to watch the cars flicker down the freeway. Humvees and ugly-butted Chevies are L.A.'s favorite way to eat up the gas, though. I wasn't going to flip just cuz I saw those dime-a-doz rides cruising through the valley.

"Laurel and Carpenter!" the bus driver called out.

Walking slow down the aisle, I held my backpack in front of me. I peered out the doors, which closed, then opened, then closed, then opened. Right outside was Yale-Westview, shiny and glorious, like a church or a Santa Monica mall.

"Time to go, sweetheart."

I got off the bus. Wandering up to the school, I spun my eyes crazily all around me. There were no signs of gangsters in Chevies and Humvees I could see. Except, those cars . . . I *did* spot them a minute ago on the freeway. My mouth went dry, even though I just spied pretty trees, singing birds, the sun rushing down from the sky like a gold-robed angel. *Get out of there, Chelle*, my brother had said. *Don't even breathe the same air as that bastard.* Get out of where? I'd like to know. I was trying to get *in* here.

9

Yale-Westview's at the end of Carpenter Street, which otherwise has billionaire houses all up and down on it. The school's tucked into a regular ritzy neighborhood, so slickster movie stars and Google richies are always bumping into its genius teachers and supersmart students. Nobel Prize winners who invented cancer cures and cell phones have graduated from it. Big-brained Pulitzer Prize–winning writers roamed these ol' halls. Yale-Westview got built in 1900, and it has 911 students, from all over the whole freakin' world. It's got eight academic halls, and two libraries, and a dance studio, and a deluxe cafeteria. You can take Introduction to Web Design and Korean, and Kiki could take a film-intensive workshop.

Y-Dub starts on a hill, the upper part of Carpenter Street filled by a parking lot where parents drop their kids off on school days. There were only one or two cars now, it being four ten on a Saturday. I stood there looking down at the green grass sloping under my feet toward the campus's chocolate-brown buildings. South of the Humanities Complex was the racing track like a giant's thumbprint. The whole place looked empty. Not even Kiki was there yet. *Good*, I thought, my nerves getting hairier by the second. *Maybe she didn't come. Maybe she didn't come like I'd asked.*

But then I saw Kiki, gorgeous against the grass, walking from the school buildings. She was wearing one of her wacky fashion getups, a pink tent-skirted dress with red splashy flowers printed on it, and matching pink tennis shoes. She had a baby blue backpack slung over her shoulder, and walked silly, half-hopping, and happy looking.

I heard a car pulling up behind me now.

Kiki looked up and waved. "Mish!"

I just stayed there on top of the crest. I was cold-blooded, my mind freezing.

I looked behind me. *Oh no, oh no.*

A giant black Humvee drove into the parking lot. A primer-painted jalopy followed along. The big, beautiful boy and the boy with the pompadour were in the Humvee. My head started to shudder on my neck like somebody was shaking me. The beautiful boy, that *was* Silver, silk hair grown down to the middle of his back, buffed up to a big-chested eighteen, and hiding from me behind his mirrored Oakleys. Tha Force and Lalo were in the ugly dump of a Chevy.

He turned into a Stone-Cold. You see him, you run.

"Silver, baby, what are you doing?" I asked, barely breathing.

His mirrored sunglasses glittered; his face looked made of rock as he got out of the car. "Staying alive, Michelle."

"S—you're scaring me, man—oh, God!"

The pompadour boy was opening the door of the Humvee. He had bug sunglasses on. He took them off so I could see his eyes.

Brown eyes, dark lashes, wiggly mouth. Silver's cousin. I'd known him when he was a wet fifteen-year-old piece of nothing begging King to be in the Snakes. Dragon Mendoza, scum bucket of the universe. But he'd grown into a bigger and meaner eighteen-year-old, now.

Two other big mothas came tumbling out of the Humvee's backseat. I hadn't seen them before, on account of the smoked windows. The boyz were huge as dinosaurs. One of them had a scar stretching from his right eye to his mouth. The other one had *Kill Ya Sucka!* shaved into his hair in fancy Gothic letters.

"Time to go, P. Get in the car now," Dragon said, with those two supersized hooligans standing behind him. Dragon took out a knife from his pants pocket, flicking it open so it glitzed in the sun. "Get in, or I'll cut ya, Michelle. I'll cut ya behind the knees so you never run again."

He *could* bleed me. Once in Montebello, I'd seen a dead boy lying flat on the sidewalk, shot in the chest by a rival. And long ago I'd learned the rule of the street: If hooligans jacked you, and got you in their car, you were as good as the grave.

Run or die!!! my mind screamed.

"*Help!!!*" My legs jackhammered into a crazy-muscled sprint, and I roared down the hill. "*Aaaaiii! Get away, Ki! Run, Kiiiiiii! Runnnnnn!!!*"

"Take out your hot," Dragon yelled as they scrambled after me. "The Remington!"

"Dragon," I heard S holler. "Hold your mud, man!"

"Just shut up and *catch her!*"

Ki didn't run away but *toward* me, and I was crying and shrieking.

"No, no, Ki, the other way, other way, away from me, *away from me!*"

"Mish!"

Her eyes bright, her hair flying. Pink dress flying right at me like Tinker Bell.

I didn't hear *or* feel it when the bullet bit the side of my right arm, but I fell down on the grass.

The big one with the *Kill Ya Sucka!* shave-job kicked me. I was on the ground, screaming "Silver!" But when I stared at S's hard face, he was a terrible stranger. The thug with the scar on his cheek wrapped his arms around Kiki like a boa constrictor. She was crying so maniacal it looked as if her face had been torn in two. They hauled us toward the parking lot, and shoved her inside the black 'Vee. Silver held me as I scratched at him, snapped my jaws at him. I screamed like a grizzly as he lifted me up, so I could see the school, twinkling. For a second, Frank flashed through my head. *Y-you must never let anyone like that touch you, Michelle. It's very important that you stay safe.*

"Frankie!" I cried out, as the big one yanked me into the 'Vee.

Dragon came up to me in the car, and hit me hard in the face.

My eyes went dark after that.

10

Wazzup homie? My boyz from Monty!
  Wazzup motha? I'll bring heat to ya!
No bad's like the bad from the 99s, sucka
No mean's like East, ya see
No rough's like whatcha gone get in 'Bello, Hello
Montebello Montebello! Uprise Montebello
Montebello! Uprise Montebello Montebello!
We burn you down ya give us trouble!!!

When my eyes opened again, they stared into a world as black as deep outer space. I was blindfolded. I'd been put on the ground, curled up knees-to-head. The floor was going *thunka-thunka* under me. My mind swirled, scattered. *Oh my God! Where am I?*

Finally, I got it: I was stuffed behind the passenger seat of a car. My wrists were tied up, too, and my ankles. My right arm felt wet down to the wrist. Blood.

Oh right, those despicables have snatched me and Kiki!

That dig-nabbity, bad-assedy music went on *blasting* in my ears.

Uprise Montebello Uprise
You mess wit us we cut you down to size
Uprise Monty Uprise
First to cross us is the first who dies

Over that tune, which I made to be Diggy-O's hometown hit

56

"Uprise! No Blood's Like the 99s," I could hear Dragon and his goonies yabbering.

"We'll get the money now," Dragon said.

"It's due in a *day*, homes—we're pushing it to the very the limit with ol' man Frederico," said one of the thugs, not Silver.

"That's why we're holding a shindig at the Fort, Biggie," said Dragon. "Put the Burner in a good mood and get our murders off his mind. You and Book are going to have to import us some good-looking women for it, too. And not just for Freddie. Hopefully some mamacitas will also fresh up our bro. Cuz, S, man, you lookin' *blues*."

"You shooting her wasn't in the plan," I heard Silver say.

"Cowboy up, crackhead!" Dragon barked at him. "You know we don't come up with the cash, it's gonna be my bones stuck in a trunk! Where's my no-*tor*-ious Stone-Cold?"

Silver growled, "Don't push me, D, or maybe my famous temper'll get visited on *your* ass."

"Aw, there the crazy eye I'm looking for," Dragon laughed. "Boyz, he's back; here he is. My Ice-Man, brr, it freezing my blood just looking atcha."

"What you going to do about that other girl?" S asked.

"I know, what a fucking pain," Dragon said. "Had to take her, though, she's a witness."

That other girl—this is when I felt something shaking around my head. It was Kiki, bundled up and struggling on the backseat right above me.

"Oh my God, *Kiki*!" I screamed.

"*Mish!*" Kiki answered.

I felt her trembling all over in *hellish* Amber Alert misery. Knowing that my Kiki was suffering made me totally bug-ass crazy.

"*AAAAIIIIIIII!!!! AIIIII!*"

"Sounds like a devil back there!" the thug called Biggie yelped.

"Get her to shut up!" Dragon hollered.

"*AAAAAAIIIIIIII!!!!!!—ugh!*" Someone had just reached over and pressed a warning finger to my lips. I could tell it was Silver, just from his touch.

"Calm down, Michelle. You'll be okay," he said. "Besides, there's no getting out of this. You're good and clipped, see. I got you."

I got you.

I got you too. . . .

At his words, a killer memory flashed through my head, and it was like from another world:

Sunny bedroom, Sunday morning. Four years ago, a week before rivals shot my daddy dead on a Monty street. I was eleven, Silver fourteen. S and I had been tangled on my bedroom carpet, reading books. I had snuggled into his chest, smiling—and then:

Creak, went the front door.

Sweetface, you hear something? Silver had asked.

I don't know. That Mama come home, S? I'd answered.

We heard two strange men talking in No Cal accents.

We doing his females if we find them?

Sure, why not?

Chi-chink. Silver and I had stared at each other as we heard a gun cocking.

It's the Limas, Silver'd whispered, his face going dead white. *Hide in the closet!*

I'd gripped onto him. *What about you, S?*

I can top 'em before they touch you.

No! You ain't as mean as them! I'd whispered. *They'll hurt you bad!*

I can be damn mean if I want, Michelle, he'd said, his voice shaking.

I'd pulled on him, desperate. *Well, you don't want. Come on!*

O-kay. Silver and I had crawled fast under my bed, wrapping our arms around each other.

From our hiding place, we could see black boots walk into my room. The men had kicked at my dresser, my books, while we stayed silent as stones.

S and I didn't let go of each other, even when the door slammed and we'd finally heard the hit men's car driving off.

I got you, Michelle, S had said into my shoulder, squeezing me. *You know that, right? I've got you, baby.*

I'd pressed against him, shivering. *I got you, too, Silver. I'll never let go.*

I'll never let you go, I've got you, I've got you. . . .

There, stuffed in the car, I started crying, while Silver was still touching my face.

"Silver," I bawled. "Why are you doing this to me?"

He spoke in a soldier's cold voice. "You know why."

"No, I don't!"

"Because you're a fake, Michelle. And a traitor."

"Goddammit," I howled. "This ain't you! *Just stop this!*"

"I told you to shut them up, not make them louder," Dragon said. "P, if you bitch anymore, I'm gonna knock ya friend into the next life."

Ki start screaming again. "*Egggggggh!*"

"Kiki, Ki!" I hissed. "Honey, it's okay!"

"Oh—my—God!" she gasped.

Wriggling around, I found her. I touched her head with my head, crown to crown.

"Don't be scared, girl, don't be scared; just relax," I said. "Shh, ssshhh."

She soothed down just to crying, while I rubbed my cheek against hers.

I tried to listen behind the music, the boyz arguing. I made out the sounds of empty roads—there was less traffic, wherever we were. The air was different out here, too. I couldn't smell anything good because I was snotty from crying, but I could feel that it was drier and hotter than either Westchester or Montebello.

Rumble, rumble went Dragon's Humvee as he headed far away from Frank, Westchester, the All-American championships, and Mrs. Markson, to someplace I never wanted to see. The desert air swept in through the windows, drying up the sweat and the blood on my body as I tried to comfort Kiki.

What in the hell had gone down with Silver? And *where* on earth were these bastards taking us?

11

"**G**ood, there's Shakira. The Fort's all clear; let's get them out."

"S, you and Bigs carry them up there. Keep them tied."

"Okay, but I'm taking off the blindfolds; they won't know where we are."

The car had come to a stop. I heard keys jingling. Doors opened, slammed shut.

Hands pulled at my head, and the blindfold fell off. Silver stared at me, black-eyed, surrounded by the brandy-colored night sky. I was frantic to see something in him that I recognized, but he was just some grim-looking masculinity as he picked me up, making my hurt arm burn. Kiki got carried by the scar-face called Biggie. While he hitched her over his shoulder, her eyes caught mine, and she was still crying.

"Welcome back to the revolution, Michelle," Silver said, as he gripped me under my knees and armpits. I was in so much pain that my legs kept kicking out, and my head was jerking back.

"I know you don't want to hurt me, S!" I wept, my mouth open and trembling. "You never wanted to be like these guys!"

Silver shook his head. "You and me are strangers these days, Michelle, so you don't know what I want. *This* is my home now, and I mean to protect it."

I snatched my head up and saw the house.

Under that spooky moon, the casa had a ghostly vampire mansion vibe. Its pointy roof was half caved in, and it had a crumbling-down side garage. There was a glossy Shakira poster in one window, showing her belly dancing. Wincing from the hot, sickly bullet-burn flaming my arm, I glanced up to see about five boyz ambling out of the bright-lit front door.

"He did it: He shoplifted Reina's kid," I heard a familiar voice say. "Man, we're going to get *bapped* for this."

"What we're going to get is what we're owed, li'l Midget!" Dragon laughed out, striding ahead of us all tall and swaggery in his cowboy boots and his ten-foot hair.

Ki and me struggled while Silver and Biggie lugged us into the house's living room. Posters of Mr. Kee, Immortal Technique, and Diggy-O covered its redbrick walls. The splintery-spiky wood floors sent up dust ghosts wherever the boys stomped, but the black leather sofas were as buttery as money could buy. While all the Snakes crowded in, I could barely hear their chatting on account of Godzilla Bose speakers blasting out this tune:

You in danger, you in danger, you in danger, my man!
You a stranger, you a stranger, you a stranger, Mex-i-can!
You better run, better run, better run from ya enemeez
Cuz you see what I seen, it'll make ya blood freeze!

One of the Snakes snapped off the Bose. Except for the sound of Kiki's muffled crying, a weird quiet filled the room. There were nine thugs in the room, and I saw that I knew most of them: not only Dragon, Silver, Force, and Lalo, but these dudes called Game, Eager, and Midget. Betrayers. Shouldn't be *touching* me. My mind went red with rage.

"*ARRGGHH!!!*" I thrashed back and forth in Silver's arms. "*Let me go!!!*"

"Goddammit, *hold still!*" Silver grappled me, making my shoulder feel like it was getting sawed by a rusty knife. "You want me to chastise you—because I will, Michelle!" I nearly kicked out of his grip. "Fuck! You're going to break your own neck!"

"Who's gonna get their neck broke is *every mothafucka in here you don't let us go*!" I hollered, glaring at Biggie, who still had a hold of Ki. "Take her ropes off *now*." I whipped my head around. "*Take them off, or I'll make ya pay!!!*"

"Oh my God, Mish!" Kiki shrieked, widening her eyes at me.

"Whoa!" Biggie yelped, giving a little frightful jump.

"Damn, I heard P gone soft, but she looking as mass destruction as Reina, man," said Eager, who was a baseball-cap-wearing, malnutrition-no-chested, seventeen-year-old antisocial.

I glared out at the Snakes through the curtain of my hair, as dangerous as a witch. Then the pain zapped through me again, and I spasmed hard, shouting out. "Agh!"

"This is an injured wildcat," Eager said, eyeballing me close. "And you know about them, right, D? They's dangerous."

"They *shot* the kid," Lalo piped up. "Look at all that blood on her shoulder."

"Who's the other one?" Eager asked, looking at Kiki.

"A civvie, her pal," Lalo said.

"N-n-n . . . w-w-w . . . r-r-r . . ." That came from big boy Game, a rebel I'd known since I was eight years old, whose face still got red and puffy from his speech impediment.

"Game's saying, 'What you go and do that for?'" translated his weenie best buddy, crew-cutted, four-foot-eleven Midget. "Game says, 'That's Princess M, and she is all nobility, D! And Reina's going to be bringing down some al Qaeda on our ass!'"

"Stupid handicap didn't say all that." Dragon spat.

All the Snakes started chattering, nervous and babbly.

"Aw, Reina is gonna get serial killaz on us!"

"Queen'll behead us, man!"

Dragon raised his hand, and they all went quiet as deer.

"Who rules you?" he asked in a real soft, vicious voice.

"You do, D," only Force answered.

"Who. Rules. You?" Dragon panther-footed around the room. He slipped an arm around Midget's neck, squeezing him scary and brotherlike at the same time.

"You do, D," Midget coughed out.

Dragon cupped his hand behind his own ear. "What?"

"You do, D," they all said now.

"That's right." He smiled, cougar-toothed. "And do you know why you looked to me after King got busted?" He pulled out this shiny, silver death's head key chain from his pocket. I'd seen it before: Mama gave Samson that death's head when he was fourteen, as a prize for leading the Snakes. *This is the mark of your Kingship, baby boy. You guard it with your life.* "Come on, now. Tell me the reason you took this away from Samson and gave it to me."

"Cuz you promised to make us kings or die, boss," Force said.

"Hell yes, I did!" Dragon said. "I gave my oath. I promised you in *blood*. So why do yous question my word?" He waved his hand at me. "What I brought you here today ain't royalty—it's ya freedom, *boyeeez*! The Burner's gonna *slave* us if we don't pay. And whose fault is that?"

"King's," they all said in one voice.

"That's right. *Samson* hid the cash we owe Burner Gonzales. And taking P hostage is the only way we're gonna get him to tell us where he put it."

Reaching over, he grabbed my face so I jerked backward in Silver's arms. "Besides, this look like nobility to you?" Dragon rattled my chin around.

I could tell, when he put it that way, that I didn't.

"Screw you!" I roared.

"Female," he said, like that answered something. "All yous scared of these Peña women, it's pathetic. Look at P here; she's no more dangerous than a kitten! So we're gonna cage her and her cute little friend, and they won't make any trouble at all if you act like men. Then tomorrow, I'll see King, make our trade. After that, we'll be free and clear. Okay?"

"Okay."

"Okay?" he said, louder.

"Okay!!!"

"Good. We are finished jawboning. Silver, tuck in our girlfriends for the night."

"Where should I put them, boss?"

"Put them in the Vault."

12

"In you two go," Silver said, after carrying me through a yellow kitchen, then up some stairs. He'd brought me to a night-shadowed attic built at the top of the Fort.

Creak, creak. As he put me down on a bed, old-person-smelling sheets crackled under my butt. Biggie plopped Kiki next to me. We sat there, communicating like by psychic thought: *Oh my God, Oh my goddammed God.*

"Get the light," Silver muttered.

Snap. A golden beam dazzled from a dusty chandelier, showing off the space. The Vault, they called it. Good name: It was a room full of treasure.

This attic *used* to be a lady's bedroom. We sat on a big, four-poster, rat-eaten sleeper, which was draped with a red comforter and had little rusted nails sticking out of the posts. There were two side tables, too, with stained-glass lamps, and on the floor lay a moth-nibbled rug and a few unsteady stacks of paperback books, grotted with a lot of manhandling. A few homemade, high-color photographs of rebels were thumbtacked on the walls, too. But that was it for junk.

Everything else there in the Vault was top-of-the-line, brand-new shiny stuff that you see in store windows and die for.

Off by the south wall, a rack dripped with fur coats, D&G dresses, Miu Miu babydolls, Chip & Pepper jeans. In front of those coutures squatted boxes heaped with Foot Locker soccer balls, Toshiba video cams, crystal-studded iPods. And there was food, too: A giant's dinner of M&M's, and a crate of Grey Goose vodka.

Well, I knew what this was. When I was eight years old, Mama lectured me on "trade": *Sugar, when you selling to dopers, ya selling to losers. See, addicts got bad credit, so you gotta get customers working retail, like Nordstrom's, or Big 5. When the junkies come up short, you just get one of ya toughest men, like Silver, say. He'll terrorize them a little till they steal from their bosses. Then they trade ya, and it all comes out equal.*

Sure, but I don't know if S would want to do that, Ma.

What the hell do you care, Michelle? That's what he's there for, ain't he?

Yes, ma'am.

Silver glared at me furious as he stood among that shiny pirate's booty. Then he pulled a long, wicked-looking knife from his pocket. *Switch.* Up came the blade, diamond-bright.

"It makes me sick just to be in the same room as you now," he hissed. "Deserter!"

"*Argh!*" I scooted back fast on the bed.

"*Frak!*" Kiki kicked out her legs as kung fu as she could, landing a good chopper right on his nose. *Whap!*

"Agggggh!" He covered up his face with his hand, squinting.

I just stared at her, stunned—because whoa, I didn't expect Ki to bring the Bruce Lee!

"I understand that you're scared, little girl, but do not do that again," Silver said in a deadly voice. "I'm not kidding. I'll tie you up, put you in a closet, and forget I ever saw you."

Kiki stared at the knife. "I'll behave."

"You will if you want to stay healthy," Silver grunted. Turning to me, he raised the blade again. His stared at me with glistening, brutal eyes, like he didn't care if he cut me or what.

But I saw his hand start shaking.

"Silver!" I gasped. "Cut this rebel act *now!*"

He stared at his hand, and willed it to stop trembling. "This isn't an act, Michelle." Tucking the blade under my wrist-ropes, Silver ripped them off. *Slit.* "I could do worse than this, I promise you. After you split me, I was in such a state you're lucky I didn't go to Westchester and burn that whole place down."

"What are you doing with the ropes, man?" Biggie asked.

"Don't worry; I'll lock them down if they try to run," Silver answered.

"Fine, your job, then." Biggie walked out of the room.

Silver cut off Kiki's ropes too, and I saw her right wrist was mashed and bloody. She began crying harder, pressing it to her cheek.

"S, this isn't you!" I hollered.

"It is now," he said, steely. "Blame yourself."

My fury buckled into sobs. "Silver, you don't have to do this! I'm sorry, all right? I am *so sorry* about your brothers, and that I didn't answer your letters when they died—"

"Aw, I already know you must not have read them." He brought his face close to mine, baring his teeth. "I poetized to you so beautifully in those notes—you would have had to be a dead girl not to be moved. And I think that is what happened. You're *dead* on the inside now, Peña. You don't have a heart, and that's why I don't have one for you, either."

My eyes locked onto his. "You know why I had to leave! I had no one!"

Silver glared at me with so much hate. "Nah, it's *now* that you've got no one."

"S, you *know* you're doing wrong to me!"

"What I know is that *wrong*'s a big word, with a lot of meanings," he spat, pulling my shirt down over my right shoulder. He frowned at my wound, rubbing some of the blood-grunge off my skin. "All we're doing is protecting our kin that's still kicking, which seems right to me. We're a day away from getting genocided, as you'd've learned if you read anything I wrote. And as you weren't going to come help us, we had to come 'remind' you of your loyals ourselves. Whether you like it or not."

Another hot, sharp pain shot through my arm, and I doubled over. "Is it true what King says about you—that you're a Stone-Cold, now?"

Shrugging, he reached over the bed, and ripped a case from one of the pillows. He pressed it to my arm to staunch my bleeding. "I just copped to my destiny. But what about you? *Quo vadis*, Michelle? Serious."

"*Quo*—what?"

"*Quo vadis*. That's the Latin language. It means, 'Where are you going?'"

Tears spilled down my cheeks. "I don't understand you, S. You talking about one of them crazy books you're always reading?"

He shook his head disgusted, like he couldn't believe how stupid I'd got out in Westchester. "It's from the Bible. That's what Peter—you know, Peter the apostle, he was asking that of Jesus. *Where you going, brother?* Jesus said, *I'm off to be crucified,* hermano. Bold, huh? And that's what I'm asking you: Where did you *go*, Michelle? You left here magnificent and came back a pitiful civilian."

His hand was still on my arm, and as I looked down at his fingers on my skin, another memory suddenly came stampeding into my mind:

I saw me at twelve, S at fifteen. We'd been sitting together, close, on my living room sofa.

I'm not like my brothers, Michelle, he'd confessed in his tender lover's voice. *But the only one who sees that is you. Ever since that day, in your room, with those Limas—you saw the real me.*

Yeah, I'd said, looking down at his bronzed hand on my arm. I'd laced my fingers into his. *I see you, S, I do. I know you in my heart.*

T-Rock and Louie don't get me, and my cousin Dragon doesn't either, he'd said. *They're all about revolution, say I've got soldiering in me natural. I say, they're my family, and I love them, but I've got to fight the beast in me. I can choose my own road.*

I touched his cheek, stroking back his hair. *She don't get me. I can't be close to nobody, she says. She says you're my soldier, and I can't be thinking I'm in love with you, S.* I'd gazed at him, feeling like I was falling off a cliff, and I liked it. *But maybe I don't want to be Queen, you know? I just want to be with you!*

I'm not a rebel except for you, Michelle. Because I love you, no matter what Reina says.

I love you too, Silver!

We'd turned our faces up, and our lips met. Our first kiss was gentle, soft. Feeling like we were floating around the room, we'd started laughing into each other's mouths . . . and when we'd opened up our eyes, my mom was standing in the doorway.

Get out of my house, Silver, she'd spat. *Now!*

Here in the Vault, I held my wet, burning face in my hands. "Oh, Jesus, I got to get out of here!"

"Yeah, you used to be something, but not anymore." Silver shook his head. "What a waste."

Kiki's freckles stood out against her tear-wet skin. "You're talking in like an accent, Mish! I can't understand what you're saying! 'Quo-Something, Stone-Cold'?"

"It's nothing, Ki," I said, weeping harder. "He's just trying to hurt me worse, is all."

Stamp, stamp, stamp. Suddenly, Dragon came all swaggering into the room, wearing a fresh wifebeater and satisfaction in his grin like a gold tooth. Biggie followed close behind.

"Bigs," D said. "You on this door all night, all day, all day, all night, ya hear? They don't get out of here till I say."

"I hear ya, boss." Biggie took his place right on the landing of the stairs.

D nodded to Silver. "Report."

"Michelle's cuffed on the arm; I've got to go downstairs, get some supplies to clean her up," Silver said.

Dragon eyeballed Kiki. "Well, this one looks better now that she ain't screaming."

I smeared the tears off my face and growled, "Dragon, don't look at her, and don't touch her!"

"Just trying to give a girl a compliment, is all," he said, smooth. "Same P as always, ain't you? You all tied up and shot and you still mouthy." His grin vanished, and he sneered. "So, you heard us dialoguing—you figured out by now why we snatched you, Princess M?"

"Money," I said. "When King did that pot deal where Patssi got axed, he kept the bank. You're keeping me hostage till he tells you where he stowed it."

"One hundred thousand dollars ain't just 'money,'" Dragon said. "We call that a *livelihood*, P."

"I didn't know it was a *hundred* K!?" I gasped. "That's a whole new order of large for you boyz!"

"Tell me about it," he said, "because it's *eighty* K we owing to Freddie Gonzales, who supplied us the chronic in the first place. You remember 'the Burner,' Michelle?"

"I don't get it, 'Burner'? Are you guys talking about a person who is, like, real?" Kiki gabbled at me.

"Half man, half monster, more like, chickie-chick," D answered. "Isn't that right, Silver?"

"I don't need a history lesson, D," Silver said.

Dragon cocked his head at me. "Because you heard how Louie and T-Rock got bapped, right, P?"

"Who's Louie and T-Rock?" Kiki asked.

I looked at Silver, my lips trembling. "His brothers."

Silver stared straight ahead. "Don't even talk about them."

"Dragon," I snapped, "just tell Reina to take care of it!"

"Reina's the reason we out in the cold, girl," Dragon said. "She says we go solo unless we title Samson—or better yet, *you*, as King."

I gripped my arm and squinted at him. "Me? I thought she cut me out of line."

"I know, funny, huh?" D said. "Why on earth would we do something as stupid as that? But we still do need you, so as to persuade Samson to tell us where he hid the green. And he better tell us quick. We need that cashola by tomorrow night."

I shook my head. "Why so soon?"

"Burner's coming down here. We're throwing the Diegos a little party. Trying to soften him, make him reconsider our extension. It's expired in twenty-four hours, now." Dragon shivered, and I saw all his scaredness hit his face like cold water. Silver looked wrung-out, too.

"Dragon, what'd you get us into?" I breathed. "What happens if you don't get the money?"

He came in close to me, lean, strong, and sweat-smelling.

"All of our damnations, *ésa*. Mine, yours, and your pretty friend's, too. Burner's going to kill us all if he don't get what he wants."

And with that, Dragon decided he'd had enough talk for the night. Both he and Silver turned around, stomped through the Vault's door. They shut it firm behind them so I heard a solid little *click* as it locked shut.

After Dragon and Silver had gone, Ki and me stared at each other pop-eyed.

"Aaa . . ." she started to babble.

I clenched my jaw, forcing myself to think clear. "Okay, keep it cool, cookie. What you trying to say? Aaa—as in, *atrocious*? As in, *appalling*? *Alarming*?"

Her eyes stuck out crazier and she got her tongue back. "Aaa—this isn't fracking reading comprehension! Some guy called 'the Burner' is going to flamingly kill us until we're *dead*! Oh my God, Mish, *please* tell me we're being *Punk'd*!"

"Ki, no, they *shot* me."

She cried harder. "Okay, okay, how do people escape when they're kidnapped? Oh—I don't know anything about real life, but movies, movies—how does the hero get out in a jam in French flicks?" Her eyes widened. "Oh, *great*!"

"What?"

"In art films, the girl always dies, usually after getting supersymbolically shot in the heart! Okay, screw high art. Um, so, okay, in *24*, the hero always gets away—because they, like, use these superintense judo moves, or they have supergenius computer experts like Chloe who yell at Tony Maneida on their Bluetooth so that he shows up with Curtis with a whole bunch of guns and they blast Jack out—"

While she gabbled in a frenzy, I scrambled up to the door and pulled on the handle, but it was locked. Biggie, our guard, thumped it from the other side as I started rattling it.

"Pipe down, P, or I'll come in there and unconscious you."

"Dammit!" My legs jittered, and I started to knock crazily around the room, desperately looking for another way out. The closest I got was finding a little bathroom right off the attic, but it didn't have a window or jack-else to crawl out of.

"Or the marines save you," Ki kept nattering, "or a nuclear bomb goes off, or you sugar the villain's car engine so he can't drive and you pedal madly away on your bicycle—"

"What? Sugaring engines?" I asked, gripping my arm again, and having to sit down on the bed when a wave of pain crashed over me. *Come on, keep her talking; she'll stay calmer.* "Um—what, like where sugar mucks it up and the car won't go? Where'd you get that tip?"

She squeezed her eyes shut. "*Charmed?* I can't remember! My brain has been eaten by zombies!" Kiki fell back against the bed. She rolled around some until she saw a cardboard box that said *Toshiba Video Cameras.* Dazed and holding onto her hurt wrist, she staggered over to it and opened it up. The box was full of incredibly tiny gold-colored cams, each about as big as a couple Nilla wafers stacked together. She picked one up and popped her eyes at me. "Oh my God, what's all *this?*"

I breathed in and out, deep and slow, to keep the pain at bay. "That's just trade. When you sell—drugs. If the customer's broke, they can pay in retail."

"And *that* brings me to my even worse problem." She began to cry again, and slapped through another box, finding film and batteries. Like on instinct, she stuck them into the camera she was holding. "Which is that my best friend is apparently a total Cylon. Because

I *knew* that you had a so-called secret life, but I thought you'd just been a band dork or had a little part-time kleptomania like a normal person! Instead, from what I can tell, you used to be like a cross between Princess Diana and the Crips—"

"No," I said, reluctant. *Might as well spill it now.* "I was never a Crip. I was a Snake. I mean, I *wasn't* a Snake. Exactly. I was second in line to inherit, like, some leadership supremacy. But then my mama cut me from the line because I didn't really have it in me. The upshot is, I'm going to have to do some fancy dancing to keep my former blood brothers from beating the hell out of us."

"I can't believe this," she panted. "W-w-we've *got* to get out of here. That hot Donnie Darko guy has it out for you. He's the worst!"

I stared at the floor, just sick. "That's Silver."

"And?"

"And he and me were in love for a long time—though my mom said we weren't allowed to be together—"

"He was your *boyfriend*?!"

"He didn't really turn gangster until I left. Anyway, I was with him until I hooked up with you and Frank." My face crumpled as soon as I said Frank's name. "Oh, Ki, do you think Frank's *so* worried? I'm scared he's gonna freak out when he finds out I'm gone! Once he found a little leftover chronic in my drawer and he went kook. For a second, it got so bad I was scared he was going to dump me. And this is *way* worse!"

Kiki ran over to me, got on her knees, and held my hands. "Mish, look at me, concentrate! We have to get out of here. How about you remind this Silver guy what great times you had together so he'll be nice to us and let us run away!"

I shook my hot, throbbing head. "We're going to have to figure out a way ourselves. Silver's gone cold."

"What does that mean?"

"It happens when a warrior's been through too much shit in battle. He won't give no quarter to his enemies, and he and D think that's what I am now, on account I defected." I choked up worse. "I can't believe it happened to S!"

"Why didn't you ever tell me this?"

"T-to protect you."

"You've got to be *kidding*." She jerked toward the door. "Wait, are they coming? What's that?"

Outside the room, we could suddenly make out the sound of footsteps clattering up the stairs, and voices.

"Get out of my face," I heard Biggie say.

"Yeah, we should go back down; D won't like us fraternizing with the prisoner," I heard Force say.

"Come on, Bigs!" I heard Midget say. And Eager, Game. "Let us in, boy!"

"All . . . right. Just for a minute."

Kiki didn't understand what was happening. She gawked at the door like some fire-breathing alien would crash through it. Then she jammed the videocam to her eye.

But I knew the boyz were coming to do an inspection on a genuine blood royal, the only uncaged Peña left in Los Angeles. I looked down at myself splayed all over a bed and bawling. It made me suddenly remember my mama, who'd took care to receive her gangsters on a throne. And I remembered, too, the advice she gave me at that party in Montebello, when I got sprayed with champagne under the magnolia tree:

Princess M, when the day comes, you demand a Queen's respect, and they will give it to you. And if you want to stay alive, don't you ever let these boyz forget that you rule them, not the other way around.

I wiped my face, pushing all my emotions deep under, in a *snap*.

"Put down the video, Kiki. These dudes got a habit of smashing surveillance cams, 'kay?"

"Oh, okay!" With shaking hands, she stuffed it in her pocket, just as they came in: Game, Midget, Eager, Lalo, and Tha Force.

"Hi, boyz," I said, willing myself to sound tough and cool.

"Hey you, Michelle," they all said, grinning with their white teeth and dimples.

I tapped my right ear with my finger. "What's my name again?"

"Princess M," Eager chuckled, while fiddling with a bootleg cherry-red iPhone.

"Princess M," I said. "I like the sound of that; it's been a while since I've gone by that handle."

"You know you the Princess, P!" Midget called out. "I told you guys she wouldn't forget who she really was."

"This is completely freaking unreal," Kiki gasped.

"Aw, P," Midget cackled. "Last time I saw you, you were just a li'l royal brat."

"P's got some power, now," Eager said, gangly as a greyhound. He scooted up to me, taking a pic of us together with his iPhone. "You see her giving D the business?"

"H-h-h-h-h, d-d-d-d-d-don't, sc-sc-scare," Game stuttered, red-faced.

"That's right, G," I said, finishing his sentence for him, real smooth. "Dragon don't scare me."

"Aw, you didn't forget old Game, neither," Midget said. "P always understood him as good as me."

"I *used* to think that me and Game, and *all* yous, was simpatico, bro," I said, deadlocking them all with my eyes. "But now I fear all yas forgot my language. Kidnapping me. That's *shameful*. It hurts me."

Eager glanced down, and said sheepish, "We just gotta squeeze Samson. We don't mean no rudeness to you."

"We'll see about that." I relaxed my pose, like to seem not just royal, but a little cousinly, too. "So what's up with you these days, Eager? You bump off a granny for that superb iPhone?"

"Yup, I'm all trickin' with the gadgets these days," he bragged. "Look, I even got a wallpaper of T-Rock and Louie; check it out." Eager showed me a pic of two black-haired boyz, shown just as I remembered them: musclier, older, and even tougher versions of Silver. At the bottom of the photo was *RIP, T-Rock and Louie Mendoza, 1990–2008.*

"That's real nice. You giving them a remembrance."

Eager's face shivered with a little cold breeze of grief, but he made himself smile.

I felt sad for those dead boyz too, but made myself shut it off. "You get so savvy with the tech, why don't you put *me* on ya phone, Eag?"

"Yeah—cool, smile, P. I'll put you on the wall." He gestured up at the handmade pics tacked up around the Vault, and I gave another glimpse to those images of boyz grinning in wifebeaters and posing with Glocks, or frowning glamorously before an East L.A. mural of Pancho Villa. "And, you know, P, I *am* the techie around here, now. Two months ago, I figured out a B of A code and hacked three grand from ATMs."

"Well, ain't you all *Mission Impossible*, Eag." I turned to the rest of the boyz. "And Midget, you and Game still tight, I see. Looking good. Reina swore you'd all grow up into some impressive savages, and she was right."

Except for Force, they grinned wider.

"Why don't you heartbreakers do me a favor and tell me where you brought us, eh?" I asked.

"Palm Desert," Eager said.

"Eager!" Force said.

"Who she going to tell?" Eager sputtered at him.

I mused, "Hmm. Palm Desert. Close to Palm Springs, that it?"

"Yeah," Midget said. "But we're far from the city."

Ki and me shot quick looks at each other.

"Our parents won't know to look for us here," she said.

Palm Desert is two hours away from L.A., I calculated. *Kiki's right, because Frank's got no clue I could be this far east. He won't be able to track me at all!* When I thought about my foster pop, my tears nearly came spilling out, and I pretended to flick dust out of my eyes. "Okay, then, Palm Desert! But it's an offense, *hermanos*, putting me in this raggedy room. I'm Reina Peña's *hija*; you got to give me my respect."

They looked at the dirty bed, the junk all over, the busted floor.

"Aw, yeah! Sure, P!"

"This is an offense, I get ya."

"She's right. Girl like her deserves to be all kidnapped in a nicer pad than this."

"Won't do."

"I need a chair," I went on. "It ain't noble, me talking to you all sprawled."

"I'll getcha a chair!" Eager jumped up. "Game, let's get the Barcalounger."

"I need some soap, too, and nice stuff—not no Ivory," I commanded. "And I need decent clothes, for me and Kiki, and somebody to clean up my banged-up arm, please."

"You're not a royal any more, Michelle, so stop giving orders," Silver said, striding through the door. He'd tied his glimmering hair back in a ponytail, and in his hands, he held bandages, cotton balls, and a bottle of Grey Goose vodka.

I swallowed, amazed afresh at his beauty that didn't match his stranger's eyes. "Look, Silver, maybe *you* stopped loving me—"

"That's right, Michelle, you're starting to get the picture," he answered.

It was like another bullet went through me when he said that, but I wouldn't show that pain, either. "But *they* still respect me."

"Then they're fools," Silver said, in an iron voice.

Just then, Eager and Game staggered up the stairs, huffing while they lugged a big, black Barcalounger into the room. "Here's your throne, P, just like Reina's!"

Silver rolled his eyes. "Jesus Christ, don't you wait on her!"

"Dude, we're just making her comfortable," Eager said.

Kiki stared amazed at the boyz fluttering all around me. "Un-frakking-believable."

"Thank you, that's very nice," I said, taking care to admire the shiny black chair Eager and Game put in the center of the attic. They set it up right in front of the rack of fancy clothes and next to the box of Foot Locker soccer balls. I settled into the cushions, careful to keep from jostling my arm, which was starting to go numb. "Okay, S, I see you brought supplies. If you're going to doc us, patch up Ki first."

"Whatever, 'Queenie.'" Silver walked over to Kiki, put some alcohol on a cotton ball, and dabbed her rope-burned wrist.

"Ow!" she hollered.

"Don't be a baby," he said, bandaging her nice and clean.

I stuck out my blue, swelling arm, and Silver made his way over to me, taking his time about it. He wouldn't look at me. Cradling my arm, he started studying it with delicate touches. For a second, he even stroked my arm with a knowing, feather-soft hand. Then he pulled it away, grumbling, "Aw, it's not pretty, but you'll be all right, I promise."

You'll be all right, I promise.

You'll be all right. . . .

I closed my eyes, as those words made another memory burn through me:

Overcast day, in a Montebello park. Two and a half years back. S and I were hanging out, watching Louie and T-Rock practicing control-fall fighting moves on the grass.

Come on, Silver, T-Rock had said. *Spar us; it'll keep ya from getting soft.*

No, dude, Silver'd chuckled. *I'm no natural-born slaya like you guys and D.*

Yo, you like all the Mendozas: born with a knife in ya teeth, Louie'd said. *Even your girl kicks ass, and I don't mean how hard she parties. Show him your moves, P.*

I'd shook my head, taking Silver's arm. *Nah, this is boring. Let's go, baby.*

Um, excuse me, S had told his brother, *but you're not going to fight her.*

T-Rock looked at me. *You still ain't told him? S, Reina ordered us to train P in fighting and stealing and stuff. You know, the Path.*

I told you, I'd said, looking down. *I don't go in for that bizness no more.*

Aw, girl, you're a natch. Check it out. Louie had lurched, cuffed me on the head. Before I knew it, I'd roundhoused him in the right eye, brutal enough to bleed him.

Stop it, you two! Silver had yelled.

I ordered you not to mess with me, Louie! I'd growled.

Sorry! Louie'd grunted, gripping his eye. *I didn't mean to offend you, P!*

Silver had stared at me. *Why didn't you say you were getting trained?*

B-because I love you, and I didn't want you to think I was like them, I'd said, shaking. I'd started to panic because I had attacked as cobra-fast as my mama would, and gripped both of Silver's hands. *Tell me I'm not, S! Tell me I'm like you!*

Silver had smiled at me so sure and loving. *It's okay, sweetface. You're not like them. You'll choose who you want to be. You'll be all right, I promise.*

I opened my eyes to watch Silver carefully cleaning up my bullet-cut.

"Silver, what happened to you?" I asked.

He just crunched up his mouth and didn't answer me.

Midget said, "What do you mean—what happened to his neck?"

That's when I saw the long, thick, white scar cutting down Silver's throat and edging toward his shoulder. I pressed my fingers to the wound, bursting into tears. "S, you got hurt!"

"Silver chastised the Diegos exterminating Louie and T-Rock, but without Reina's backing him, it was an almost-suicide," Midget said. "D had to pull him out of there, and he was still an ass-hair away from the Reaper."

"Oh my God, Silver, honey, I didn't know— *Ai!*"

Silver had just poured the vodka straight onto my shoulder.

"No one wants to hear it, and that'll shut you up," he said.

"Ooh," the rest of the boyz said. "*Got* to smart!"

"Not so bad," Force sneered.

"Girl got shot!" Midget finished his sentence for him. "Baptized by fire!"

I clutched my arm. "S, is that it? You nearly died, and now you're a Stone-Cold, and ya hate me?"

Silver's mouth was a tight line as he finished wrapping me up with gauze and tape. "Yes."

I tried to hold his hands. "Oh, S! Don't say that!"

"Be careful not to hero her too much, boyz," he said, standing up, away from me. "Remember, Michelle just spent the last two years trying to forget your names."

Without another word, Silver stomped out of the room, brushing by Kiki, who skittered out of his way. I jumped a little as S banged the door shut behind him. *Wham.*

"Like I said, he's been real moody since you left, P," Midget said. "He said you didn't love him or us no more."

If it'd been Queenly, I would have hung my head and done some funeral crying over the Silver I'd known. But I heeded my mama's example and toughened myself into a dry-eyed, in-command Princess. I was sweating all over in the effort not to show a scrap of fear or how Silver's hate was bruising me worse than any beating.

"Well, that's not true," I said when I was able.

14

Hours later, when the Snakes had left the Vault and it grew close to morning, I wasn't Princess M anymore. I was just me, snuggled up next to Ki in that busted, dusty bed surrounded by all that stolen treasure. We'd buggled all the way down deep under the covers. Ki kept on that diggie videocam like a night-light, and it propped up the comforter tentlike while she filmed her giant, tearful eyes and quivering lips. I reached out and held her.

"Ki," I said.

"I wanna go home. I want my mommy. I want my daddy."

"You'll see them soon." She was so scared she was going back into her tinier childhood. "You're going back to your ma, and to your pa. No one's going to hurt you. I'm going to get you home no matter what I do. Okay? You're my girl, Ki. You're my girl."

"Oh, Mish, don't leave me alone with these guys," she said. "I don't have anybody but you."

She crumbled in my arms. I'd never seen her like that before, and it scared me.

"Come on, can you sing it? Ki? Just let me hear it."

"N-no. I can't."

"Come on, let's hear it. You can do it. . . ."

It took some nudging, but after a while, she finally crooned for me. In a cracked, unsure voice, she started sob-whispering our song.

My favorite song in the world.

Ki and Mish gonna dom-i-nate
Those li'l girls gone beat your butt
You push them down; they don't hes-i-tate
Cuz they never, never, never give up. . . .

15

Dream-fog, dream-memories. Was this real, or was I asleep? I saw myself in the backseat of T-Rock's red Corvette, hugging Silver.

I love you, S, I said. *You know that, right? I don't ever want to be apart from you; I'm crazy about you.*

Silver smiled. *I love you too, baby. I loved you since before I can remember. Since before I was born.*

We have to be together, I said, kissing his cheeks, his lips. *No matter where that is. Right? You and me will always stick. Always! Even if we have to leave this place—*

Michelle, why are you shivering?

I can't be here anymore! You have to run away with me.

He frowned. *Run away?*

I threw my arms around his neck. *You know she has plans for me. I can't fight her. That's why you have to come with me.*

Where? he asked.

I don't care—Oregon. Alaska. Far away.

He touched my hair. *But my brothers; and Dragon, he's my cousin—*

So what? I asked. *We promised each other: We'd go our own way!*

He nodded. *That's true. But we're still loyal to our kin. All of us, we're one another's country. And who knows, maybe one day, we could change things around here for the better. You could, I mean. Because in a way, I see in you just what Reina sees.*

What do you see? I asked, gazing into his dream-dark eyes, kissing him deeper.

Just then, Silver pulled away from me, wavered, and started to fade.

Silver?

I opened my eyes, which were wet and burning. I stared up at a wood ceiling. Yes, a dream. That had really happened, more than two years ago. But this was now, and I was in the Vault. Somebody was talking and shaking my shoulder. Kiki.

"Wake up, Mish! We've got to get out of here! My mom's going to be so flipped out!"

"Huh?!" I sat straight up, still crying. "What's going on?"

Kiki had washed and changed into a yellow dress that'd been hanging in the Vault. She still had that camera, and started filming me with it, though the camera whacked around because of how hard her hands shuddered. "Well, let me think. Oh, we're totally abducted. We could be, like, killed at any moment. You have been completely lying to me for two years about who you are. I don't even know you. That's basically, you know, the update."

"Oh, Ki, okay, just give me a second. I can't think straight yet." I blinked the tears out of my eyes, then rubbed my deadly sore arm while moving quick over to the bathroom. I was already starting to sweat again, my neck getting tense. I washed my face until I felt calm enough to talk. "Okay, I'm better," I said, when I walked back out.

"So?" Kiki asked. "What's the plan?"

"I swear, I'm working on getting us out of here," I said.

She marched over to the Barcalounger and flopped into it. "Oh, thanks, P. I feel so much better now!"

I looked over at the front door, twisting up my eyes as I tried to cogitate. "Look, I get you're mad, but please don't fuss—I've got to figure out how we can walk out of here, and not get *carried*, you know?" I moved over to the door, to see if Biggie still guarded us on the other side. Getting down on all fours, I peered under the door, to see Biggie's two big New Balances. And that sight made me go from sad to instantly *pissed*: "Oh, dammit! We can't be stuck here! Frank is going to panic attack his *ass* off!"

"Okay, I am really completely furious," Kiki said. "But the bigger thing is, I just don't *get* this. When you first showed up at Rosa Parks looking like an almost regular girl—what, was I so totally high on Dexatrim not to see who you really were?"

I stared at Biggie's foot, hissing as quiet as I could, "Is there a knife in here? Something sharp? I swear to Christ, I'll shank him—"

"What's 'shanking?'" Kiki pressed the heels of her hands to her eyes. "Why didn't you tell me you knew these guys!"

I squinted through the keyhole. "I didn't tell you because I was worried you'd freak, honey. You know how you are."

"What do you mean?"

I cleared my throat. "You know, all smart and nervy and spastic and stuff—I knew you'd *wig*."

"No, I'm not really," she sputtered. "I'm a totally normal, regular person!!"

I looked over my shoulder at her.

"Well, I'm working on it! And, actually, on that point—okay, I'm just telling you this finally! My mom says that I sort of let myself live in your shadow, and that I just really shouldn't anymore!"

"God, Kiki! Do we have to talk about your self-esteem problems *now*?" I peered at the clothes on the hangers and dashed over to them. Quick-changing from my grunged Che Guevara sweater and garbaged jeans, I slipped into a pair of black Nike warm-up pants and a red lululemon T-shirt. Then I took a hanger wire, unbending it. I moved back to the door and poked the wire into the keyhole. "Look, you don't live in anybody's shadow!" I wiggled the wire deeper into the hole. "You're great, and smart, and really, really normal, okay?" I started whispering again, jiggering the lock. "All right, here we go, I've almost got it—" My heart was jackhammering, and my breath came out in short little scared puffs. When I opened up the door, I was going to *push* that sucka down the stairs.

"You know how to pick locks?" Kiki whispered back.

"Shh!" I said. Then I mouthed, *Get ready to run, okay?*

Kiki jumped up from the Barcalounger. *Okay!!!*

Clack. The door unlocked, opened—and suddenly I saw boyz climbing the staircase.

"Hey, Bigs," Eager said. "You lookin' *tired*, my man."

"What, you all want to see them *women* again?"

"We just checking on P, bro," said Midget.

"Shoot!" I pulled the door back, shutting it as silent I could.

"What?"

I scrambled to my feet, hurly-burly. "They're coming to see me again!" I waved my hands madly at Ki, because she stood in front of the throne. "*Get away!* Give me the chair. I've got to look dignified!"

"Dignified?"

"These boys are gonna *hurt* us if I don't make them respect me, Kiki," I jabbered.

She wriggled her nose at me. "What? You are being so galactically bizarre—"

"Move!"

She scatted away from the throne, sat on the vodka crate, and I jumped into the seat. I smoothed my hair, and tucked in my shirt, all tidy. *Breathe, Peña! Don't freak!*

Knock, knock, knock.

"P?"

Knock, knock. "Princessa Eme!"

"It supremely grosses me out when they call you that," Kiki whispered.

"Hush down!" I gasped. "And pull your skirt over your knees."

She pulled it down, more modestlike. "What do they *want* with you?!"

"I don't know—we're going to find out." I pulled the sleeve all the way down on my right arm, to hide my bandage there. *Michelle, remember to never show an inch of frailty in ya. Cover up your wounds, because as my daughter, you the baby lion of the jungle, and all the jackals gonna smile if they smell blood.* I tightened my jaw, focusing on Mama's long-ago counsel.

"*Okay,* you can come in now, boyz!"

16

In they came: Eager, Midget, Game, Lalo, Tha Force.

"Hey, P!"

"*Princesa!*"

"Brought ya breakfast burritos I made."

"Need anything?"

"How about a ride home?" I looked at them stern in the eyes.

They wrinkled their noses. "Come on, P, you know we can't do that—"

"Fine. But how about you give your respects to my friend, too?" I ordered.

"Hi," they all said to Kiki in a chorus.

She only looked at the ground, and tried to appear all inconspicuous.

I smiled like I had an appetite, and made myself munch the burrito Lalo placed respectful in my hands. "Thank you, Lalo. So, what's the word?"

"Coming to see the monkey in its cage." Force grinned at me nasty.

"Shut up," Lalo, Midget, and Eager all barked out.

"Ooh," I said, forceful. "My mama's gonna *cry* some tears when I tell her how you boyz' manners is grown so foul, Force! Back in the day you *vatos* was *knights*."

Game whacked Force upside the head.

"Ow!"

"Yikes!" Kiki said.

"*Gracias* for that, G." I said.

He winked at me. "W-w-w-w-welcome."

I settled back in my throne. "Where's Dragon?"

"Gone to Chino with Book," Midget said.

I said, "Book—what, is that the other big goon? Crazy shave-job?"

Midget nodded. "They's interrogizing King about the money, to get you out of here."

I forced my voice to stay chill when I asked, "Silver with them?"

"Nah, he's downstairs reading, like usual," Lalo said. "*Autobiography of Malcolm X*, I think."

"What bookworm *should* be doing is running the numbers," said Eager. "Get us our percent. That's why we're here—"

"Will you all stop ragging on that?" Force sneered.

"Just cuz you're getting your cut before us, ya don't wanna hear nothing—" Eager yakked at him.

"What you all squabbling about?" I asked.

"It sounds like money," Kiki said, in this soft and timid voice.

"Hmph," they all grumbled.

"How *are* you chickenheads making it these days, anywho?" I asked. "Ya still bizzing weed, as usual?"

They rolled their eyes. "Nah. Not right now."

"If you're not dealing drugs, how'd you rent this crib?"

Eager flipped up the visor on his baseball cap. "Dragon bought it for us."

"D ain't old enough to buy a house, Eager," I said. "He just turned eighteen—"

"Anybody can buy anything they want with money, P," he replied. "The Burner sold it to D after he got kingmade. You know, before he cut us off cuz we couldn't pay back what King stole—"

I said, "You boyz now owing Freddie Gonzales a hell of a lot of money, from what I understand."

"Yeah, but Dragon came up with this business *plan*, like." Eager kicked the Foot Locker box. "About two months ago, he was going on about how we could make enough to pay back the Burner *and* get rich. Except, we ain't seen a penny yet."

"And why's that?" I asked.

"Something's rotten, you ask me," Eager said. "I was trying to tell the boyz that Dragon's digits look *funk-ay*, but they don't take their advices from me."

I crossed my arms in front of my chest, like my arm wasn't killing me at all. "Let's hear Dragon's plan."

"So, D told each of us we had to pitch in three Gs into what he calls the Snake investment fund," Eager started to explain.

"He told you to pony up three *thousand* dollars?" I asked. "But without weed, the only bank you got is Monopoly."

"Yeah, we made it, you know, snatching handbags, pickpocketing, and me with the ATM gig," Eager said. "D told us we'd be all earning back fifty K."

"That's a ton of moolah, man," I said. "Smells fishy."

"Yeah, it sounded pretty good," Eager said. "D told us all we had to do was bring in some new bloods, and they'll pay three Gs each, too. That's how we make the money, off the membership fees."

I shook my head. "Did Dragon tell ya how many new rebels you'd have to blood into the Snakes to make fifty K?"

Eager looked nauseated. "I showed D the equations, but he says it ain't no dilemma."

"Will you just shut ya nose?" Force asked. "Everything's on the up and up. Snakes never lie to their brothers."

"Always a first time, Force," I replied. "And this is it."

Kiki looked at me and nodded.

"Ki?" I asked.

"I *think* this is called a pyramid scheme," she said. "Mrs. Elmer told us about them in math. They're totally nasty; people can lose everything."

"Shut up!" Force said.

Kiki's lips turned white. "I'm sorry!"

Midget frowned at Game, then me. "What the fuck is she talking about?"

"You should treat her with more respect," I said, and gave them a sly smile. "Kiki's just telling you that you been conned, my men. Because, dudes, there's no *way* you could each earn back fifty K from three-thousand-dollar membership fees. It's simple addition. For nine of you to make fifty each, you'd have to get in, what, 150 new gangstas, each of them with three spare K. And that just ain't going to happen."

"What?!" Everybody but Eager yelled out. "Conned?!"

"That ain't right!" Force yelped out. "That's screwy girl-math, man!"

Eager squeezed his eyes shut. "Nah, it ain't."

"Don't we get a *little* money?" Lalo asked. "I wanted a car, like what Force and Game is got."

"That's right," I muttered. "Force has a car, and Game too? Parked outside."

All the boyz slumped their shoulders and moped very miserable. Kiki sat on the box of Grey Goose, touching her lips nervous, all frail and exhausted.

As for myself, though, I started to feel pretty good! Suck on *that,* D! I jumped out of the Barcalounger and strolled around the Vault, past the boxes of video cameras, Grey Goose, iPods, MP4s, designer duds, and new soccer balls.

"Aw, stop all that whining." I nudged the crate of MP4s, then kicked the box of iPods. *Keep them liking you,* I thought. *Make them see you're on their side. They'll let down their guard and then you and Ki can run.* "Lookie here. I see some toys might cheer ya up."

Eager squatted in front of the Foot Locker box with the soccer balls, holding his head like it'd go rolling off his neck. "Dragon says we can't touch that stuff."

"I'll bet he *does* say that, Eager," I said. "I'll just *bet* he says you can't touch all these goodies. Just like he says you're gonna make fifty Gs easy as pie."

I rummaged through a box of shiny-boxed new iPods.

"P . . ." Eager said, like I was a wicked girl, but he sort of liked it. "P, *no!*"

I tossed an iPod to Lalo. "Whoops! How'd that get over there?"

Lalo stuffed the iPod down his shirt. "I didn't see nothing."

"That iPod's gonna cost you your *head,* Lalo," Eager said. "D wants to give all this stuff to the Burner tonight, hoping it'll cool the situation down."

I grabbed a leather Sean John jacket, tossing it to Eager. "All D has done to you is lie and get your ass in trouble. Maybe it's time you start thinking for yourself. Snatch all this booty and just *scoot,* know what I'm saying? Leave the liar holding the bag—"

"Yo, that's some insurrection," Force said.

Eager held the jacket up. "R-right. I—can't. . . ."

"Damn, she's got a point, man," Midget said. "D ripped us off!"

Eager murmured, "I did always kind of want this thing. . . ."

While the other boyz watched all breathless, he slipped it on.

"Oh, yeah, that's style!" Eager marveled. He swaggered around the room, while the boyz grabbed at him, cackling. "Ooh, ooh—ooooh! How I look?"

"*Pimp!* I want one!" Midget said.

"Any more iPods in there?" Force mumbled.

"S-s-s-s?" Game asked.

"Sure there's sneakers." I laughed. "Anything you want, boyz!" I hurled out black Diesel puzzle sneakers, mirrored Republica sunglasses, a candy-red Biebel skateboard, and a big silver chain-looking L.A.M.B. necklace. . . .

"*What* is going on here!?" a voice suddenly called out.

Silver stood in the doorway, muscles bumping big out of his shirt as he flapped a paperback in the air. Biggie peered at us, too, checking out the garage sale like he wanted in.

"Do you know how much this stuff is *worth*?" Silver threw the book at Eager's head. "Get your grimy hands off it!"

Biggie eyeballed Eager's jacket. "That's cold, ya digging in Dragon's trade."

The Snakes stared at Silver, holding their little treasures.

"Put that all back, I said!" Silver hollered.

Biggie walked over to Eager, hit him on the shoulder. Eager took off the jacket and gave it to him. Biggie put it on, smiling so his scar went shiny and crooked.

Eager rapped out, "S, we've been chatting with P here, and we got to ask: Where *is* our money? No more dallying—we got to know!"

Silver suddenly looked like he got a bug up his nose. "Ah, geez—"

"Where's our fifty Gs, Silver?" they all hollered at once, so loud that Kiki jerked and nearly fell over.

Silver shot his eyes over to me. "*What* have you been talking about up here?"

"The Snake investment fund—that's what it was called?" I asked.

"Yepper," Midget answered.

Silver looked mortified. "I caught that much. What'd she tell you?"

"What you always used to tell back when I knew you, S," I said. "The *truth*!"

Silver glared at me again, then said, "Boyz, I can explain—I *told* D not to play games with the digits."

"You *knew* he was cheating us?!" Midget hollered.

"Yes," Silver admitted. "Dragon told me he'd make it right after the danger had passed, so I kept my mouth shut. He thought you wouldn't fork over if you thought it was just to pay a debt!"

"Well, we wouldn't have!" Eager, Lalo, and Midget belted out at the same time.

Silver screwed up his reddening face. "You think I want the Burner to get a fucking dime of your wad? He killed my brothers! I want him dead! But I'd do *anything* right now—including lying and stealing from you tightwads *and* tripping on my old lady—*because he is gonna kill us!*"

All their shoulders sagged. Every single one of the boyz gave a big, sad sigh.

"Dang, dang, *dang*," Midget said. "Money's gone."

They moped like goats, as my mind ticked. *How can I use this against D? Because I've got to get Ki out of here; I don't need more clues to know this boat is gonna sink fast.* My eyes landed on the box of soccer balls.

"Hey, Silver," I said, hatching an escape plan on the fly. *If I can just get them outside, and steal a pair of keys while we're goofing around, maybe Ki and I can get out of here. But S is the one I've got to convince. How am I going to do that? He hates me now.*

The answer came to me: *You have to make him remember the old days.*

I said in a breezy, easy voice: "I've got to say, S, I leave you guys alone for two years, and you turn from the hardest-core rebels in Montebello into the sorriest-looking bunch of numbnuts I ever did see." I legged it over to the Foot Locker box, nudging Eager aside. "Back in the day, we were all laughing, joking, kicking it."

Silver muttered, "No time for jokes right now."

"What I'm saying is, we were *one another's country*," I pressed. "We all loved one another. We didn't pull stunts like this."

His mouth dragged down. "Maybe you didn't notice, but these are grim times, calling for some harsh measures."

Bending down to the Foot Locker box, I picked up a soccer ball. I walked up to him, holding it like a gift.

"I did notice, baby."

"Do *not* call me that," he said, in a rough, splitting voice. He put his fists up, pressed them to his forehead, and groaned. "Oh, God! We are in so deep!"

I said, "Look, I understand you're pissed at me—" I stared into his dark angel eyes, and my words faltered. "A-and—"

I'm not very good at this. I don't know how to put up an act with him. He knows me better than anyone.

I gave a short cough and lowered my tone: "And I know you don't want me anymore."

His eyes stayed on my face, and his cheeks flushed. "That's—right."

"Still," I went on, taking a step closer to him, my face turning hot. I was now talking to him in my old sweetheart's voice, and it felt dangerously right. "I want to see you smile again, okay? I can't stand seeing you like this!"

All the boyz were standing around, studying us. Kiki frowned at me. *What are you doing?*

Silver shook his head. "Michelle, maybe you don't get it! We're going to be *wiped out*!"

I smiled at him, gentle. "Not right now, we ain't. And I'm just saying, you boyz need to let off some steam, seriously. So, just, come outside with me, kick the ball around. Let's pick up a game like we used to, back in the day. It won't hurt anything."

"You want to play *soccer*?" Silver asked.

I papped the ball in my left hand. Then I started bouncing it on my knee.

Pap, pap, pap.

He scowled, but kept his eyes on the ball. "Forget it."

Still, Silver watched close as I started to skittle the soccer ball around—bouncing it on my knee, dribbling it rapid-fire from ankle to ankle. I hadn't played the sport in about two years, but the moves came back to me natural. It made my shoulder hurt like a motha, though.

"Check it out!" Midget said. "Girl's on fire!"

I kept up my soccer girl act for a minute, two minutes. And it worked.

Silver's mouth started to tweak in a rusty smile. "You're playing me. You're not just trying to get me out there on the field because you miss kicking it with us."

"No, I do miss you," I said, my heart shattering against my ribs. "I hate how you're acting, but I do—" *Oh, God, that's the truth.*

He clenched his jaw, making a move to walk out of the room. "Never mind this, I've got to go downstairs, take care of business—"

I blurted, desperate, "Just come on, dammit! Remember how we were?!"

He halted mid-step, his hand on the doorknob.

"All I'm asking for is a little ball," I said. "It's totally harmless. We need a breather. All of you do. We all used to have a good time. We *were* family, like you once said. And that ain't changed. Let's just go have a little fun, remind ourselves how it used to be."

He stared at the floor. "'How it used to be.' How it *used* to be was the only thing that ever mattered to me." He looked up at me, and then, there it was: I saw an old tenderness flicker through his eyes.

I've got him, I thought. *I've caught him.*

Or—maybe I wasn't so sure. Maybe *I* was the one getting dragged back in. Because, oh, I wanted to be in those big arms of his, and have him look at me like that for hours and hours.

"Come on, S, let's go out," Eager said. "It'll just be for a goof."

And Midget: "It won't hurt nothing, man, and we could use a couple laughs."

Silver stared at me, his gaze moving from my eyes to my mouth.

"Fine, fine, enough already!" He finally caved. "But just for a minute."

17

The next thing I knew, I was standing in that grassy vacant lot outside the Fort, staring up at a soccer ball that was flying right down to my head.

"*Saque de puerta*, Eager!" I bellowed.

"Bring it!" Eager hustled up to me from the other side of the field.

"Intercept her!" Silver cried out, his face shining. "*Defensa!*"

The ball shot down right onto the sweet spot on my forehead. *Wham!*

It ricocheted right to Eager's zippy-kicking feet.

And we were *off*. Three boys on my team, two on Silver's, we zigzagged down the gold-grass field. Ahead, I saw Game's wild, toothy smile. Force laughed almost like a non-evil kid. Midget let out an Indian whoop, while Lalo ran slow, belly swinging.

Eager hurtled to Midget, Silver's goalie, the ball spinning between his heels. Peering past him, I spied the crumbling-looking mansion, with the poster of Shakira in the window. Kiki sat on the Fort's porch steps, watching us while being guarded by Biggie. In the side garage sat a dinged-looking brown Ford, and on the front yard squatted the Chevy. The house sat just off a long, black highway stretching to Palm Desert. As soon as I had a pair of car keys, *that* would be me and Ki's route back to L.A. "Punch it, Eager!" I yelled out, acting like I wasn't doing surveillance but playing soccer normal.

"Sock it in the pocket, P!" Eager hit the ball with the side of his foot, spinning it my way, just as Silver swooped me.

"Ready to dance, Michelle?" he asked, shadowing my every move as I started to tap a wicked defense.

Silver was so close that it was almost like we *were* dancing with our old natural rhythm, and I felt less in control than ever. "I know you don't *really* hate me, S," I said, my nerves all a-jumble as I skittered the ball between my feet. "You're just putting on an act—"

He clenched his mouth and stole the ball from me. "You are such a piece of work."

I shoplifted it back, as my wounded shoulder cramped harsh. "You're lying to yourself if you think you do hate me. Nobody ever knew me like you. And nobody ever knew you like *me*."

"No, I never knew you," he said.

"You *really* believe that?" I asked.

Pap, pap, pap. He scooped the ball with his heel, toggled it. "I don't just believe it. I *learned* it, the hard way."

My voice went tight with emotion: "So nothing that happened between us means anything? Like don't you remember—S—that time with the Limas, and we were *so scared*—"

"Don't—"

"And you said, *I got you, Michelle*, and I said, *I got you too*—"

"What *I* can't forget, baby, is the last day I saw you—"

I winced. "S, please, let's not go there—"

But it was too late. Suddenly, the ball, the boyz, the vacant lot disappeared, and I saw that last day too:

Two years ago. In the park again, sitting on a bench. Silver had held my face, his eyes shimmering.

Michelle, you can't go to Westchester! he'd said. *You can live with me and my brothers!*

I told him, *I can't be here no more; I asked you to come with me.*

He looked as if he'd been shot. *Did you fall out of love with me?*

No! I'd said. *But I won't wind up like her! I will if I don't break clean from you all.*

But remember what we swore? Silver asked. *That we were different.*

We lied to ourselves, S, I'd said. *We're not different, but you can't see it.*

You're killing me, Michelle!

I'm sorry, I'm sorry! But I can't see you again.

"Ugh, ugh," Silver and I both grunted now.

We were still scissor-legging each other in a competition for the ball that was getting brutal, fast, and sweaty.

"I should have kept you locked up in there," he said. "I can see all you want to do is mess with my head."

"I guess it's easier not feeling anything, isn't it, Stone-Cold?" I pickpocketed the ball from under his toes.

He just nabbed it back. "Dead men don't feel, Michelle. You already killed me worse than a war."

"Oh damn you, I am losing my patience!" I felt my eyes blaze. "Fine! If you're dead, then I guess that's why you suck so bad at soccer."

He nearly chuckled, but cut it off. "You think this is funny?" he huffed. Our faces were an inch apart. Our lips were nearly touching.

"No. This comedy ain't funny. You are breaking my *heart,* boy. But I'll tell you what *is* a laugh, S."

"Oh, help me, I can't wait to hear."

"It's funny how even when I've got more buckshot in me than a stuffed bear, you *still* can't beat me," I said.

Curling my lip up wicked, I bapped the ball hard with my heel—straight across our goal line, whizzing it past Midget's flailing arms.

"Goal!" I yelled.

"Damn!"

"Hail the Queen, handsome!" I locked eyes with him so my heart gave a powerful *thunk-thunk* skip, but then I reminded myself, *Peña, you are on a mission right now; stop mooning at him!* Giving him a casual slap on his back pocket, I felt the pockets on his chest. They were empty, though—no phone, no keys. "Score one Peña!" I yelled, running back to my side of the field before he could clue in that I'd been frisking him.

"Sucks, man!" Midget shouted behind me, as Game hoisted him on his shoulders. "Woo!"

I papped the ball up at him. "Eager! Come kick this in!"

He ran down the field. "Sure thing!"

"Good man." Ignoring the pain in my wound, I whapped him all sportsbuddy-like on the chest—felt his empty shirt pocket—and his hip and butt—where I felt his iPhone in his jeans. As he turned around, I tried to slip the phone from his pocket, sneaking my digits in easy. Eager darted away too fast for me, though. *Shoot!*

"*Patada!*" Eager yelled.

The ball came zooming over to me. I juggled it while a crowd of madcap gangsters steamed up to my tail. Soon that squad of scoundrels and me were all shoulder-to-shoulder, cursing, tackling, and tangling our legs together. Brushing my hand on Game's back pocket, I felt a set of keys. Just as Silver snatched the ball from me, I light-fingered them up my sleeve.

"Whoa! Woo!" I hollered. "Silver got it!"

Eager, Lalo, Force, and Silver went stampeding down the other side of the field.

Game and I stood there, about ten feet away from Midget, who was at the goal.

"You play a good offense, there, G," I said, watching Eager swipe the ball from Silver, and everybody race toward us again.

"It's o-o-o-o-okay you took them," he said, quiet enough so nobody else would hear. "You can have th-th-th-them."

"Took what?" I broke out in a hot, panicked sweat. "What are you talking about?"

"M-my car keys. Mine's the Ford; it's in the garage."

"Oh, G. How did you *know*?"

"I ain't in love with you, so I can see you pretty clear, girl. I-I saw you trying to lift off Silver right away."

The keys pressed cold up my sleeve. I smiled at him grateful. "You ain't stuttering so bad right now, G. You know that?"

"S-s-sometimes I forget to be nervous. Then I speaks normal."

"Dragon make you nervous?"

He slowly grinned. "Just cuz ya stutter don't make ya stupid. That D-d-d-dragon's a devil. Which is why I ain't in a m-m-m-mind to keep you and that Kiki girl around here, see? He'll get y-y-ya hurt, bad. Though don't mistake me, things ain't much worse than they were before. K-k-king w-w-w-was a killa too—" His eyes shot forward again: "Oooops—look out !!!!"

I turned around to see Eager and Force barreling headfirst toward us as they fought each other for the ball. "Gonna whip ya ass!" they grunted at each other.

"Wait!" I yelled, trying to scoot out of their way.

Too late. *Thud!* Eager and Force skidded on the field, but couldn't stop themselves from slamming into me and G. Eager sailed above me, hand-flapping like a freaky Spider-Man. Force somersaulted on Game's belly before crashing into my backside. As Eager and G flopped on me, too, I felt my legs slip. I went tumbling, arms stretched out, flat on my stomach.

"Ai!" The keys shot out from my sleeve and into my hand, glittering under the sun.

The rest of the boyz came rushing over, scared looks on their faces.

"P! You okay?!" Midget asked.

I hollered, from the fresh throbbing in my shoulder.

"Michelle!" Silver hurled Eager, Force, and Game off me. He bent down next to me, scanning me with his hot eyes. "Back off! We're playing too rough with her."

"I'm okay," I wheezed.

"Stay still," Silver said.

Reaching down, he touched my shoulder to check it. Gently, he ran his fingers down to my wrist. I had a sudden, way-too-vivid recall of all the days he'd put his hands on me and wrapped his body around mine. The tender look in his eyes. *I love you, Michelle. I love you.*

I squeezed my eyes shut. "Silver."

That's when he saw what I grasped in my hand.

"What's she got a hold of?" Force gabbled out, half his face green from grass stains.

Lalo peeped over Force's shoulder. "They's some keys, man."

"Are those *Game's* car keys?" Midget asked.

Force untangled himself from Game by punching him in the gut. "Looks it to me."

"Mish, are you okay?" I could hear Kiki calling out from the Fort's porch.

I kept gripping onto the keys.

"D *told* us she's a sneak!" Force said. "Trying ta fool us, get away."

"Not trying to snow one over on the Snakes, was ya, P?" Eager asked.

"Course she's snowing ya, asshead!" Force spat.

"Why do you have Game's car keys, Michelle?" Silver asked, in a colder, quieter voice. "You steal them?"

"*Yes*, of course I did!" I lifted my eyes, slapping him with my look. "Silver, you know this is crazy, and that you have to let us go!"

"*Mish?*" Kiki called out again, her voice getting screamy. "You get hurt?"

Silver didn't answer me. But suddenly the rest of the boyz looked scared.

I thumped my chest, howling. "Why are you all treating me like this! Ain't all yous and me been amigos since we's just itty-bitties?"

Slowly, all of them nodded but Silver and Force.

"Then *please* let us go before D gets back! Silver—Silver look at me. I am so sorry about your brothers. I'm so sorry about every-thing. But you can't keep us here!"

Silver sat back, his face hidden by his hair.

"I'll come back and see you," I swore. "The first thing I'll do is talk to King—and settle things with Reina for you! I still love you all; don't you idiots know that? And I'll be loyal to you again—I promise it! But I got a foster dad, Frank Redman. He loves me, too, except shit like this wigs him *serious*. And I really don't want to vex him too bad." My eyes started overflowing.

"Mish!" Kiki ran up, Biggie thumping after her.

"B-b-b-b—" Game said.

"Biggie," Midget said. "Even if we let her go, he'll stop her from running."

"He's strong," Eager said, unsure.

"What are you guys talking about?" Force wheezed. "You ain't let-ting no hostage go cuz we play a little *futbol*! Dragon'll whipya!"

"Force," I said. "Dragon *cheated* you!"

He started blinking really rapid, like everything was getting crazi-fied in his head.

"You got to keep faith with your family!" he blathered. "Right Silver?"

Silver reached up to touch the scar on his throat, and didn't say a word.

"N-n-n-n-n—" Game said.

107

"Not faithful like this," Midget finished. "Hurting P—that was foul, not faithful."

"Oh, no, are they messing with you?" Kiki screamed, reaching us.

I felt the circle of boyz loosening toward me, opening up. They still looked worried, but didn't lay hands on me. Maybe they'd even help me if Biggie put up a fight. I could drive Game's car out of here. . . .

I looked at the keys in my hand. "Ki, let's go."

"What, what's happening? Where are we going?" Kiki's forehead wrinkled, and she turned. "Wait—that's . . ."

Just that second I heard a deep stereo bass bumpin' in the distance. "Oh, no."

Dawng dawng dawng.

A flash of shiny black appeared on the road leading from the house to the city. Diggy-O's rapping floated out the 'Vee's rolled-down windows:

Uprise Montebello Uprise! Uprise Montebello Uprise!

Make the men fear and the women cry

In the next beat, Dragon had pulled his beast-looking Humvee up to the house.

Silver lifted his hair from his face, so I saw his bleak, rough eyes.

"Baby," I said. "Please. Help us get away. Maybe later, when D's not looking—"

He stared at me, his mouth broke-looking from grief. "How could you have left me, Michelle?"

Peering up at Dragon, he glided his hand over mine. I thought he was caressing me, until he pried my fingers open, hard.

"S—don't!"

"You're not going anywhere until we get that money," he said, closing his fist over the keys.

18

Dragon stared at us out of the Humvee window. He'd been pretty Frankenstein-faced driving up to the Fort, but as soon as he saw me out on the field, he got a powerful glowering look on. Before he could get all Satan on me, though, he jumped out the car, running to the other door. He pulled out Book from the front seat. Book came wriggle-sliding out of the Humvee. Blood stained him bright and shining.

"Ah, ah!" Book screamed.

"Biggie, help me!" Dragon roared.

Biggie and the pipsqueaks were already running to the Humvee. Biggie picked up Book under the neck and knees. I saw then that Book had a long, ragged cut through his shirt, and the blood flowed out. He kicked out his legs from agony, and roared.

Big-eyed Kiki had backed away from our grass-stained dog-pile. I scooted to her, and saw that she half-hid the video camera behind her skirt. She was aiming it at Book.

"You've got to put that away!" I hissed. "Thuggies don't like their crimes to get on film unless it's *Girls Gone Wild*!"

"Okay!" she whispered, and tucked the camera back into her pocket. "Oh my God, do you see him? It's awful!"

"He got it in the side," we heard Dragon say to Biggie. "Get the first aid we got in the basement—see if you can stitch him."

"*Ai, agh!*" Book screeched as Biggie carried him into the house.

Dragon made his way over to us. His neck and chest gleamed with Book's blood.

"What happened to Book?" Midget chippered out.

Dragon ignored him, staring at me with evil eyes. "*What* is she doing out here?"

I said, "Dragon, we were just—"

D twisted up his face and yelled at me *hellish*: "*I'll take out a tooth for every word that comes out of your mouth right now. It's a promise!*"

"Just try it, *sucka!*"

Silver clapped his hand over my mouth. "I'll put her back in the Vault, D. Don't worry about her."

"Mish!" Kiki called out. She ran up to Dragon and faced him, feet apart. "*Do not hurt my friend!*"

"Shut up," everyone answered her—not Dragon, but the rest of the Snakes.

Little drops of sweat sparkled on Kiki's upper lip. She looked as scared as if she was looking at her own death. But she didn't budge.

"I just had a rough morning, so maybe you shouldn't be messing with me right now, *chica*," Dragon growled.

She breathed shallow: "I've seen what you can do, Dragon. I know that you're *bad*."

"Damn straight he bad!" Tha Force cawed out.

"But you know what else I see?" Her eyes shone with terror tears.

A pause. He studied her. "Okay—I bite. What?"

"That you're good, too, Dragon," she said. "That you're *good*."

His eyes shimmered—and his mouth softened, nearly curled. "Pretty li'l thing, you get a hold somebody's crack? You trippin'?" he tried to joke. But his voice faltered.

"No, I can see it in you," she said. "I'd bet anything that you've actually got a heart. You don't want to hurt us. It's not who you really are."

"You think you know who I really am?" Dragon asked, and oh, it *shocked* me to see his face suddenly turn emotional-red as he met her stare. I thought he'd either hit her or kiss her feet. But before he could lose his mud, everybody else began to laugh.

"Yeah, right!" Tha Force guffawed. "D's heart's tenda as Jesus's, baby! Amen, give me some of that lovin', Dragon!"

"You laughing, homes?" Dragon seethed. "Book could be dying inside the house right now, so shut up!"

"Mmm!" I yelled under Silver's hand, but he just grabbed me up tighter, pressing his chest against the back of my shoulders.

"Michelle, I'm not trying to hurt you," he whispered. "But you have to stop this, or he'll go Ciudad Juarez on you *and* her."

Wiping the human feeling off his face with his sleeve, Dragon lifted his bloodstained hand. He pressed a finger to Kiki's lips.

"Quiet, cutie," he said. "I know you being all a cowgirl there for this garbage you call a friend, but sticking out your pretty neck for her ain't good for your health."

"Don't touch me." Kiki yanked her head away.

"You know who I will touch?" D turned from her and scanned the boyz. "The body who thought it was a good idea to let P out."

The boyz' laughter died down quick.

"We was all playing some *futbol*, man," Midget said. "It ain't right to keep P cooped up, dawg! She's a Peña!"

"You questioning me?" Dragon moved up to him, smooth and slow. Midget was still on the ground where the dog-pile had been, and looked up, his cheek twitching.

Dragon hit Midget hard across the face. *Smack! Smack! Smack!*
Midget held his cheek, crying, "*No, D!*"

The other boyz turned rock-faced, but Game hollered. "*D-D-D-Dragon!*"

Silver's heart whacked against my spine as he said, "Dragon, it's my fault. I got worried about Michelle, thought I'd give her some air. It was a mistake."

Dragon shot Silver a cruel look, but he stopped hitting Midget.

"Stop crying now, you *fucking* disability!" he said to Game, whose face was wet. "Can anybody here tell me why I'm so mad?"

"Because you the boss, D," Force answered. "'N' we didn't follow your orders."

Dragon pointed at me. "No. It's because if she gets loose, then I don't got *nothing* to protect you."

"Dragon, what are you saying?" Silver asked. "What went down today, man?"

Dragon hesitated. He took a good long look at S, who still held onto me. "You tell me. I ain't gone six hours and this turns from a hostage situation into a fuckin' picnic? Is P messing with your head, Silver? Making you forget your oath to them that's *loyal* to you?"

"Dragon, tell me you got that money," Silver insisted, moving his hands down to my arms. "*Tell* me you saw King in the pen and he told you where the cash was in exchange for Michelle. And now it's all over, and we can just let them go."

All of us watched silent as D's eyes went red once more, and his face flinched. But then it was like he got a hold of himself: He shook his head, breaking out in this crocodile smile. "Yeah, sure I did, S."

"Serious?"

"Yeah, I got the money from King. I met him in the pen and told him we had his sister. And he gave up the location of where he'd hid the bank."

"He *did*??"

"I said so, didn't I!?"

"Then what happened to Book?" Silver asked.

"We had some complications, which you do not have to worry after—because you got to concentrate on what we gonna do with the Burner—"

"I don't understand—" Silver pressed. "And why aren't you arranging a trade?"

Veins stuck out of Dragon's forehead. "Hear me! Never mind all that now! Because, listen, all of you! This game ain't done! We are on the Burner's clock! So hup to it *right now* and get this girl out of the open air. Though I got the cash, we *still* need Michelle Peña locked up safe as crown jewels. Because this ain't no ordinary female— Michelle is a royal captive, and so she is worth your *life*. You play games with your life?"

Silver was looking at him confused, and so were Midget and Game, but the rest of them shook their heads *no*.

"So you mind me," he went on, blazing-eyed. "Or I will beat you, *and* bad, but only cuz I love you. This girl Kiki got an insight into me, ya badasses, because I love yous like yous got my own soft heart beating in ya. I only seek to save *your lives*. So know I am telling you the God's honest: If you disobey me by even one move, then we are gonna get hunted to our graves, I *swear* to you."

Whatever lies he'd been blustering before, you could tell by the terror in his eyes that he wasn't lying about *that*. Everyone instantly got so scared that no one breathed a word about the three Gs D'd stolen from each of them. Nobody asked about who had cut Book, either, or where the money was, or why, if Dragon really had it, he still wasn't letting me and Ki go.

Dragon looked back down at Midget. "You hear me, boy?"

"You won't get no argument from me, boss," Midget forced out the words, the left side of his face already bruising.

"You hear me, Game?"

"Y-y-y-y-y-ou—"

"He says yes, D," Midget lied.

"Good." Dragon thrust his chin out. "We got a party to throw for the Burner, to show him our respect. It's in five lousy hours, and it better be the popper of our lives. I got Diggy-O himself coming out here to make things swing. *And you gonna spit-shine this house!* I want kegs, weenies, burgers." He thought for a second. "Oh, and I want you to get a *big* box of sugar, to make those sweet cocktails the Burner likes so bad."

"Highballs," Lalo said. "I can muddle them with a little mint, for flava—and for ya apps, maybe make some mini-tacos, too, with like some turkey-pork and habaneros—"

"Right, *whatever*. And I want the rest of you to get your girlfriends out here to the desert, and quick—the jigglier the woman, the better."

Everybody just stared, like they were waiting for more orders.

"*So, what you waiting for?*" D hollered. He slapped his hands together. "Make it happen!"

They all scattered like mice.

19

After D's speech, Silver and Midget carted me and Ki back to the Fort. When we passed by an office next to the living room, we peered in to see Biggie holding a shirtless, bloody Book down on a sofa. Book was screaming, his *Kill Ya Sucka!* shave-job turning hell-red.

"Aw, man," Silver put me down. "It just feels like this is going wrong."

"Ya think?" Midget muttered.

"We've got to help Book," Silver decided.

We shuffled in there. Decorated with another black leather sofa, and a wood table stacked with papers, this room was where Dragon ran the Snake business, I guessed. On the sofa, Book's head thrashed back and forth, while he held onto his blood-soaked side.

"*Aghhhh! Aghhhhh!*"

"Who cut you?" Biggie asked, his hands quivering as he patted Book on the arm. "You run into some Diegos or something!?"

"It was King! He escaped jail! He's out looking for P."

As soon as I heard those words, my heart slammed crazy in me: *Wham—wham!*

"King's coming?" I breathed.

"But D said that King was in the pen," Silver blustered. "And that he gave you the locale for the dough!"

"Is he talking about your brother, Mish?" Kiki asked.

"He broke out of minimum," I gasped. "And now he's coming for us, Ki!" My knees almost buckled with relief. "It's going to be okay!"

She stared back at Book, only half listening. "Mish, this guy's hurt really bad."

"He found us on Orwell," Book choked out. "Caught us right, *ugh*, coming out of the apartment." His voice got thinner, softer, and his eyes rolled back in his head. "He gonna get us, and it'll be a *massacre*."

"No, King doesn't know about us here in Palm Desert." Silver's mouth pressed into a white line. "But—I don't get it, why did D say he was still in jail? And, what, did Samson just start fighting you after he told you where the cash was hid? That doesn't make any sense. Wait, Book—oh my God—"

Book had just passed out, his face looking halfway to a corpse's.

"Oh, no, I got you homes!" Putting his slender bronze fingers on Book's chest, Silver studied his cuts. The worst one was about six inches long. It stretched over the right ribs to the belly, spilling out more blood over his hip. "Okay, Bookie, honey—oh—I don't know how to take care of slags this bad!"

Biggie started bawling. "Could he die?"

"No," Silver croaked. "He's our family. Nothing's happening to you, boy. We love you; we'll take care of you—"

"He needs a doctor," Kiki said.

"Dragon said no docs," Biggie gagged out. "They call the police, we get nabbed."

"Oh, Silver, my brother's gonna kill you all," I said, amazed, as the reality started to hit home, and I got almost scared for them. Though Book was looking all bloodishly apocalyptical, I tried to draw my strength from some advice Mama once gave me: *Michelle, ya remember to never give no mercy to ya enemeez; ya rejoice over your power and their weakness.* "Yes, that's right! You all better *run*! And S, seriously, you should hightail it into some really good witness protection, because Samson and Reina will make you pay *blood* atonement for what you've done to me! But . . ." I frowned on Biggie and Silver weeping over Book. "Silver, hey, why are you messing around? You got to put *pressure* on that cut. Hold him under the armpit, disinfect the wound, and then sew it up! Come on, man, don't be bungling around with his circulatory system; he'll flatline on ya in three minutes."

Midget slapped his hands on his eyes. "He's gonna buy it, man!"

"No, Michelle, you're right." Silver pressed on the cut, hard. "Biggie, get alcohol, that vodka we got in the Vault. And bandages. We got thread? And a needle? And fetch a Bic!"

"Lalo's got that sewing kit. What he used to size down that 49ers T-shirt."

"Get it."

Biggie ran off. Book's face went from brown to green to white.

I shook my head. "Uh-oh. In half an hour, he's going to be deader than George Washington."

Kiki nudged me hard. "Mish, *help him*."

Silver darted his eyes at her. "What, does she know what to do?"

Ki said, "Her foster dad's a doctor; he showed her how to sew up wounds. I mean, he only gave her one or two lessons, but still, maybe—"

"Yo, Book here can croak like a toad," I said.

"I wouldn't help Book if I was you, neither, P." Midget looked like he'd upchuck from the iron-smell of the blood. "But maybe you could just do it anyway!"

"Mish, it's *wrong* if you let him bleed out like this," Kiki said.

I said, "*Wrong's* a big word, Ki, with a lot of meanings. Isn't that right, Silver?"

"No, *she's* right," Silver said. "You just said that you still loved— us. That you were loyal to us. Were you lying?"

"I love you, not *this* weasel!" I croaked.

Tears ran down Silver's face. "Then if you can help him, do it for me, Michelle!"

"Now don't get all complicated on me, S!"

"You've been playing my heart since the second you got here," he said, rough-voiced, and grasping Book's limp hand. "It is *time* for you prove to me that you're still a good soldier."

"But you always fucking said we was nothing like them!" I sputtered.

"And you always knew that we *were*," he said. "So this is it, Michelle. You've got to make a *choice*."

"That's not what I'm saying!" Ki yelled. "You have to do this because you're not anything like this guy. Maybe he and Dragon are psychos, but you're *good*. And that's why you're not going to let this—idiot—die!"

Biggie rushed back into the office with his hands full of supplies. "I got it!"

"Listen to them, P!" Midget yodeled. "You're good! Help him!"

Remember to never give no mercy to ya enemeez—I stared at Silver, who was looking at me exactly like he did that day I left for Westchester, when he'd hoped so hard I wouldn't turn my back on him. My mom's words faded away. "Fine!"

I glared down at Book, who was jerking, though still unconscious.

"Hold him down; don't let him move—and know that I ain't no expert, okay? Frank only taught me about ab lacerations on a Raggedy Annie! Okay, Midget—string up the needle." I opened up the Grey Goose Midget had brought, and poured it on my hands to disinfect my digits. I next poked around Book's ribs, making sure King's chopping didn't go so deep that he'd have internal bleeding. "Pour some vodka down his gullet so he doesn't thrash around. And the needle's got to be disinfected with a lighter flame."

"I'm on it," Midge said, tipping the bottle down Book's throat.

Behind me, I heard Kiki rustling with her videocam in her pocket again. But I was too busy to care.

I stitched Book. The needle flashed in and out of his side, while he moaned, then fainted again. I started with a U-shaped suture, then finished by sewing a square knot at the bottom of the wound. There came a time, after the first two passes, when I left off being scared and focused on my work as intense as when I studied for the decathlon or when I whupped Money in the 800m. I sewed him up almost as tidy as when I'd first-aided that Raggedy Ann.

"You *do* have to take him to the doctor, though," I said when I was just about done. Book was as flabby as a fish on the sofa. "There's all this blood gone—look at his face. His color's bad. Could be in some, like, shock, too."

"Aw, you did it, though, you really did it!" Silver cheered, grabbing hold of me.

I held his hand. "I think I did. Oh, Silver, I might have pulled it off."

"I'm so proud of you, baby!" he said.

A love-pain shot through my heart. "I'm—glad. Though after what you did to me, I know I shouldn't give a damn, S."

"Ugh, this was the most disgusting thing I ever saw," Kiki gargled.

"I wish Dragon'd let us bring him to a doc, though," Biggie said.

"Well, maybe you shouldn't ask D for permission," I spat.

"You shouldn't ask me what?" Dragon suddenly said behind us.

We snapped our heads around. In the doorway, D's right shoulder was stained black with Book's blood, and his eyes were hollow.

"I told you to put them upstairs, Silver," he growled, grabbing me by the collar.

"D, come on," Silver said. "She took care of him."

Dragon winced at the sight of Book. "That's what I came in here to do. Okay, good job, but it's time to go, P. You're going to have to get yourself freshened up." He grabbed my arm.

"Let go of me!"

"Watch her shoulder!" Silver said.

Dragon ignored him, mutterering something about the nefarious stubbornness of women before dragging me around once again. He pushed me up the stairs and shoved me into the Vault; I stumbled over the Barcalounger.

"Leave me be, D!" I tried to throw a swing at him, but he danced back on boxer's toes.

"Don't think you'll start a fight," he said. "You've got to be in one pretty piece tonight."

"Wait, *hermano,* why are you acting like this?!" Silver ran into the room, with Kiki and Midget coming up after. "Clue us on what happened with King!"

Dragon just stuck his hand in his pocket, bringing out his silver death's head key chain. He threw it to Silver. "Stop your chattin' and get my Humvee washed. Tell them to use that expensive wax I bought what's in the garage."

"Why?"

"We owe interest on our debt now, and I am hoping like hell that the Burner'll take this for the extra we owe," Dragon said.

"Book told us King sprung himself," Silver pressed. "Is that true?"

D sighed. "Yeah, we met up with him in Monty."

"Why'd you say otherwise?" S asked.

Dragon snatched his head at him. "To keep your eye on the ball, kemosabe."

"But you *got* the money?" Silver said.

"I told you I did, didn't I?" Dragon's voice took on some menace.

Midget's face was still red from getting slapped outside. "Well, if you got money now, I'd like my three Gs please, Dragon."

"What the hell you talking about?"

Silver grimaced. "Oh, gawd, the boyz were just getting a little curious about the cash they—you know, donated to the cause."

"Yeah, we was wondering about the Snake investment fund," Midget said.

"Aw, hell, I blew that dough at the track." Dragon glared into Midget's slitted eyes. "Just trying to keep *your* ass alive, punk!"

"You are dastardly, man," I said. "You're a cheater, a kidnapper, and to look at Book, a bad babysitter, D. You are *rotten*."

Dragon moved his look to Kiki. I saw him take in her prettiness, her wayward hair.

"I'm not, really, cowgirl," he said, in a lower voice. "Kiki, that's your name, right, lovely thing?"

Kiki and I snatched nervous looks at each other.

"Like you said, I'm a good guy," he went on. "I didn't hurt you— not really. Hope not, anyway." He cleared his throat. "Cuz I'm a nice, gentle, good-boyfriend type of man. Just by way of your information. If you make my acquaintance, you'll see that."

"Boyfriend?" I yallered. "You must be joking, palooka!"

Kiki fluttered her hands around her ears. "Okay, just because I don't think you're 100 percent evil doesn't mean we're going steady. You need to understand that I would rather drink Clorox than go out on a date with you."

"Kiki, I'm just telling you something about me." Dragon stared at her, intense. "In case you ever want to know."

"She *don't* want to know!" I yelled.

His eyes went flat as he turned to me. "P, shut up, and comb your ratty hair. Wash off that BO, put on makeup, and look like a normal girl. Midget, where's that girl-crap trade we got?"

Midge said, "Uh, it's back here, I think, behind the Xboxes—"

"Get it for them."

Midget scatted to the back of the attic, while Dragon beelined for the trade clothes. He rifled through the fluff-skirts and the slinky corsets, finally throwing a couple of hoochie dresses on the bed.

"You'll dress proper, too, for our festivities." He gestured at Silver. "What you standing around for? Get the Humvee shined. Burner's coming in a few hours. And go get Force, too. I want him manning this door."

"Force? Hold on, I still don't get it," Silver said, mortal serious. "You say you got the money. Why do you still want to keep her here?"

"You are beginning to try my nerves, Silver." Dragon slipped a look at me and then S. "And I see what's inspiring you to this rebellious questioning, too, don't I? Damn, you got a *weakness* where she's concerned."

"Answer me, D," Silver said.

"Fine—out of friendship, I'll tell ya: I'm hosting P just one more night, so as to defend her from harm," Dragon said, as smooth as he could, though I could see his eyes getting shifty. "This has become what you call an explosive situation, and we don't want our little girls to get hurt. We got Diegos coming over; Samson's on the warpath. And if P gets hit by some friendly fire, then it's our asses on the line. So we're just going to guard her this evening, as a friendly precaution. And while she's in protective custody, why, all she'll be doing is partying with us like old times."

"I can take care of myself, Dragon!" I sputtered.

Dragon slapped Silver on the shoulder. "S, I see you got some confusion about my strategy, dude. But, let me remind you: Do you recall when the Diegos cut you and I nearly got my head blown pulling you out of that battlefield?"

Silver let out a long breath. "Of course."

"Why would I do that?" Dragon asked.

"Man, come on—" Silver shook his head.

D squeezed him harder on the arm. *"Why?"*

"Because we're soul brothers," Silver finally admitted.

"And that's why you know that you can trust me, don't you? With your life."

"Yeah, I do," Silver said, in a torn-up voice.

D went on, "And that's why you know, too, that I'll look after what's yours, bro. So, you just go take care of the 'Vee, and in a matter of hours, we can just look upon this as a day that started bad and ended good. Okay?"

It took a minute, but S nodded.

"Don't buy it, baby," I said, holding out my hands to him. "Look at me—look in my eyes. You can't trust him! Help us get out of here! There's something wrong."

"It's okay, Michelle." Silver hesitated again, then said, "Dragon is the only person in the world who never burned me. He'll do what he promised."

"Listen to *me*; you can depend on *me*," I said.

"Oh, is that so?" Dragon asked, happy at my slip. "Hear that, S? You can depend on her. Except when she dumps you for some white-man in Westchester."

Silver just stared at the ground.

"Oh, God," I moaned, hurting because what D said about me was right.

Dragon pointed at me and gave me a fake-confident smile. "Calm down, P. Everything's gonna be okay; you and your pretty pal just sit tight. My boyz'll fetchya when the party's started."

"I'll see you in a little bit, Michelle," Silver said. His tone softened then, just a touch. "It'll turn out okay."

I ran my hands through my hair, fighting off panic.

Dragon and Silver thumped out, just as Midget emerged from behind the clothes, holding a pizza-sized cardboard carton in his hands. He pulled out a glossy black box with *CHANEL* stamped out on its cover, and threw it on the bed. "There's other chick stuff back there, too, what we got from a Beverly Hills haul. Sort of stupid, you ask me. Who going to pay for all that sissy trash?" He started to stomp away.

"Midget," I said, right when he crossed over the door. "Text my dad: 213-555-4323. Tell him where I am, Midge!"

He stood real still, his back to me.

"Call my mom!" Kiki begged him. "It's 424-555-7859!"

"Midget, where are you, boy?" D yelled from below. "We got a party to throw!"

Midget peered at me over his shoulder. "You heard Dragon; it's all set up. Why you in such a hurry to scoot for?"

"Damn, Midget," I said. "Anyone with a nose can tell the garbage D's shoveling stinks bad. I've got to get Kiki out of here!"

"Yeah, D's a wily one. But I only stick my neck out for my tribe. Are you with us now?" He stuck his chin out at Kiki. "Or you running with a new crowd?"

My eyes grabbed his. "What do you think?"

This little happiness suddenly tugged up his mouth.

"I saw what you did for Book. I think you doomed to be a Snake for life, baby."

"Midget!" Dragon bellowed out, just as Force came running up the stairs and stood in the door. "I got jobs for you to do!"

"Better get cleaned up, Princess M," Midget said, tilting his hat as he walked out past Force. "I got a feeling tonight'll be a rough ride."

Force rested his hand on the door handle, smiling at Ki and me with half his mouth. "Yeah, have fun getting pretty, girls. And don't think about getting all smarty-pants on us again. I've been assigned to keep my eye on you, P. I'm going to be standing right out here, by the door. I don't want no trouble from you females, ya hear?"

"Bite me, man," I said.

Force gave me a nasty little grin. "I will, you give me cause."

Click went the lock.

20

I stared at the door. "That Force is sure getting himself some big ideas. I'm worried that if I don't watch him close, he's going to try to earn his stripes with me."

Kiki put her hands over her face. "We're supposed to get ready for a *party*?"

"Dragon likes you, though, Ki," I said. "And that's good news. You earning his favor could keep you from getting hurt."

She gripped her bandaged wrist. "Mish, it is so not good news that Hellboy wants to take me to the prom."

"Yeah, but hopefully D isn't lying, and the Burner'll get paid, and we'll be out of here soon. But what's even better for us is, if Samson really sprung from Chino, he'll radar right down here. No stopping him. If somebody gets in King's way, he'll *run* that sucker down."

She tweaked out a melancholy grin. "He sounds like you."

I tilted my head at her. "Nah, what?"

"That's how *you* are when you race. Or remember last year when you crushed your competition like bugs in the America's Sweetheart poetry contest and Mandy Adams threw up on the stage from the stress—"

"Hey, King's not anything like *me*. Him and me—that is, *he* and I, we're totally different. We're apples and . . . grenades, you know?"

"Okay. Yeah." She laughed a little.

"Oranges and Uzis, girl." I cleared my throat; my voice had gone shredded. "Okay? You get that?"

It didn't even seem like she heard me as she looked around the room, shaking her head. "Did they kidnap us only yesterday? It seems like longer."

"Yeah. Just, give me a hug, okay?"

She put her hands on my shoulders but stopped. "You're covered with blood."

It was true: Book's gore stained my arms, my shirt.

I stammered, "O-oh, I'm a mess. Thank God Frank's not here, Ki. He'd have to get himself a *lifetime* of shrinkage if he saw me looking like this!"

"Mish, oh, are you crying?"

"Nah . . . it's just dusty up here."

She pushed back the hair from my face and took a long look at me. "Hey, I know Frank would be really proud to see how you sewed up that guy."

"You think so?"

"Yeah." She patted my cheek. "Though he'd probably be less stoked to see how getting pistol-whipped has *completely* screwed up your pH balance. You need a facial, stat."

I laughed and cried at the same time. "Oh, now you're making jokes, Miss Brave-and-Zesty?"

"Just bad ones. But it's a start. I'm beginning to get the feeling that I'm going to have to get a little tougher to get through this. So let's just get you cleaned up. Me too. We'll feel better. How does that sound?"

"Like a good idea."

She looked at the hoochie-mama dresses again, and the expensive makeup case. Then she peeped at all the Beverly Hills rags and shiny woman stuff sparkling around us. Even in her scaredness, a little fashion madness glittered in her eye.

"And what do you say, maybe we can find some decent clothes in here?"

*

Kiki wrapped herself in a towel as she started to rummage through the cartons of trade. "Look at all this stuff; this is *crazy!*" She gave a look at the door, behind which we could hear Force grumbling and shifting his weight from foot to foot. "You think he'll come in here when we're changing?"

"Ya ain't thinking about peeping us, are you, Force?" I called out. "Cuz I'll break ya face."

"I don't want to look at your ugly butt," he hollered through the door. "My only mission is to slice and dice ya if you try anything tricky. I ain't kidding about that, P."

It was hard, but we tried to ignore him, if just to keep ourselves from going totally nuts. I'll say, though, the clothes and fluffy junk did help to distract us. During the hours we "shopped" the Vault, we pawed through boxes of golden L.A.M.B. perfume, smelling of white musk, and onyx-black bowls of spicy Agent Provocateur body oils. Spiderweb-thin underwear from Stella McCartney peeked out at us from tissue-frothy boxes. Silver Prada handbags with bone handles and chubby steel chains clanked in sleek silk bags. We stumbled over Narcisco Rodriguez high-heeled shoes like little towers of spun sugar, and peep-toe platforms . . .

"Pretty fancy doodads they got here," I said, raising my eyebrows at some fairly skimpy lingerie.

"These are Christian Louboutin," Kiki gasped, holding up a pair of red silk stilettos.

Scrubbed clean of all Book's blood-scum, I skittered around the attic, spritzing perfume, and silver-glitter body crème. After Kiki fished out the prettiest foofoo, she plunked on the bed with that Chanel box. It had a big mirror and shimmered with rose-colored rouge, parrot-green shadow, gold dust, and fire-red lipstick.

"That's some pretty dapper goop, Ki," I said, a little befuddled. I never wore makeup more than once or twice in my life.

"Goop?! This is *French*. Because, okay, you've studied history and stuff? But I've studied fashion. I mean, don't get me wrong: Being kidnapped is beyond terrible. And these gang people are so gross, except they have a-*maz*-ing taste." Kiki shook a little moon-colored dress at me. "We are in a girl's Fort Knox here, Mish!"

She kohled her big eyes, fluffing out the lashes with a brush, then kissed her lips with magenta gloss. It doesn't sound like much—but actually, all that fussy painting of hers took a *long* time. From the window, the blue daytime darkened into charcoal and blood pink. Music pounded from downstairs, already. When she finished, she did look real spiffy.

"Oh, man, you are *so* beautiful, Kiki," I said.

She pinched her little locks so they stuck up perky. "Now you."

"Yeah, no, I don't think so," I said, ducking away from the makeup brush. "I don't think I look very good all fancified. I'm cool with just some cherry-flavored ChapStick and a little mouthwash—"

"Oh, stop fussing and hold still."

Her feathery fingers brushed my face. She stroked my eyelids with her thumbs, dabbing my mouth with the flame-colored paint. Pencils tickled over my brows, my lashes. Gawd, though, I thought I was going to collapse asleep on that bed from the boredom. Fluff, fluff, puff. She hooked giant silver hoop earrings into my ears. My hair was glossed with clouds of flower-scented foam, parted neatly with a comb. Meanwhile, the window had turned black from the night. Voices bubbled up from downstairs—girls hooting, men yelling. A lot of cars had been driving up, too.

"Okay, enough already, I'm turning into a half-wit sitting here while you goo me," I said. "Give me the mirror."

She widened her eyes. "No, don't look yet." Slowly sifting through the white cotton, black leather, and feathers hanging from the racks, she plucked out an apple-red tulip-skirt dress with a round collar. She slipped on the red gown, throwing a little gray capelet over her shoulders.

"That looks nice," I said.

She stuck her videocam into the tulip-skirt's side-slit pocket before dancing barefoot like a model. "Do you think it's sort of Sofia Coppola?"

"Who's that?"

"Oh, Mish! *Marie Antoinette*?"

"That movie with all that pink barf you made me watch?"

"Actually, the only time I remember seeing pink barf on TV was when you made me watch the Olympic trials, and some sick sprinter chucked up a bunch of Pepto."

"Aw, yeah, now *that* was cool!"

"All right, now for you. Oh, *perfect!*" She rummaged around until she found that moon-colored dress again.

"What's that?"

"Marc Jacobs!"

"You know, I just like a nice pair of jeans and a T-shirt and some good Nikes."

"Just try it on."

Didn't take me too long to slip into that dress, on account it had as much fabric in it as an Ace bandage. I gasped at my boobies poking up and a big harlotty slit sexualizing my left thigh. "This dress has got some *air*-conditioning!"

Kiki slapped her hand over her mouth.

"See," I moaned. "I look stupid."

"Nope. You don't."

She grabbed the makeup box, propped up the mirror.

Oh no! Hey-ho! Glam-o-rous!!!

Hair spilling like smoke down my shoulders, dusky eyes, diamond-sprinkled collarbone. Bandage on my arm making me look tough. Rockin' bod.

A little too rockin', you ask me.

"I don't know. . . ." She handed me the Narcisco Rodriguez shoes with the shiv heels, and I teetered on those high-rises like a flamingo. "Almost not having any clothes on is sort of too sexy, don't you think?"

"What's the problem? You look like a freaking movie star!"

"Nah, this is all *Scarface*, Ki, you don't understand. This is dangerous."

"Don't you like it?"

I nodded. "I do, that's the dilemma."

"What do you mean?"

Knock, knock, knock.

Both Ki and me froze and stared at the door.

"What do they *want* with us!?" she hissed.

"I'm afraid to find out," I said.

"Coming in, dummies," Force said.

"Hello . . . ?" Force, Eager, and Lalo poked their heads through the door. They wore spanky, ironed new button-downs and nearly black jeans. Lalo had shaved off his purple bangs so as to be handsomer, and his eyes boinged out of his head when he spied me.

"Oh, P, seeing you look like that's gonna grow me to *manhood*!"

"*Yo!*" Eager yelped. "Dang, I thought you was—for a second—"

"Yeah, I know," I said.

"W-who?" Kiki asked.

"Her mama, Reina," Lalo said.

"Why'd you guys come up here?" I asked.

Eager stretched out his arm, giving me his elbow. "You've been summoned to the Burner's shindig, m'lady."

"More like you've been ordered to appear," Force said. "D says I'm your bodyguard tonight. *And* that you coming if we all have to drag ya by the hairs."

"Woo wee!" Lalo yelped, a little drunk. "*Boogie!* I'm the bartender!"

"Or maybe we could just stay up here playing Barbies until, you know . . . *your brother comes to get us.*" Kiki whispered hopefully in my ear.

Burn it up, burn it down, turn ya heat on tha clowns, I suddenly heard someone rapping from downstairs.

"Is that Diggy-O?" I asked.

"In the flesh," Eager said.

"Come on, P, it is time to par-tay," Lalo yawled. "Remember all that dancin' ya used to do? Ooh, you was *wigging*, P!"

"Dancing?" Kiki asked. "You don't dance."

"Nah, ignorant! P's all *disco*," Lalo said. "She cuts *loose*. Especially when she on the ganja!"

"Never mind all that," I said.

"You were only thirteen the last time you lived with your mom," Kiki said. "You couldn't have been all reefer madness at *thirteen*."

"Ha!" all three boyz barked.

"Poor P," Eager said. "You forgot tha Life. You's gone all civvie and stressed."

"All right, enough chatter, time to move it, P," Force barked. "Get downstairs."

"What's stressing me out is *you*," I said, staring at Force. "Why are you all stuck to me?"

"I've been given some dominion over you, girl." Force whipped a knife out of his pocket and sprung the blade. "Now, we can do this easy, or we can do this hard."

"Hey, *hey*, watch it now!" I said, my whole body clenching *right* up. "What's that for, tough boy? You don't need to get all hectic on me!"

"Don't do that—" Kiki started shuddering, hard. "Why don't you just leave us alone?"

"If she's really your friend, I'd do it the easy way, P," Force said.

Eager and Lalo shook their heads. "Damn, calm down."

"Ya all better get *used* to me exercising some supremacy around here," Force sneered at them. "I'm rising in the ranks."

"Fine, fine!" I said, standing in front of Kiki, though frightened as hell. I *knew* that a meathead like Force would just love to get promoted by bleeding me dry. "No need to get huffy, baby. Put that knife away."

"You going to be a good girl, then?" Force said.

"Sure," I said. "Whatever you say."

"And you *see* that I got some rule over you, don't you?"

"'Course I do, Mr. Big Man. You the boss. Let's go jubilee."

"That's all I wanted to hear, P." Force tucked his knife back in his pocket. Opening the door, he gave a mock-respectful little bow. "Ladies first."

21

Burn it

  Oh sa-weet chica!

Burn it up, burn it down, Honey's here

To paint da town

Music like fire in my ears. Bass thumpin' behind my ribs. Desert heat sweat on my naked skin. With Force and Ki close behind me, I walked down the dark stairs, willing my legs to behave in them unnatural high heels. My hips swayed in a natural, old-school beat under the velvet of my dress as I made my way into the living room. Hundreds of people grooved in the center of the reefer-perfumed, stained glass–colored dance floor.

"Now don't be dreaming about running away," Force said in my ear.

"Oh my God, look at this," I murmured.

It was like walking out of a time machine and into my glorious, *perilous* past.

The room shone with blue lights, red lights, and gold. The colors washed over the band that was raging at the far west side of the room. Diggy-O was a short, heavy, sunglass-wearing pachuco jumping like a jackhammer while he screamed into a mic. A lizard-skinny cholo with a Latino 'fro played bass, and there was a monster man thrashing away on the drums, all covered with Aztec tats and with like ten piercings sticking out of his Villaraigosa-handsome face. The sofas had been pushed to the sides, and the floor shimmied with hip-thrusting dudes and about three times that number of lolas. Except for Dragon, Silver, Biggie, and Book, I saw all the rest of the Snakes down there, most of them begging the females for some tongue. Dragon'd shipped in like sixty girls who wore butt-hugging bandage dresses and looked like they'd shake pom-poms while they had sex.

Also, I spied about forty Armani-wearing gangsters who I remembered from meetings Mama let me sit in on when I was young. These had to be the Burner's men—about twenty years old, twenty-five. The Burner ran the Diegos, the big club which started down in San Diego but superquick spread to L.A. They and the 99s were sometimes partners in crime, though lately dead rivals. I didn't see the Burner, though. All I could make out in the crowd was his crew dancing with the chicas. In this case, "dancing" mostly meant feeling up the trucked-in girlies.

Outside roared the *vroom vroom* of motorbikes driving up to the house. Peering out a window, I made a squad of Humvees, Caddies, and even a Bentley parked up on the front lawn. One losery-looking dude smoking a pipe (not the Sherlock Holmes kind) dawdled by the Bentley. Farther off, two rhinoceros-ugly, 'roid-muscled thugs charged up to the Fort's side garage in red-flame-painted Harleys, and they had primped-out hussies riding the bitch seats. The girls wore these matching denim vests over their boobies, and they'd rigged up the denim with little lights, like Christmas lights, so they sparkled like rodeo bimbos. Apparently, the loser smoking crack by the Bentley said something impolite about the girls, because one of the rhinoceroses jumped off his Harley and started beating his head *rigorous*. Then the other helped him, while the girls clapped.

I grasped at Kiki, who was glued to my hip. "Aw, Ki, we shouldn't be here."

"No kidding," she blurted.

Fear made my throat ache. "These are some dangerous folks. Don't let any of them touch you."

"I wasn't planning on it!" she wheezed.

"Hey, Michelle!" That was Midget yallering at me from the dance floor. "Princess Eme's here!"

Upon hearing that, all the rebels, lolas, and old-timers turned to stare at me.

"Look, it's Reina's kid. . . ."

Suddenly, it got *dead* quiet. Even Diggy-O got the vibe, and the music tweaked, stopped. I saw all their faces moving, their eyes slitting down at me.

"Um, why do they all look like they could totally bump you off right now?" Kiki asked in a warbly voice.

"Cuz most of them *are* probably deciding if they should shoot her as a Judas or give her a friendly slap on the behind," Force explained, sidling right by me. "We'll find out what they settle on in a minute or so."

He was right. If I made a wrong move, they'd tear me right up.

Act like a Princess or these jackals'll smell blood!

Heart whacking, I looked all those desperados in the eyes, as confident as Cleopatra. Then I gave the mob a Queenly nod.

A long moment passed. Eyes popped; grins widened.

"P!" everybody screamed.

Bam bam! played the music again, with the monster man slamming on the drums. Diggy started ad-libbing into the mike:

Princess P is back with me!
Princess P is an emergency!
Princess P looking hotter than hell
Princess P ring ya bell
Oh, Oh-oh, ring ya bell!
Oh, ay, ring ya bell!

"*Oh, ay, ring ya bell!*" the crowd repeated back, as a monster-mash of gangster men and googly-eyed girls crushed up to me and Ki, pushing Force to the side.

"P, yo!"

"They saying they had to 'nap you, but you lookin' pretty sharp anyways."

"How's your mama? She's still running our competition tough from the pen, but you take care to give her my best, sugar."

"Back at you, old man," I said, sweating ice as I got smushed up in the arms of this hugely pumped-up and long-bearded Diego called Hellacious Diaz. A vicious arms dealer, I knew him to be, but I forced myself to smile. "Don't forget to say hello to my friend, Kiki. And you make sure to respect her, homie—"

"Sure, I give honor to a pal of ol' P's," Hellacious boomed, massaging Kiki on the shoulder with his iron-tough hand. "What's yo' name, P's pal? You like Mexicans? You must, right? So, come on, let's go outside and I'll show you my Indian, sugar!"

"Seeing your Indian sounds super fun, but I can't, because I'm too busy looking for my purity ring, which just slipped off, and I'm really busy looking for it—" Kiki gacked.

Force barked, "And I can't let her out of my sight anyways—"

"An Indian's a motorcycle, sugar-sugar!" Hellacious shouted. "One of the *finest*. It's in the garage—in case it rains, you know. Come on, you'll *love* it. It's cherry!"

Kiki gripped onto her hurt wrist. "Please don't say 'cherry.' I find it kind of weirdly terrifying, so—could you just not talk to me?"

Force bugged his eyes at us, keeping his tabs, but Hellacious batted him away. "What's this fly buzzing around me?"

"I got to make sure these dogs don't dash, man," Force said.

"Aw, you ain't gonna run from me, are you, cutie?" Hellacious laughed at Ki. "Come on, sugar, let's get you a cocktail."

"No, not for her, she doesn't drink," I said, Diggy-O's beat pounding in my ears as I surveyed the room. *Where is King? Dammit, if he jumped Chino this morning, he should be here right now!*

Hellacious pulled us over to a table stocked with liquor, fruit, salt, and a big bag of C&H sugar, where Lalo was making highballs. Force followed us, breathing all over me.

"You'll have a tipple, won't you, P?" Hellacious said, eyeballing me and handing me a sweating glass full of booze. Sharing drink was an act of courtesy among villains, and if I refused, it would brand me as a vulnerable outsider.

"Sure. Salud," I said, looking in his eyes the whole time—a must when toasting a rebel. I downed the drink in one glug.

"Woo!" Hellacious hollered. "Girl can take her hooch like a man!"

"I think it's always a really good idea to drink alcohol in situations like this," Kiki said, rolling her eyes around the room.

"Now you," Hellacious said.

"Hey, I told you no," I said. "Rules is different for her. She's a friend of mine, see? Under my protection. Don't crowd the girl."

"Aw, don't be all uptight," he said.

Kiki did a backbend as Hellacious hoisted a glass to her lips. "No, no," she sang out. "I heard that highballs gave you blackouts and really bad bloat—"

"Hellacious, cut that out!" I said to him.

"Yeah, maybe you shouldn't be messing with them," Force said. "D doesn't want them getting mussed up."

"Yes, could you not touch me?" Kiki said. "You guys are seriously freaking me out—"

"And they *are* in some fine form. Sugar's so cute," Hellacious said, starting to bear hug her really tight.

"Hey, *hey!*" I yelled, punching him in the ribs.

"Ow!"

"Stop it!" Kiki suddenly roared. I'd just been about to roundhouse him again, but she beat me to it: Ripping herself out of his grasp, she slammed her knuckles into his nose. "*Fuck you!*"

She and I stared at each other, mouths opened into big *O*s.

"Ki!" I gasped. "Are you okay?"

"Is *she* okay?" Hellacious said, massaging his beak.

She glared at me, then spun away from us and ran away through the crowd.

"Wait, don't do that!" Force yelled, snatching his eyes at her and then me, trying to figure which one to stick to. "Come back here!"

"Ki! Kiki!" I yelled.

I rushed after her, Force chasing me. I slipped past the people, ducking under elbows, past wiggling hips. Then, *wham!* I slammed right into Silver.

"Whoa!" he said. "Where's the fire, girl?"

"It's Kiki; she's upset," I said. But even though I was hellishly nervous over Ki, I just *had* to do a triple-take: Silver looked so beautiful in his blue shirt, his hair flowing down his back as soft-looking as ink in water. His muscles thrust out tight under the cotton of his blue button-down. Inside the collar I could see his broad, hard chest, and his bronze throat brightened by his scar. "I-I've got to go get her."

"Okay, but find me later. I've got to talk to you about something." Silver put his hand on my cheek—but then squinted at Force, who was practically mugging me. "Damn, Force, you still playing hall monitor?"

"Just keeping my eye on the ball, Silver," Force said. "Like you should be."

I didn't hear the rest of their spatting, because I pushed away, running through the strobe-lit, pulsing mob, so Force lost sight of me.

"Hey!" I heard him, over the sounds of the crowd. "Where'd you go?"

Stumbling past the kitchen, a little bathroom, I turned into an unlit, empty hallway. I looked over my shoulder—Force and his little knife hadn't found me yet. I padded up the hall and found myself now up by Dragon's office. But Ki hadn't gone this way: She wasn't in the side rooms, the dead ends, the corners.

But then I made out two men talking. Low, tense voices.

"You've got one more hour to pay up," one of the dudes said. I peered through the shadows. Ahead, I saw a stripe of lamplight. That was the door to Dragon's office, and Dragon was holding a meeting. I'd heard the other man's deep voice talking to my mama a long time ago, and remembered it still. Frederico Gonzales. The Burner.

"Freddie," Dragon said, smooth sounding. "I got thousands of dollars in trade upstairs; I got a Humvee—"

"I don't care about ya trinkets, D."

"We gonna work this all out, man. Listen—" Dragon hesitated, just for a beat. "I got a secret weapon."

"And I got a not-so-secret weapon here in my holster."

"I'm telling you: You're gonna be satisfied."

"Then show me the cash or admit that you're bluffing."

I slipped off my high-heeled shoes, so I wouldn't make any sound.

Then I crept in closer to hear every single word.

22

I tiptoed to the door crack. Inside the office, there was now a blue-and-red Mexican blanket on the sofa where Book had bled a river not six hours before.

Oh, no! A thin, cold knife of fear sliced through my chest.

There was the devil they said would kill us all.

The world-famous Burner sat on the sofa, not ten feet away from me. He was like five foot ten, and with this glossy, curly black hair he wore in a lion's mane spilling back from his forehead. He had a big, handsome brown face, pockmarked, and a mini-goatee. His devastating peepers were dark, long-lashed. White teeth like a Siberian husky. And he looked all the scarier-hotter on account of his Armani mobster clothes: pressed charcoal three-piece suit, a Guatemalan scarf, and a black mink coat, slung over the sofa.

Dragon stood before him, wearing a pair of black cotton trousers and a red sweater. He put his hands in his pants pockets, then pulled them inside out. Empty. He shrugged.

"I didn't get the money from King, Freddie."

My breath died in my throat.

The Burner shook his head. "Too bad I put on my nice suit, because this is gonna get messy. Do your soldiers know you're broke? Because I noticed they ain't acting like boyz who are in the line of fire."

"No," Dragon said. "I lied to them that I got the dough. They wouldn't like what I've got planned. Because, Freddie, I told you: I've got your payment. It's *her*. She's the one hundred thousand dollar *girl*. She's worth *way* more than the bank I owe you."

"You selling me Reina's daughter?" the Burner yukked, in his growly voice. "That's a high-maintenance filly you tendering. You got some bold balls!"

"I know Queen's still giving you a beatin' on your L.A. connections," Dragon said. "A taste of little Peña might sweeten the humiliations the big one's put you through. And bro, I can sell her to you fully loaded. She's under protection all night, so as to make sure I deliver her in prime condition."

The Burner reached into his jacket, pulling out a big, black gun from a holster, and it looked powerful enough to kill a horse with one shot. "Your deadline is in, let's see"—he checked his watch—"fifty minutes, and after that, *everything* in this house, including her *and* you, belongs to me. Why should I buy what I already own?"

"I'll give you special rights over a couple boys," D said, desperate. "You can punish them harsher than's called for. Say, Midget and Game."

"You think I'm interested in damaged goods? The only bread in here I wanna toast is Silver."

"Silver's not for sale." D's voice betrayed a shiver of fear. "When I called you about this payoff, you pledged an amnesty on him for cutting your soldiers."

The Burner said, "Boy, S was dead the second he laid hands on mine. I only played with the idea of giving him a reprieve when you were promising a swift return on my dollar. But now, all options is off the table but one."

"Freddie, if you burn me, you burning years of business coming to *you* instead of Reina, and you too smart for that."

"There's something to what you say, boy. And it is a *threat* to my empire."

"I can turn her," D blurted out.

"*What?*"

"Michelle. I can bring her to your team. I'll put Silver on the job to turn her against Queen. He's a machine now, a *true* ice-man."

The Burner cocked an eyebrow at him. "Even where the girl's concerned? I thought he was soft on Queen's pup."

I saw Dragon's hands tremble at this hard truth; he hid them in his empty pockets. "Sure, it'll take some convincing; she's a real pretty thing. But she threw his ass over, and I got a talent for reminding him of that—and what he owes *me*. So don't you worry about it; I know how to work S. He'll do what I tell him and bring her to your door gift-wrapped. And he'll figure out a way to make her like it, too."

"That sounds like a tall order, my man," the Burner said.

Oh my God, I thought. *Would S really help* slave *me? He can't have turned* that *cold—but I don't know!*

"Aw, the girl's like all women, of two minds," Dragon went on. "She's already back in love with him; I can tell. Probably never stopped. She'll be easy as cake, Freddie. She'll be *your* soldier in no time."

"*Agh!*" I gagged furious in the shadows.

The Burner stared at him for a long beat before breaking out into a shining grin. "That would be something, wouldn't it?"

"It'd be the end of the 99s."

"Well, I'll admit, you've caught on to the game of the jungle fast. So. You giving me Reina's kid? What about the other one? The *morena*."

Dragon shook his head. "No, the black girl's for me."

And, well, that last bit pretty much did it for me. *Oh, hell no!*

I got up careful, quiet. Padding down the hall, I was crazy as *goddamn*. My hands stretched out like I was a blind girl trying to feel my way through the dark.

Kiki.

I had to find her, get her out of here. Safe. And fast!

Dashing out of the hallway, I passed a blonde girl and a hulky man making out like wild wolves, just off that little bathroom. I looked up and saw Force scrambling up to me. "Where the hell you run off to?" he hissed. "I was running around outside in the fuckin' dark looking for you!"

Made super strong by my terror, I grabbed him by the neck so hard he went limp for a second. The man and girl looked over at me.

"Come on, lover," I said, pulling Force into the bathroom.

"What?" he gasped. "What are you doing? You hate my guts!"

I yanked him into the john, closed the door. "Oh, yeah, right!" I closed my fist and slammed it in his face.

"Ugh!" He staggered back and started digging in his pants pocket, whipped out his knife. He slashed it in the air, giving me a wicked little slice on the neck.

"Ai!" I clasped my hands together into a big fist and slammed his wrist as hard as I could.

"Shit!" he said, as the knife clattered to the floor. He glared at me. "I'm going to beat some brain damage into you!"

I reared up and brought my skull down hard as a hammer on his nose.

Wham! Wham! Wham!

"Ugh!" Force stumbled to the floor, and I grabbed the back of his neck. Raising his head, I smashed his face into the toilet seat.

Whack!

Mr. Big Man dropped like a stone by the toilet, quivered a little, and passed out.

I scooted out the door, pawing the blood off my neck. The man and girl doing the bump and grind were too busy with the big fornicating to notice me rushing down the hall.

Kiki! Where are you?!

Kitchen—bedrooms—another bathroom. There she was! Standing in the living room, by the bar, she glared superscandalized at a bunch of dudes doing body shots off some loose womanfolk.

"Oh, God, there you are!" I said, grabbing her. "Come on!"

She pulled her hand back. "Yeah, so, I don't want you to do that anymore, Mish."

I boggled at her. "What?"

She blew out her cheeks. "Order me around! Not listen to me! I'm sick of it! That's what got me here in the first place."

I clasped my hands, nearly hysterical: "Oh, do not tell me you're having a hissy *now*, Ki!"

"Yes, I am, and it is *extra crispy*. Because I finally really got it. My mom was right! Having less confidence than a sea slug is so *not cute*!"

"Will you just shut up right now and listen to me?!" I belted.

"You shut up!" She crunched her forehead. "Wait, did you cut your neck?"

"They're going to hurt us, Ki," I breathed. "Dragon's selling me to the Burner."

Her eyebrows popped straight up. "'Selling' you?"

"They're splitting us up, too. I heard them talking. We are *gone*."

As the intelligence penetrated her noggin, tears shot out of her eyes. "But, you said your brother'd rescue us!"

I was feverish, my legs jumping. "That clock's run out of time. We've got to find a car, drive away."

We both stared out at the room, trying to figure out what to do. Diggy-O was getting set back up after a break, while folks cruised to the dance floor. To my right, I saw Silver James Deaning in a corner, all by his lonesome and brooding. To my left, Lalo mixed drinks for a crew of girls at the bartender table. Standing next to them was Eager, trying to take glamour shots of lolas with a freeboot diggie Canon, while they ignored him. As consolation, Lalo made him a highball, with rum, whiskey, ice cubes, and some sugar he poured out from a pink-and-white C&H bag.

"We could sugar their engines!" Kiki rapped out superfast, zeroing in on the table.

"Sugar their engines?" I stared over at the pink-and-white bag of C&H. "Oh, *right*—it gunks up the cars; they don't work—the guys couldn't follow us—"

She slapped away a tear. "Listen, you figure out how to get us a ride out of here, and I'm going to get the sugar, go outside, and pour it in all the tail pipes—"

"You are?" I piped out. "Oh, okay! Good! Just don't let them see what you're doing."

I had to raise my voice as Diggy-O started playing "Uprise!" but changing it so it was a Diegos song instead of a 99s tune. Scoping out the crowd moving on the floor, I looked for Silver again. He was still in a corner, just watching the crowd while standing in a pool of blue and gold light.

In my head, I could see Dragon throwing Silver the death's head key chain: *Go get my Humvee washed up. And tell them to use that expensive wax I bought what's in the garage.*

And D's words to the Burner were still fresh in my ears: *I'll put*

Silver on the job to turn her against Queen. He's a machine now, a true ice-man. He'll do what I tell him and bring her to your door gift-wrapped. And he'll figure out a way to make her like it, too—she's already back in love with him. Probably never stopped.

"Mish?" Kiki asked.

I put my hands on my thighs and bent at the waist, dizzy and faint. For a second, I couldn't do anything, not barely even move.

"Mish, what's wrong?"

Silver will be in deathly trouble if the Burner gets his hands on him. I stared up at Kiki. *But Kiki could get hurt if Silver betrays us. I don't know what to do!*

"What's the plan?!" she jabbered.

I breathed in; I breathed out. I swallowed down my tears so hard that my throat clamped down painful. *Use your brain, Peña. What would Reina tell you?*

I squeezed my eyes shut. The answer was clear and easy.

Reina would say you'd be a damned fool to trust Silver.

"Kiki," I said, panting, forcing myself to speak. "I'm going to steal Silver's keys. Okay? I'm going to con him into thinking I want to get close to him."

"Do you think you can handle it?" she asked. "I've seen how you look at him."

"Yes. Just don't sugar Dragon's black Humvee," I told her, arranging my hair so it covered the cut on my neck. "I'm going to steal its keys. So, go do it, baby. But remember, not the Humvee!"

"I told you: It's covered. You just do what *you* have to." Ki tugged down her jacket and ran over to Lalo's table, where the boys listened to Diggy's rap:

No blood's like the Diegos, hey-now

No mean's like South, ya see

No rough's like what the 9s gone get in 'Bello, Hello

Montebello Uprise Montebello Montebello!
We burn you down ya give us trouble!!!

Everybody went totally wild. Diegos jumped into the air, thrashed their arms. Snakes slam-danced like punkers. Lalo, Force, and Eager turned away from the booze table to pump their arms in the air, singing along to the lyrics.

Kiki sneaked by them, snatching the bag of C&H sugar, with nobody the wiser.

I waited till she ran out of the house, toward the cars in the yard.

Then I made my way over to Silver.

Uprise Montebello
Yah, uprise my clever fellow
You in more danger than ya know
Woman hunting you, bro
Got tiger eyes and she so sly
She'll catch ya if ya slow

I made for Silver like he was a cat and I was a coyote and I was going to grab him in my jaws. Back in Monty, I had seen Mama work her sex-ambition so hard hombres begged to kiss the gold heels of her shoes. *Men gonna be helpless before you, too, baby, when ya a little older. Ya got the Peña way of moving, but I want you to keep it locked tight for now. Ya too young yet, but you'll know when to bring it out.*

It was time to bring it out. I tiger-walked toward Silver, hip-swiveling, lip-glistening, holding my head high enough to touch heaven. The horde of sexy dancers hijinksing to Diggy-O's tunes parted for me easy, the same as the story of the Red Sea parting for old Moses. Because I guess I was beautiful right then. I could feel it. Everybody turned their heads to follow my cat-slinky ways, including Diggy-O, who started ad-libbing those "Uprise" lyrics about me while I crossed the floor.

Right before I got to my target, I passed by Eager, who was lip-mugging a blonde wearing a long, red Spanish shawl draped over her shoulders. I eyeballed that cover-up. Giving it a good tug, I yanked it off her, and took it with me.

"Hey!"

I scorched my path to S, dragging him to the center of the dance floor.

Silver and I glowed under the blue and red lamplight. The air between us swirled with sweet-scented ghosts made by cig and weed smoke. His mouth was a plump slice of fruit I wanted to eat.

"Come on, let's step outside—like I said, I've got to talk to you about something," he said.

"Not right now, Silver."

He looked down at me, finally noticing my dress. "What are you *wearing*?"

"What, don't you like it?"

"Yeah. But—you look older, though." He swallowed. "You're beautiful, Michelle."

My heart boomed in my chest, but I didn't answer. *Don't screw it up, Peña!*

I raised my hands over my head, shaking the red shawl behind me.

Woman hunting you, woman wantin' you, Diggy-O sang. *But take it slow, Montebello. What looks fine could be the end of the line. So take ya time with unripe wine.*

Silver couldn't pay attention to Diggy's warning when I moved my hips and my head back and forth like a girl possessed.

I brought my hips forward, and my long caramel legs peeked through the dress's slit. Throwing my head back, I felt my hair splashing against my spine. And then I started to move my hips, in this way I got a gift for: *fast.* That's how I used to dance with S in Monty, when I was younger. But now I was like an Arabian seductress. My body shivered, banged out. I flashed the scarf behind me and started to yip out these little screams: "*Ai! Ai ai ai ai ai ai ai!*"

Silver's face turned lovelorn and hungry while everybody else shouted, "Do it P! There's the ol' P! There's the old dancing chica!"

Next to us, Hellacious kookily twisted. Eager and Lalo knocked their heads together. The two rhinoceros-ugly 'roided out Harley thugs slobbered all over their hot pants–wearing hussies. And through the window, I saw Kiki jog up, dust on her skirt. She held a crumpled C&H bag. Her eyes were shiny as a cat's as she threw the bag away.

Silver held my hands, his voice strained and sad: "Listen, if you really want to come back to us, I've got to tell you some things first. About me, and what I've done. I want you *know* me, Michelle. All the things I wrote you in those letters—"

Oh God! I squeezed my eyes shut, trying not to let my love weaken me, then flung the scarf around his shoulders. Moving like that made my bullet-cut burn, but I didn't show it. I pulled him toward me, so our faces were just a breath apart. Twining my arms around his waist, I slid my hands down his sides, his hips, squeezing him— and patting him down to see where those keys were.

There they were: in the back left butt pocket. With my superquick fingers, I slipped them out, hid them under the scarf.

But I'd pressed so close to him that our chins now touched, and our cheeks. My heart started collapsing like an ocean wave, and not just from my fear.

Silver took in a ragged breath. "Michelle." He laced his fingers through mine. "You're waking my soul up, and it hurts, girl."

Touching his collarbone, I stroked my hand down to his hard, muscled chest. "It should, after what you've put me through."

I tilted my chin. My mouth grazed his. He held back, breathing hard. Then, as if he were falling from a long, deadly height, he lowered his head. Pressing his soft mouth to mine, he was shaking. He tasted like apples, clean. I opened my eyes, to see the dark lashes feathering his cheeks.

He came up for air, and looked at me as lonely as a murdered man.

"I'm not who I was, baby. I've done some things, and they broke me so I can't be fixed."

I grasped him harder. "S, forget the confession; I heard about what you did to those Diegos. All I need to know is, can I trust you? Time was, I could with my *life*—"

His eyes darkened. "What I'm trying to tell you is, the times have *changed*. I'm all messed up!"

"Man, forget that!" I yelled. "This is not the time for you to get all tortured inside, okay!?"

"I'm just trying to explain—"

"We've got to get out of here!" I shook the keys in the air.

He slapped his pocket. "The 'Vee—ha, my brothers taught you that trick."

"Hear me, S," I said, my eyes hot with tears. "There is no deal. D didn't get the money from King."

Silver took in a scared breath. "What are you talking about?"

"*Dragon doesn't have the money.* I just heard him begging Freddie Gonzales. That's why he wouldn't let me go, and he's had Force shadowing me all night. But he doesn't want me as a hostage anymore. He's lost control of King and knows he won't be seeing that hundred K. But he's come up with an even better plan for me now."

Silver stared deep into my face. His forehead twisted. "Oh—oh no."

I put my hands on his chest. "You *see* I'm telling you the truth."

"Goddammit! I knew something was wrong—"

"Dragon *lied*, Silver. *Again*. That's why I'm getting you out of here, plus Midget and Game—they're in danger. We all are. Dragon sold us to the Burner. And Freddie's got big eyes for you, too. Your amnesty is done."

"Wait—'sold' you?"

"Dragon slaved me, S."

S's cheeks paled to white.

I pleaded, "We've got to go. Come on, baby, let's get somewhere safe—you and me—you and me back together—we'll figure it out! Just come with me!"

Silver looked around at the people in the room. "I guess what I was trying to save was lost a long time ago—I just couldn't admit it." He focused on me and tried to smile. "You have to go now. I'm so sorry I brought you here. But I'm going to fix it. I've got to go get Dragon's hot—"

"But the Burner's got it in for you!" I flung my arms around him, sobbing. I pressed my mouth to his cheeks, touching his hair. "S, you've got to come with me! I won't leave without you!"

"Baby, no, you've got to skip out." He kissed me again, all over my face, my eyes. He saw the cut on my neck, touched a drop of blood there. "Oh God, Michelle. Never mind what I said before. You can trust me. *I got you.* Remember?"

I kissed him again, harsh and reckless. "I got you too!"

"Not this time. But I love you." He looked away from me, and a terrible, death-hunting look that I never saw before entered his eyes. "Just run—*now!* I mean it!"

He bolted fast through the crowd, disappearing in the shadows and smoke.

"S!" I screamed. "Where you going?! Don't leave me!"

Pushing through the dance floor, I yelled his name again and again. Wading neck-deep in shimmying hustlers and skirt-twirling girls, I twisted around, searching for him. At the front of the house, I suddenly saw Ki standing at the open front door, staring at me crazy because of all the sexy hip-wiggling she'd just seen me do.

"Where did you learn how to do *that*?" Ki asked, when I rushed over to her.

"Oh God, oh God!" I said. "Silver!"

"What's wrong?! Did one of them hurt you?"

I stared at Kiki. *Okay, I can't crack up. I've got to get her out of here!* "Ki, did you do all the engines except the Humvee?"

"Um, yeah. A lot of them. Then one of these Diego guys came staggering out to the front yard, and I got freaked out."

Using the scarf to hide the keys from any evil eyes, I pressed Dragon's skull-and-crossbones key chain into Kiki's hands. "Get to the car; I'll meet you out there. But I've got to go back and get Silver and Midget and Game, bring them with us."

"Let's just go *now*! Those guys are going to totally snitch on us!"

"No, I've got to get the boyz! Remember how I showed you how to double-clutch that day we ditched and I took you around Beverly Hills in Frank's Lexus?"

She waggled her head. "What, that day I was yelling about how we didn't even have a learner's, and you were drag racing all Vin Diesel?"

"Yeah, that's it." I pointed at the Humvee, glittering like a big-top three-ring circus there on the scabby front lawn. "Listen to me, if I ain't—I mean, if I'm *not* out there in *three minutes*, you drive that puppy out of here."

She blinked so fast at the 'Vee it was like she wanted to fly out of the desert using her eyelashes as wings. "You want *me* to drive that army thingy?"

"Yes!"

"Okay, okay, how hard can it be?" she jabbered. "I'm a strong black woman. Right?"

"R-right!

"*Frakking* right! But you hurry up!" She dashed out.

Bolting through the room, I searched through the crowd for Game and Midget. Beautiful women thumped their patooties to the music alongside men with tear tats. Eager batted his lashes at them. Hellacious smooth-talked a girl onto one of the big black sofas. Lalo ate a hamburger and laughed.

Where are they?!

Running up the stairs, I didn't see anybody but a drunkenly unconscious Diego. I scooted up to the Vault. Nobody there, either, but I took the opportunity to yank on the socks and Nikes I'd got 'napped in.

Back down the stairs, *there* were Midget and Game munching appetizers.

"Hey! You've got to come with me—"

Midget held out his paper plate, full of Lalo's mini-tacos. "P, chill. Have one."

"Where's Silver? *Where is he?!*" I nearly screamed.

"Thought he was with you." Midget said. "Jeez!"

"Oh, Mary, help my Montebello ass!" I prayed.

Thupt-thupt-thupt! Suddenly, over Diggy-O's racket, I heard the Humvee motor coughing into life, and the sound of Force yelling: "Boss, boss!" Mash-faced from my beating, Force staggered from the bathroom into the living room. "She's getting away!"

I dashed away from Game and Midget. Through a window, I saw the black 'Vee bumping past three cars before blasting down the road.

I jumped to the open door. "Kiki! What are you doing?! *Don't leave me!*"

The music stopped, Diggy-O cutting off mid-syllable like he'd been choked.

"Hello, Michelle," I heard the Burner purr.

Breathless, I turned around.

Past the mob, him and Dragon stared me down. Dragon looked like he'd been punched in the gullet. The Burner, though, was real fluffy-tailed at the sight of me in my nekkid dress.

He raised that gun he'd been swinging around at D. "Looks like your debt has come due, Dragon—"

"*Don't you touch her!!!*"

Silver rocketed through the crowd, holding a Remington in one hand, his dark hair flying like a thundercloud as he launched himself straight at the Burner's head.

Wham!

Clinging onto the Burner's neck, S tried to force the muzzle of the gun in his mouth, but seven or eight Diegos flew from all directions, fists spinning, knives flashing and slashing through the air at his head and chest.

"*Arg!*" the Burner roared.

Bam! Silver aimed his gun at a gigantic, big-bellied Diego, shooting him in the shoulder. Another Diego pounced on him, slicing down a knife, but Silver grabbed his blade, then pivoted and slashed his arm. Red liquid scarves twirled in the air. Swinging his leg in a vicious judo move, he kicked the brains out of a bald, bearded gangster who was aiming a Colt at him. Next to that guy, a smaller Diego, with bandy legs and pocked face, tried to run away. Silver stuck his knife straight in his thigh, and the man went down on his knees. I was screaming crazy. Silver looked like a demon, red as hell, white stripe of teeth. He spun again, and kicked unconscious two more dudes standing awkward, helpless, and stupid between him and the Burner.

"Stop it, man! *Stop it!*" Dragon was shrieking, as Game hollered, incoherent, trying to reach S through the crowd.

The Burner raised his black shining pistol level to Silver's head.

"*Silver!*" I howled.

Silver twisted, grabbed the pistol.

Bam!

I screamed at the white smoke, the bright flash of blood.

"*Go, go, go, go, Michelle!*" Silver bellowed.

Bam! Bam!

My last glimpse of him was bathed in red, circled by sparks, white and black fog. His face flickered in the scarlet light. His eyes were white. In the next heartbeat, he disappeared.

And then this fast girl was out the door, running wild into the dangerous world.

Boom *chaka chaka, boom chaka chaka, fast girl oh you* fast girl, fast girl. *You gonna take it* fast girl, yeah you fast *bad* girl—

Fire burned in my legs and a whirlwind twisted my mind as I raced past the garage. Worldwide racing records broke under my feet.

Save me, somebody! Save me, Lord! Help me!

I sprinted under the moon quicker than wishes and prayed to a God I stopped believing in when my whole family disappeared from me. *Jesus, help me save myself!* I aimed for the desert sand, and then the long black road heading away from this hell.

"Hey—hey!" Boyz yelling behind me.

Ratatat tat tat—sound of dress-up man shoes clattering on the Fort's porch.

Ka-thunk! Noise made by the tumble fall of some boy slipping on the sand.

But I didn't look back. You don't look back. I didn't even look back when I heard Money fall during the 800m, because a runner is blind and deaf except to everything in front of her, everything in her way.

"*Michelle!!!*" the boyz screamed at me."*P!!! Gonna get you!*"

Black road before me. Hunting it, flying toward it—

Behind me was the *grrrrr-ank!* of sugar-gunked car engines starting, failing. The *whap!* of men beating on the car hoods. The sound of Dragon hollering: "*Bring her back here! Bring 'em both back!*"

Kiki! I saw the Humvee ahead of me. Its yellow taillights sparkled too far away. Kiki shrieked, "*AAAAAAAAAAIGGHH!*" inside that car. *Slam slam* went my feet on the sand, never slipping, never falling. I sailed clean over two scrub brushes. Hurtled like a jackrabbit over a cactus.

Here's the road!

Wham! I hit the pavement. There was sand, cactus, and grass on either side of the black highway. And behind me, maybe two hundred yards away:

Pap pap pap pap pap pap.

"Catch up with her! She's just a—"

It was the Diegos mostly was my guess. Burner ordering them to hunt me like an animal. And they were men. But me, I'm—

Female, Dragon had said, like that answered something, as he'd patted my cheek. *This look like nobility to you?*

Was I faster?

I'm a girl. I'm a girl.

Am I faster?

What do you think?

Hell yes I'm faster.

The Humvee was dead ahead of me now. I chopped up to it, closer, closer. *Got to catch up!* But Kiki kept speeding forward, far ahead of my reach. I suddenly saw her start to stick half her body out the window in a crazy panic. Head first. Shoulders out. She stretched her hands out to me, the video camera glittering.

"Mish!" The wind blew back her hair; her eyes were streaming. "I didn't mean to go! I was just starting it! And then it started to move! And I was driving it! But I can't stop it! And, *aaagh!*"

"Stop the car!" I blasted out.

"*I can't! I don't know how!*"

I thrashed through the air. "Slam the brakes!"

"Which one is the gas and which is the brake?"

"It's the left pedal!"

"*Which* is?!"

She clambered back down, stomped on something. Not the brake, the gas. The Humvee rocketed away.

"*Waaa!*"

"*Kiki!!!*"

Behind me, I caught this sound: *Vrrrrooom. Vrrooom vroom.*

And now I had no choice *but* to look back.

Three black, shiny, demon-quick motorcycles burned up the road.

She didn't sugar the bikes!

Dragon hunched over on Hellacious's Indian and gunned it straight for my ass. Just behind him, the two rhinoceros-looking Harley-riding thugs bore on down me like beasts. The wind blew back Dragon's pompadour into a tumbleweed. With the X-ray vision blessed upon me by my horrification, I saw that one of the rhinos had a tarantula tattoo on his left cheek.

"Help!" I screamed. But Kiki was too far ahead to save me now.

The motorcycles sped up, reached me—they were on both sides of me. The rhino-looking Diego with the tarantula tat rode my left. The other rhino and Dragon rode my right. The black paint of all three motorbikes glistened as gloomy as the vampire sky. High beams shot out a gold halo, lighting my way.

"Woohoo! Hey-you! Girlieeeeeeee!"

The rhinos reached out, slapped at me while I ran. *Whack, whack.* Hands hitting my shoulder, my head. Animal terror strangled me. I kept shredding the road. The tarantula tat snatched at my butt but missed and punched at my ribs instead. They were both guffawing.

"Stop it! Stop it!" I shrieked.

"Just grab her!" Dragon called out.

Kill or be killed! ripped through my mind.

I looked to my right. I looked to my left. Both rhinos were evenly matched up on either side of me. If one of them took a quick turn, I could make them into asphalt pudding.

I waited for the rhino on my right to get an inch up, matching noses near exact with the rhino on my left. *Now!*

Bearing straight left, I scooted behind the tarantula tat, circling his motorcycle and zipping onto the sand-and-packed-dirt desert bordering the highway. The rhino on my right gunned too hard after me, hitting the tarantula's bike. His front tire went right into the other Harley's right wheel.

Ack-hup-thump. Aaaaggghhh!

Both boyz flipped their motorcycles. They crashed, in a head-splattering, bone-splitting explosion.

I kept moving. Into the desert, into the cactus-spiked sand. I veered far enough off that I lured Dragon onto that slippery territory, where I might take the upper hand.

"Come here!" Dragon yawled out. "Burner'll kill everybody here if I don't bring you to him!"

Golden car lights ahead. Was that the Humvee turning back? Diegos coming to get me?

Dragon's bike whirred rougher, grinding as he skidded over the sand. Ahead of me, there was nothing but more sand and sharp, bumpy cactuses.

I ran straight for a gnarly cactus that was about a hundred feet away. I judged it stood about as high as my ribs. Thick as a sequoia. Behind me, I heard Dragon's bike getting closer.

I bet I blocked his view of where I was headed. He'd be keeping his eyes on my back.

One second, two seconds, three seconds to lift off: I pounded right up to the cactus—*hoo wee!* Hurtling it with one smooth jump, I cleared it complete, landing hard on the other side.

Slam! Dragon's motorbike slammed right into the cactus. *Suck it!* The front wheel spun sideways into the dust. *Wha-wham!*

Dragon crashed, the bike flinging violent from under him as he screamed.

I slowed, slowed, stopped. Hands on my thighs. Breathing harder than a suffocated girl. Going to barf up my brains. I fell to the ground, my knees crumbling.

A car barreled up toward me.

Bright car lights blinded me. The car charged closer up. I could barely see it—gold or silver, skidding to a stop with a big *screech!* Two men ran though the dust. The Humvee was stopped on the highway some distance up.

"I'm gonna give you a taste of my temper before them bastards buy me, D," I said in a chill, deathly voice, crawling toward him.

Dragon lay on the ground like a shot dog, half under the motorbike. He had red stains on his cheek and his bangs clumped up with his head-blood. Blood streaked his neck. His arm flung sideways over his body. His feet splayed far apart.

"I wasn't going to hurt you," he wailed, tears mixing red with the blood.

I stood up and kicked him in the ribs. *"You killed Silver! You killed him! You killed him!!!"*

"No, I didn't!"

"You sold me to the Burner, dawg! *I heard you do it, sucka!"*

"I would've got you back. I would've seen you was safe. I would've made sure. Burner was going to rip all of us. He's *gonna.* My boyz!"

I kicked him again and again. I would have kicked him all the way to hell, too, if I hadn't heard the most unlikely combo of voices calling for me that second.

"Chelle!"

"Michelle, kid!"

163

There, like a dream sent me from the God I'd lost faith in, was Frank running toward me, fear creasing his skinny, fine-boned, handsome whiteman's face. Next to him ran Samson, big-chested, bush of black hair, fire-eyed with worry. Kiki ran after, screaming and crying.

Dad! Samson! I couldn't pick, running to Frank *and* my brother— but Samson was already bent on D's destruction, pulling away to get down to business. So I rushed to my foster pop.

"Frank! I think Silver's dead! Silver's dead! Help me, Frank!"

Frankie's green eyes crumpled. His face had gone white as paste. I clutched onto him, taking in his skinny cheeks and his sweaty brown hair, his shaking green bean body.

"It's okay, Michelle! Oh, Christ, I've been going crazy worrying about you!"

Behind us, Samson said, "You hurt my sister, D, and that is a treason punishable by death."

Dragon didn't debate. He knew King was right under the law of tha Life.

"Oh no, wait! What is he doing?!" Kiki shrieked.

Samson bent over, putting his hands onto Dragon's throat. As Dragon got that knuckle necklace, he looked over at Kiki with these gigantic loverboy brown eyes.

"Don't do that!" Kiki howled. "Stop!"

"Samson, don't!" Frank hollered, trying to shield me from the violence by gripping me harder.

Kiki cried, "Mish! Tell him not to! Tell him not to!"

I kept my cold, cold eyes on D, as a flood of tears ran down my face.

I did not say *stop*.

Samson was in blue jeans and a too-small Harvard sweatshirt. Frank's. As he curled over Dragon, he was half in shadow, half lit by the motorbike's high beams. The veins stuck out of his head. His hands clung onto Dragon's throat, gripping. Dragon's eyes popped. He scratched at King's hands helpless. "*Aaaghghgh!*"

But then, my brother shuddered, like a cold wind got into his blood. He fell back, let go. "No, *no!* I'm done with that. I ain't going to double my sins with you, you bastard!"

"Sssssssss," I hissed. "Samson!"

"Can't, Chelle," he said. "Even though you want me to beat him dead, I just can't do it, baby."

"Ugh! *Damn you!*"

Kiki's head snapped as she stared in shock at me.

"Oh my God, just leave him alone and let's get out of here!" Frank yelled.

"Agh!" Dragon didn't need a second invite. He staggered up, grabbed the bike.

Vrooom!

Still clinging onto Frank, I watched Dragon skitter through the sand, toward the Fort. Far off, I could hear the sound of sirens.

Woooo-oooooo! Woooo-ooooooooo!

Blue and red lights shimmered closer. The sirens got louder and higher.

Whoop. Whoop.

"Those motorcycle guys—*what happened?*" Kiki squeezed her eyes tight, blinding herself to that tangled-up hump of rhinoceros boyz splattered on the road behind us. And oh, *yes,* they *were* an awful-looking moaning heap of red-skinned flesh and busted-up motorcycle metal. Out of that pile of messed up manhood stretched a hand. You couldn't tell which rhino that hand belonged to. But it waved up toward the sky, like it had a white flag in it.

"I wish they were dead for what they did to S!" I screamed.

"Oh, that's terrible, Mish!" Kiki said. "You don't mean it!"

"Give them to me now, *I'll butcher 'em!*" I doubled over, holding my face. "*Oh, Silver, Silver, Silver, Silver!*"

"What's she saying?" Frank asked.

"Oh, girl!" Samson's mouth twisted in disgust when he checked out the rhinoceroses. "You is a killer, Chelle! You're a chip off *tha block!*"

Tears and sweat shone on Frank's cheeks. "Michelle, you can tell me. Did they touch you? This dress they made you wear—did they *hurt* you? If they—took advantage of you . . . I'll get you help—"

"I'm sorry I'm wearing this hoochie dress, Frank," I sobbed. "I didn't want you to see me in it! It don't mean nothing! You don't got to worry! Nobody raped me; they just shot me, is all."

"*What?!*" Quick, he started to undo the bandage on my arm. "I don't see a bullet in here—oh, Jesus, you're going to need stitches, and antibiotics. How did these people even get a hold of you? Your brother came to see me this morning. Samson said he'd heard rumors about you being *somewhere* in Palm Desert and would I help come look. And then, not long ago, thank God! I got a text message from some person called—something—strange—Midget? And then we found you!"

As the police made their way up to us, Kiki stared at me, suddenly seeing the secret bad in me with her big, glowing eyes. And while the police busied themselves with the rhinos, Samson snuck into Dragon's Humvee, then drove off.

I crushed myself into Frank so hard he'd have bruises the next day.

"Frank, tell them there's a boy," I blithered, "shot, in the house—"

Frank told them.

"Oh, I love you, man. I love you, I love you, Frank," I gasped into his chest.

"Shh, shh," he said again, but suddenly that old awkward sound came into his voice. "Um, oh. Okay. Just calm down. This has been such a terrible night. But it's over."

"Frank?"

He cleared his throat, tensing up. "Just . . . it's all right. We'll take you to the hospital."

Frank felt like a block of stone in my arms now. I said, "No, I don't want nobody to touch me—just you, Frank, you take care of me!"

But leaning his head back, he grimaced, and turned away from me. "Oh, God. I can't handle this."

I let go of my grip and stared at him, but he didn't look at me. I moved toward Kiki. She wouldn't meet eyes with me, either.

The bright black sky and the police lights kept thrashing overhead. The sand under my feet was loose and crumbling. The whole strange world felt cold and dead.

I hugged myself, tight, tight. My throat was so full of weeping I could have choked. I squeezed my eyes shut and saw Silver's horrible face when he got shot.

Then I couldn't take it, and threw myself on Frank again.

"I don't care. I don't care. You came for me! Just take me away from here, Frank!"

"Of course, of course! You're going to be okay; you'll be all right!"

"Take me home. Take me home, Frank! Just *please* take me home!"

RACING WUNDERKIND FLEES CAPTORS IN A BRAVE DESERT DASH: NINTH-GRADE RUNNING CHAMP KIDNAPPED BY GANG MEMBERS ESCAPES ALIVE, BUT IN SERIOUS CONDITION

BY ANITA ROTHMAN

SPECIAL TO THE *LOS ANGELES TIMES*, JANUARY 8, 2009

Emerging from Palm Desert after two days in captivity, All-American track and field hopeful Michelle Peña suffered from a pistol wound, dehydration, and shock, say local authorities. . . .

JUNIOR DASHER "DOING FINE," FOSTER FATHER SAYS, BUT WON'T BE COMPETING IN KENTUCKY

BY CELIA MURPHY BROWN

DAILY NEWS, SPORTS SECTION, JANUARY 13, 2009

All-American Track and Field Championship officials today declared kidnapping victim Michelle Peña "unfit" to compete at this week's Kentucky races as a result of the trauma the ninth grader suffered during her ordeal in Palm Desert. . . .

KIDNAPPERS' TRAIL GROWS COLD IN THE INLAND EMPIRE

BY ALEX O'NAN

SANTA MONICA TIMES, SPORTS SECTION, JANUARY 14, 2009

Palm Desert police officials, in conjunction with the FBI, have recalled half the agents out searching for the gang ringleaders who kidnapped youth runner Michelle Peña last week. Though seven members of the "Diegos" gang were apprehended in their desert hideout, all have invoked their right to remain silent under the Constitution's Fifth Amendment, thus eliminating the possibility of their imminent cooperation with the police. Without any guide to the location of their leader, Frederico Gonzales, authorities admit that the chances of capturing the gang's inner circle decline as each day passes, and say they will not "waste manpower" on what may be a fruitless hunt. . . .

LOCAL PREP SCHOOLER TAKES THE GOLD IN THE ALL-AMERICANS
BY FELICE JIN
LOS ANGELES TIMES, SPORTS SECTION, JANUARY 17, 2009
Yale-Westview Cougar Lisa Smithson thrilled the Kentucky crowd on Wednesday when she took the gold in the 800-, 400-, and 200-meter races. Her sweeping victory was barely dimmed by the marked absence of her closest competition, kidnap victim Michelle Peña. . . .

27

I was a dead girl for the couple weeks that passed after Ki and I got rescued. Once I got back to Westchester, King had told me on the phone that Silver hadn't made it out of the Fort alive. I spent the next two days slipping out my bedroom window and searching for him or any other soul in Montebello who would tell me different, but they'd all gone into deep hiding. After that, I got even more scared for him, and Silver's beautiful, black-eyed face ghosted me so painful that I couldn't do much but lay in bed as a deep gloom swallowed me. I stared blind at the ceiling when Frank nailed my window shut and said I was too messed up to run the All-Americans or do a decathlon scrimmage. And I didn't even care when Frank told me five days later that Lisa Smithson had taken all the golds at Kentucky. Let her have them; didn't matter to me anymore. The only time I drummed up enough gumption to so much as lift my head was when I tried to call Kiki. But she didn't seem to want to talk to the likes of me, and every time I rang her up, I just got rolled into her voice mail.

After those two weeks, I'd sunk so low that I could practically see the whole shiny world float far above me, and so far away that I wondered if I'd ever catch up with it again. This is when Frank tried to have a showdown with me. He came into my room, where I was clutching that pink Prada heart-goob key fob that Ki had gave me after my All-American regionals. I'd put my keys on it, and was holding onto it, something like a baby blanket, but I guess different. A best friend memory key fob blanket.

"Michelle, how are you feeling?"

Frank reached down and touched the little scar on my neck, the stitches on my shoulder. Poor old boy, he was doing his best, though he was worn-out. He had circles under his eyes. Could have used a haircut, too.

"You need a makeover, Frankie."

"You are giving me some cause for concern, dear." He tried to smile, but just looked more worried. "This is worse than the last time you had a breakdown. And I'm finding myself a little bit at a . . . loss."

I waved a weak hand at him. "Aw, you don't got to stress on me or have a panic attack over me or nothing, Frank. I'm gonna be real well behaved, real soon. You're gonna be surprised. Just as soon as, you know, I get a little rest."

"You've been resting enough. It's time to get up!" He boomed out his voice, trying to sound all energetic and super positive. "Why don't we go out? Come on; let's go on a run."

I shook my head, a tear dripping down my nose. "Nah, I'm gonna sit this one out."

He ran his hands over his mouth. "We *can't* keep going on like this, Michelle, seriously. Tell me about this boy who got shot—who died. Maybe that'll help."

The tears poured down me. "I don't know what happened, man. I was looking for him, but I couldn't find Silver nowhere. And Samson said he's—" I couldn't say it. *Dead.*

"Michelle, I don't want you talking to your brother. He always gets you in this stage of agitation. Not to mention the fact that he's a fugitive."

"Yeah, right," I murmured, rolling onto my side. "Sam was telling me how he escaped from mini-sec posing as an electrician. Stole a cap, a jumpsuit, and a clipboard, and just walked out. Imagine that."

"I'm out of resources here," Frank went on. "You need to talk to *somebody*, even if it's not me. What about Kiki? She always made you laugh."

I gulped air. "I don't know what's going on with her; I can't get her on the line. I guess she's *really* busy."

"Okay, right . . ." he said, trying to think. "Her mother did say she didn't want—"

I tilted my head at him. "Huh?"

He squinched his eyes up. "Nothing. It doesn't matter. What do you say let's just get that phone I bought you? We'll ring her up again. I think it would be really good for you to talk to her."

"Nah . . ."

But he got the new pink iPhone from my desk, scrolled for Ki's name, and then put it to my ear.

Ring, ring.

"I told you, she's not picking up, dude."

Ring, ring.

Click.

And like a present from Saint Flo-Jo, I heard her live voice: "Did you get one?" Kiki bellowed, talking rapid-fast.

I flapped open my mouth. "She answered, Frank!"

He waggled his fingers at me. "Well, say something!"

"Hello? Ki?"

"Did you get one?!"

"Ki? That you?"

"Yes!"

"Did I get a *what*?"

"Oh—my—*God*—an interview!"

"An interview?"

"For Y-Dub!!!"

I sat up, brushed the hair out of my face. "What—you made the first cut?"

"Ten minutes ago!" she said.

I hesitated. "And—you're not mad at me?"

"Never mind that right now; did you get an interview?"

"Who cares about that?" I said. "I got to know if you hate me, Kiki!"

Silence, for a second. "I don't know," she said. "I'm not supposed to talk to you or see you. But—I don't want to talk about that right now. Check your e-mail!"

"Okay." I scrolled down my forty messages from Monroe Park and RP's assistant principal and academic dean, and Coach, and Principal Fisher, too. "Um—oh, yeah."

"Yeah what?" she breathed.

"Yeah—yeah. I got one; it's here."

"*Oh my God!*"

I looked at Frank, fluttering my lips at him like a fish.

"Michelle, what?" he asked.

"Frank, look, look!"

subject: **Invitation to Michelle Peña to interview for MLK scholarship**

from: Yale-Westview

date: February 18, 2009

attachments: Yale-Westview map

driving instructions

Dear Michelle Peña,

Yale-Westview Academy is happy to offer you an invitation to interview for the Martin Luther King Awards scholarship on Wednesday, February 27, 2009, at 3:30 p.m. The interview will last for approximately one half of an hour. It will take place at the Roth auditorium, on the Yale-Westview campus. Attached to this message are driving instructions and a map. Please also call to confirm your attendance: 818-555-7869.

Sincerely,

Dean Alexandra Peterson

"That is completely amazing!" Frank rapped out, turning pink around the eyes.

"*Woohoo!!! We got interviews!!!*" Kiki screamed some more.

"Yeah, yeah!" I croaked.

Frank gripped the edge of my blanket. "Michelle, I know you're happy about this. Right? Come on, you can just give me a little tiny smile, right?"

"Well, you like it, don't ya Frank?" I asked, trying to creak out a human-looking grin. "If I go to Y-Dub, you'll dig that. And I'll be with Ki. So, I am happy. Um, right. No, I *am*." I squeezed my eyes shut, convincing myself. "Yeah, this makes things better. It's great; it is—it's really, really, really great!"

28

"**W**hat do you *mean* you can't take me to the interview?" I asked Frank a week later, on that Wednesday, February 27, 2009, at around 2:30 in the p.m. Him, me, and Squiggy stood by the kitchen counter. Frank was dressed in a blue button-down and chinos, looking all normal and low-key. I'd dressed up in a monster mock-up prep-school girl costume, with a navy Brooks Brothers blazer and a red-and-blue plaid skirt that made me look like I belonged on a box of some defunct Christmas cookies. "You promised you'd be there with me, dawg. I've got to have your prepster expertise to help me slam this."

"I have a consultation," he said, touching his fingertips together and looking at me over his hand-teepee, "with the best psychologist in Los Angeles, who is squeezing me in."

I took in a breath. "But I thought maybe you were just joking around before when you said you were going to a head-shrinker on account of me."

"Oh, no, I was completely and totally serious. And if anything, I need it even more, now!" Frank's hand-teepee crunched up as he started to wring his hands together. "It's nothing to worry about. I'm only taking some time out for myself. I know it's hard, but I'm just going to have to put myself at the top of my to-do list today, Michelle."

"You ain't wigging—I mean, you're not upset because of *me*, right, Frank?"

"Oh, the etiology's more of a gestalt."

"Huh?"

He said, real careful: "The last few weeks have been somewhat *challenging*. And I'm just looking for a little advice."

I tried to wink at him frisky, like he wasn't giving me the chills. "If I didn't know any better, I'd say that *was* because of me, then. And I told Ki that you'd get a little nervy because of us getting 'napped—and me wearing that dress and stuff. But I know that really, you and me are okay, Frank. Right?"

Frank gave me a nice but tired smile. "Look, Michelle, like I said, I don't want you to worry. I just have to rethink this whole foster care business."

I stood real still. "Rethink it?"

"Well, yes," he said, nervously yanking his shirt down to smooth it out. "This isn't really working."

"What's not working?"

"I don't think we should talk about this before the interview."

I stared at him.

"Oh, dear, erm." His little green eyes looked at me super soulful. Then they started fluttering and he rolled them up white in his head. "I'm having issues with, you know, our *dynamic*."

"'Dynamic'? What you talking about? That sounds like a cereal."

"Michelle, listen, of course, you and I—we're—and—I feel, I feel . . ."

"F-feel what?"

"Uh, really, very, absolutely, you know . . . ." Desperate, he looked at his watch.

I started biting my nails.

"Oh my God, look at the time," he said. "Listen, the important thing is, I am so hugely proud of you for getting this interview. And—you are going to be *fine*."

You gonna be fine without me, okay? I suddenly heard my mom's voice echo in my head. *You forget me and put your money on somebody else.*

Then I heard the voices of my other foster parents, too, other ones who dumped me, Mrs. Carmichael, Mr. and Mrs. Gold.

You're going to be fine, Michelle; don't worry! You should just find foster parents who can handle your . . . personality.

Frank went on, "This is perfectly regular adult stuff! Not anything you have to worry about. I just have to think about, you know, being a foster dad to you."

I didn't say anything. All my words were stuck in my craw.

"Michelle, hey. I told you: It's going to be okay."

I didn't say anything. Staring down at Squiggy, I petted his butt with my shoe-toes.

"Michelle? . . ."

"Aw, that *burns*," I murmured.

"Oh, Michelle, don't look like that!" He grabbed his head. "Oh, God! If you really need me to take you, I'll take you!"

Finally, I managed to get it out: "Nah, that's okay, Frankie."

"Seriously, never mind. Let's go. I'll find another specialist."

"Oh, calm down." I made my voice breezy. "It's no bigs. Agh—erg. I was all just overcompensating. You go shrink out; I'll get to the school another way."

He peered at me close, like I was an amoeba under a microscope. "You promise me? I wouldn't do this if I didn't have to."

"I promise. I got this one."

He stuffed his hands in his pockets. "Oh, good! You're going to be okay, right?"

"Yeah," I grunted.

He nodded. "All right, good, good. But don't be ridiculous about getting there yourself. Helena's going to take you."

"The *maid*?"

"She's coming over in about a half an hour, hopefully sooner. So. Let me just give you a—little h-h-h-h—" He couldn't say *hug* beyond the "h" sound, so just patted me on the shoulders with his fingertips. "Okay! We will talk about everything tonight! And you're going to do great! They're going to love you!" He got up, snatched his jacket, and then scrambled down the hall. "Bye! I'll make this up to you. I promise."

"Wait, Frank?"

But I heard a slam, and he was gone.

Looking down at my blazer, I tugged it smooth, like Frank messed with his clothes when he didn't want to feel anything. My throat made some gacking noises, though.

No, no crying! Stiff lip, stiff lip, stiff lip—you got an interview! I stood in the kitchen, shaking and swallowing everything down. I thought of Helena driving down here to fetch me in her Pontiac, and shook my head. *Hell no, I don't want your maid to take me to my Y-Dub interview. No way!*

Hustling to my bedroom, I got my iPhone. *Ring, ring ring.*

"Chuy's Monster Garage," came a voice on the line.

"King there?"

"Who?"

"Samson, I mean," I said.

"Hold on, kid; I'll see if I can find him. . . ."

Rattle, rattle went the phone. And then:

"Hey, Chelle! . . ."

29

"**H**urry, Samson, we are going to be *laaaaate*," I crowed about forty minutes later, while barreling down the 101 freeway in King's used forest-green Range Rover. "My interview's at three thirty. And Ki's was at three! I've already missed seeing her before she went in!"

Driving with a pinkie on the wheel, King flashed his mirrored sunglasses at me. "Keep ya wig on; this Rover got so much horsepower, we'll be there in plenty."

Man, but my brother looked tough. Bronze skin, that blackbird hair, and his muscles bumped powerful out of his wifebeater. The blue Snake tats twinkled on his neck, and the Colt on his right bicep shone like a jewel. He looked just about as fetching as that Rover, which had authentic leather seats, and custom smoked windows hiding the brown-and-gray ugliness of the L.A. roads.

"Where'd you get this rig, anyway?"

"Traded it for the Humvee, after liberatin' it in the desert. I knew if D's boyz saw his car around town, I'd taste trouble. Once in a while, I even squat in our house in 'Bello, park this on the street, and the Snakes ain't sniffed me out yet."

"Nice ride." Reaching down, I tinkled the keys in the ignition. They hung from the silver death's head key chain, which he'd stolen along with the 'Vee. "I see you got your death's head again. This is supposed to belong to the head of the Snakes."

"I bet D's missing it. You know, if I wasn't trying to live in the right, Chelle, I'd find that Dragon, split his head open with a shovel, and then I'd bury him and Silver in the desert for what they did to you."

Hearing Silver's name, all I could do was stare out the window.

"S's already buried, from what you told me," I finally said, an edge in my voice.

King stuck out his chin. "Silver's dead, like I said to you before."

"Yeah, so, when was the funeral?"

"Um—last week. Or, I don't know—I didn't go. But, why even talk about him? The way Silver wound up, he was pure poison to you; he'd lead you straight to hell—hey, you all right? You got crazy eye all of a sudden."

I scrubbed my face with my hands, trying to smash the tears back into my blowhole. "You're right! I can't think about this right now. I've got to be all positive! *Arg*!" I started to bang my head, like football players do to get revved up for a game. "I'm going to dominate that interview! You know? *Agh*, I'm going to be super tough! In—what—"

"Like ten, fifteen minutes."

"Yeah, right. Oh! That means Ki's doing her interview right now. Hurry it up, please, King."

He swerved the Rover through the lanes, nice and easy. "Nah, no rushing. Doesn't get you there faster. Patience, that's what I learned in the joint. See, *agape*, it means, I am a patient, good man. A *good* man. A gentle man. A *gentleman*. I got a job, I got a squat, I got some money—you need money, Chelle?"

"No. Frank's taking care of me. For now, anyway."

"What do you mean, 'for now'? That Frank's being good to you, right? He all loves you, what you said."

"Yeah . . . I don't want to think about that neither. What do you think, they gonna ask me about presidential politics, or the eco-geo-system of the Low Countries, or they just gonna do a psych profile on me, which I sure the hell hope not—"

"Oh, guess things aren't going so well, huh?" King asked. "That's too bad. Maybe Frank don't dig you cuz a how he's all homo, huh?"

"Man, no, do not call him that," I said.

"That's cool with me he gay. See, I'm growing up in the world, Chelle." King talked with both of his hands while he drove. "I'm all tolerance, and that agape love, and I'm all reading that Gandhi, see, Chelle? I got myself some hope, yeah—hope in my heart—hope in my soul, *yes* Jesus—"

I slid my eyes over at him. "You going to church, ding-a-ling?"

"I sneak into Kenny's congregation, out in Burbank. But I don't make myself known because he'd *bust* my hump, on account I all skipped that low-sec joint he practically had to noodle the governer's poodle to get me into. Anyway, I listen to the preacher lady they got there. And I read, too. Emerson, and Thoreau, and that Dalai Lama, and the Mahatma, and it is opening up my mind to agape, and living in the right, and whatevah . . . um, hold on, sister-sister, I got a hankering—will you look under your seat?"

"What? Wait—you've got to get off the freeway here. This is the turnoff. Laurel Canyon. Hurry, hurry."

King skidded off the freeway, and we motored onto the little streets and suburbs in Studio City that led up to Y-Dub. "Okay—got it—but go under your seat, Chelle. I've got a little bag there."

"A little bag of what?"

"Just get it."

I reached down as we started to pass by mansion-type houses with big green lawns and oak trees. Under my caboose, like King said, there was a little plastic bag. I lifted it, to spy it had six big fat doobies in it, and a little lighter, too.

"What is this—*weed*?" I gabbled.

"Hand it over."

"You're talking about living in the right and Jesus, and you are smoking weed?"

"Nothing wrong with a little *weed*, Chelle."

He took the bag from me, plucked out a doobie, and lit it, all while "driving."

"Get your hands on the wheel!" I blasted him.

He puffed, and laughed. "You an old lady already."

"Mama *kill* you. Remember when she beat me for tokin'? She said we never do drugs. We should *sell*, but not *do*—*not do, but sell*."

"Yeah, but she's in jail, Chelle! And I don't go for her advice anymore. I live by my own code. The one that Kenny taught me."

"He taught you to smoke weed?"

"Well, not that, but, he's a little conservative, you know." King puffed a couple more times, holding his breath. The Rover pulled up past some more mansions—and Yale-Westview Academy came into sight. We chugged up to the parking lot, where Ki and I had got snatched just weeks before. I could see the brown tops of the school buildings, and glimpse the racing track, the big green playing field.

My hands gripped tight on my knees. "Just stop the car! I'm gonna smell like chronic in my interview!"

He let out a big blat of ganja-scented air, hitting the brakes.

"There ain't a thing wrong with mowie-wowie, Chellie. Herbal's peaceable, see. You smoke a little chronic, and you won't feel like pulping up tha heads of them Diegos—like the ones you nearly turned into fertilizer, baby, when you smoked 'em in the desert on them motorcycles. Ugh, what a business that was."

"God, just stop talking, King! You are driving me nuts today!"

"See, uh-uh. You *dangerous*. Me, no more. I just toke a tiny hit, and it ain't nothing aggressive. People don't hurt each other on pot, understand."

"It's *illegal*."

"Illegal? There's *medical* marijuana; you heard that? So how wrong can it be?"

"What do you mean?"

"The only wrong in the world is hurtin' other folks, baby. That's it. And ganja don't do that. I use it to cure all my rage, see; it's *medicine*, see. It's civil *disobedience*. You know, John Lennon smoked herbal, Chelle."

"Who's John Lennon?"

He laughed. "Jesus probably smoked pot, Chelle, and Gandhi, too. I just toke a little and, and, and—am I being a bad influence on you?"

"*Yes*."

He laughed, really hard. "Sorry, I know this is serious. I love you, though, Chelle. Gawd, I love you, baby girl. You my only family. In the *world*." He got excited, his cheeks glowing bright and his smile wide as a rainbow. "And you gonna *whup ass* on this interview today, mothafucka! You gonna get into *Harvard* and get A's on all your tests and you gonna be *president*, bitch! I am so proud of you!"

I hopped out of the car and ran away from it. "Shut up, shut up."

"I'm just gonna park the car, Tweedle-Dee."

"Just stay there; I'll come back when I'm done."

I sprinted up to the parking lot, which was full of cars, I guess of the parents of the kids who'd come today for MLK interviews. There was a Rolls-Royce, and a Lexus, and two black Humvees, and a burned-out Toyota, and a Chevy pickup. And I saw Kiki's mom's purple Avalon there, too.

Running past all of them, I made it down to the grass field, and toward Y-Dub's brown buildings, my heart smashing like an earthquake inside of my chest.

I had five minutes to go.

30

I rushed down into the beautiful kingdom of Yale-Westview Academy, with its emerald field, its gorgeous racetrack, and its kick-ass palaces where preppies work to turn themselves into smart, rich, successful—*somethings*.

I legged it toward the brown brick buildings. As it was Wednesday, the field had lacrosse players crushing each other's skulls, and on the racetrack, girls sprinted. Getting closer, I spied the pink, punky hairdo of Money Smithson as she pounded up the gravel, leading up a pack of bionic Anglo females who looked like they could kill bears with their naked hands.

Money saw me—she and I met eyes as I swept down the green hill with my blue blazer fluttering out in back of me like a superhero's cape. She stopped running, putting her hands on her hips as the other girls rushed past her.

"Hey! Michelle!" she called out. "Good luck!"

"Th-thanks!" I yelled. "Congrats on Kentucky, Money!"

"Thanks back!"

I dashed, nearly race-speed, into the quad. On account I'd come snooping around Y-Dub before, I had a pretty good notion of the campus. But I still got a little lost. There were maybe one hundred millionaire kids milling around, on some kind of break. The quad was made of red brick, with green trees, the leaves of the trees tipped in silver-gold from the sun that just seemed brighter here.

The prepsters were dressed in navy suits, and blue striped ties with shamrocks on them. Most of them had tweaked the outfits, sewing patches on the jackets, and frills, or plopping on funky hats.

As I came hurtling into their world, they turned around, spotted me.

"Disadvantaged civilian alert," one of the Y-Dub females said. She was this big, Viking, rock'n'roll model type with ice-blonde hair, black eyeliner, a T-shirt that said *Sex Pistols*, and big safety pins stuck through her reconstructed blazer.

"Whoop, whoop," said her friend, a heartcrackingly pretty red-head who was some freaky species of hippie-prepster, with a boho crochet beret and leg warmers under the plaid skirt.

"You guys, be sensitive; I mean, we just read *House on Mango Street*," said a dark-haired girl wearing fingerless lace gloves and lots of goth mascara, her neck bleeding with a probably temporary tat of a heart stabbed by a knife.

"Excuse me, where's the—the—" I had the Y-Dub invitation e-mail and map in my jacket pocket and I took it out, scrackling it nervous in my hands.

"*Quo vadis?*" said the rock'n'roller.

"Torie, it is beyond uncool to status her with Latin," said the goth.

"What'd you say to me?" I asked the rock-n-roller.

"*Quo vadis*," she repeated.

Where you going, Michelle? I heard Silver saying in my mind.

"I'm headed to the MLK interview, for the scholarship," I said.

The rock'n'roller raised her eyebrows at the redheaded hippie, impressed.

A lanky, good-looking Anglo prep-boy with fancily mussed brown hair nosed his way into our circle. "It's at Roth Hall."

"Yeah, that's it. Where's that?"

"You go left, then right, then right, then left, then left, then right, then right, then left," said the hippie.

"Blythe!" said the goth.

"No, I think it's left, then right, then right, then left," said the rock'n'roller.

"Don't listen to them," the goth said. "They're just being jerks."

"Hey, kid, you just go straight, and then go right," said the prep dude, pointing past the quad and toward a set of buildings.

"You messing with my head, boy?" I asked.

All of them laughed, and started jabbering jokes in what I think was Russian.

"Thank you." I skedaddled for the direction he'd pointed.

Dashing past the glass-walled library, I got a glimpse of its thousands of books on Latin, Chinese, English grammar, African history, Japanese. I scrammed by the gym, with its state-of-the-art NordicTracks, gold-plated ThighMasters, aromatherapy whatchamacallits. I blasted past the caf, with its probably organic everything.

I turned right, just like the boy had told me.

Before me glittered a large crazy-modern-looking building made of steel and wood and glass. In front of it muddled a small crowd of Sunday-dressed minority or wheelchairing kids and their parents, who'd showed up for their interviews extra early. I knew I was in the right place even before I saw a bronze sign saying *Roth Hall* right over the tall, brushed-steel doors.

Kiki came out of those doors, with her mother, Mrs. Markson.

"Ki!"

She was dandied up in a little green dress suit; her skirt went down to her knees, and her long, prim jacket had daisy-shaped buttons. She looked thinner than she should have, and wore a pink and green feather bracelet around her right wrist.

"Where have you *been*?"

She hugged me, and I hugged her back, strong.

"Hello, Michelle." Mrs. Markson's dark natural hair floated like a cloud above her slender neck; her silk, tawny business outfit hung elegant on her perfect body. Her glossy, beautiful eyes dug into mine.

"Hello, Mrs. Markson. Ki, how'd it go?"

"I think it went okay," she said. "They asked me about if I wanted to go scientific or artistic if I made it into their program, and I was like, 'Ummm, I'd rather have the ice cream than the root canal, thank you.' And then they said my video essay was a cross between Mira Nair and David Lynch, and I was like, 'I think you've missed the Buñuel references.'"

"What video?"

"Oh—my personal essay. For the application."

"But we turned in a written essay in November."

She said, "No, I turned in a visual like three days after—you-know-what happened. With the footage I shot? So, they saw it, and I guessed they liked it, because they said they had like an *amazing* media lab, and computer graphics, and they like—"

"I'm going to begin fining you again for every time you use that word," said Mrs. Markson.

"Oh, sorry, I'm just nervous. And they have a screenwriting work-shop, once you hit eleventh grade; you can take that as an elective. And they asked about what happened to us, too."

I squinted at her. "What, us getting 'napped?"

"Yeah," she said.

"How did they know about that?"

"My video."

"Oh, right." Some serious anxiety started to whirl in my chest. "What'd you show them, Kiki?"

"Just what happened," she said, looking at the ground.

"It's inappropriate that they even brought that up, considering everything you've been through," said Mrs. Markson. "They're just compounding the trauma. They're using you as a sideshow. Good media value, you know, if you get in. Overcoming obstacles and hardships and all that garbage. 'Disadvantaged.' I'm a registered nurse!"

"Mom, it was okay."

"They should take you because you're brilliant. The *entire* conceit is insulting, and I told them, too. Oh, I told them. You're not going to any school that doesn't *really* value you. If they want to take you because you were exploited by this girl's family, because you had a crime committed against you, because you're *black*, they can take this scholarship, and they can shove it—"

"Mom!"

"'Exploited by *this girl's* family'?" I repeated. "What girl's that?"

"*You*, of course." Mrs. Markson sniffed at me.

"My family didn't do harm to anybody." I took a step away from her.

"Oh, really?" Shoving up the bracelet on Kiki's arm, Mrs. Markson held up the rough-looking wrist-scar to my face. "Then what's this, Michelle?"

"If you're gonna be worried over something, Mrs. Markson, I'd be worrying about her weight, with all respect."

"You *presume* to tell me what I can see and don't see in my own daughter? Her issues aren't something that you fling in her face like that! What kind of child are you? Were you raised in a *barn*? I already told your father—I mean, your foster father—that this was *over*—"

"You told what to who?" I asked.

"Mom," Kiki said, "calm down; please calm down."

"*I saw your rough draft, Kiki,* so I know *exactly* what happened up there."

"Mrs. Markson, I would never hurt Ki; you're getting the wrong impression about me," I gabbled, even while I noticed that the kids around us peered at us strange. "I just want her to be doing super all the time. She and I are best friends—"

But even while I was saying that, I heard somebody shouting behind me.

"Hey, hey-ho! Chelle!"

Mrs. Markson's eyes lifted from my face.

"Who's that?" Kiki asked. "Mish, your brother."

"Oh, no," I said.

"*Woo!*" King stagger-shadowboxed his way up to me. "Man but are there some *white* people here." He spotted Kiki with his stoner-red eyes, smiled wider. "Looky here—yeah, *you!* I recollect you! You that peewee I saved with the foster gay in the desert, hey? How's it going, girl? You here to wish my *hermana* good? She gonna get this scholarship. Aw, she so smart, my sister Mi-*chelle*." Snatching Mrs. Markson's hand, he pumped it up and down. "Hey, good-looking old lady, peace to you, too, mama!" He peered around at the school. "Man. Education. That's good, that's good. That's good, education. I, you know, I *celebrate* this."

Mrs. Markson sniffed at my brother. Her eyes turned into two volcanoes.

"That is *it*, Kiki. I already told you not to have any contact—that if I even got a *hint* that you had anything to do with gang members—"

"Mom, come on, he's just a—"

"I see what he is."

"Mrs. Markson." My heart shook like rain. "This is my brother. This is Samson. He doesn't have any harm in him."

"Not no more," Samson sang. "I learned how to behave myself in solitary confinement, see. I learned some ethics in the pen."

Mrs. Markson didn't even look at me. "Kiki, you have one minute. *Hear me?* You'll wrap this up. For *good*. And then we'll go home. I'm going to the car."

Mrs. Markson walked away from us, her suit glowing in the sun, and her high heels going *click clack, click clack,* as she disappeared around a corner.

Kiki's veins stuck out in her temples, in her neck. She pressed her eyelids with her fingers, like to keep her forehead from blowing up.

"Ki," I said.

"Hey, who died, man?" Samson asked.

"Kiki," I said again.

She shook her head. "I don't know if I can do this. I thought I could, but I don't know."

"You can't do what?"

She opened her huge hazel eyes, and tears welled up. In the next second, they were streaming down her face. "Be friends with you anymore."

"But we *are* friends. Don't talk like that!"

"I have to, because I'm thinking it. And saying the things that I really think is kind of a resolution that I've made. Like the fact that I am so, so mad at you for never telling me that being friends with you was, like, a biohazard!"

"I'm sorry, Kiki!"

"About the fact that you lied to me about being in a gang, or the fact that I don't even know who you are?"

"You do know me; don't you remember us?" Desperate, I grasped her hand and began to rap to her, our old song:

Ki and Mish gonna dom-i-nate
Those li'l girls gone beat your butt

"Stop it." Kiki pulled harsh away from me.

You push them down; they don't hes-i-tate
Cuz they never, never, never give up!

"Don't, just don't—shut up!" she yelled.

"Please don't be rude to my sister," King said.

"She can be rude to me," I said. "Just talk to me, Ki."

"I don't know." Kiki squeezed her eyes shut, tears trickling down both sides of her face. "You don't get it. She was right. I hate her for saying it, but it's true: You're not always great to me, Michelle."

"What—what?"

"And also, I don't know if you ever noticed this, but *we don't have anything in common*." She dug into a pocket in her skirt, pulling out a new BlackBerry that she must have got in the last weeks. "I'll show you the video, and you'll see."

"See what? I was there!"

Her fingers danced over the keys. "But just so you know I didn't hurt you, I'm sending you the one I turned into the school. You'll see, I didn't trash you to them—"

"Never mind that right now!" I gasped. "Just, can you forget what your mom says about me, and we can go back to the way we were? You don't get it; I'm losing *everything*—"

Kiki's eyes plunged into me. "You don't have a mother, Mish. You couldn't understand."

She walked away from me.

"Kiki!"

She turned around the corner and vanished.

"Ki?"

I felt light-headed and so empty; it was like I'd been robbed of myself.

Samson put his arm around me. "Chelle, you got everything going for you; don't look like that."

My heart started to bust into pieces. "Oh—"

A woman came out of the brushed-steel doors of the Roth auditorium. King turned around, checked her out. He gently pushed me toward where she stood. I could barely see, because my tears were blurring everything. I could kind of make out that the woman was white, with brown hair and glasses and a beige pantsuit. She held a clipboard in her hand.

My heart went *crack crack*.

Crack! Crack! Crack!

"Michelle Peña," the white Y-Dub lady said.

31

Roth Hall was as big as a church, its foyer's ceiling shimmering with copper. As I forced my legs to follow the whitelady down a corridor, I saw the building had tall windows, made of multicolored stained glass. They poured blood-purple glittery lights down onto my hands and my clothes, which reminded me of Silver and so only supersized my wiggification.

"Through here, Michelle," said the whitelady after we'd twined through another hallway. She put her hand on a door. Her brown eyes were large and kind. Wrinkles shot all through her soft, peachy face. "My name's Ms. Peterson, and I have to say, we've really been looking forward to meeting you."

"*Why?*"

She tilted her head, confused at my tone. "Because your application shows so much potential, of course."

I didn't answer her. I was too busy willpowering the tears that had the potential of shooting up through my nose to go back down my throat.

"Well, let's just go in and have a chat," she said.

The interview room was large, with a long, cherry-colored wood table. Three menfolk and two whiteladies sat around it. One of the ladies had frosty blonde hair and wore a pantsuit made out of stripy wool. There was also a tall black man, wearing a blue baseball cap. The rest of them were Anglos with brown hair and glasses. Behind them, there were more windows, showing the sunshine flowing over every leaf, every red brick, and every blessed poindexter who got to go to this school.

I sat down.

Their mouths started moving. The lips formed words, and their eyebrows shot up and down their foreheads, making them look grandly sincere. The only problem was, I couldn't hear a single word they were saying because of the roaring in my head.

When the lips and eyebrows stopped moving, I could tell the menfolk and ladies at the table had stopped talking. They shot worried looks at each other.

I pressed my knuckles to my eyes. Oh well. A good runner knows when the race is blown way before the finish line, and this race was dead as soon as the gun went off. I was a damned disaster.

"I really wanted to go here," I murmured to myself.

"What's that, Michelle?" Ms. Peterson asked.

I started sweating like a monster. "I wanted to go here, you guys. Honest, and for real. I *did*. I wanted it so bad. I wanted it like nothing ever before, not even racing. Not the decathlon. Not even my mama getting out of prison."

"Well, that's . . . *great!* That's what we're asking you about," exclaimed the blonde lady with the stripey suit. She was one of those hand-talkers, swiping her fingers through the air with every word. "*Why* you've been drawn to apply to Yale-Westview."

"I thought if I went here, I'd earn my place," I replied, in a scratchy voice.

Ms. Peterson was writing down what I said on a piece of paper. She lifted her pen up. "That you would—I'm sorry, what was that?"

"Earn my place, ma'am."

"Earn a spot at the school?" one of the whitemen said. He was short, with thin brown hair, wearing square glasses without frames. "I'm not quite understanding. . . ."

"But I was about as mistaken as them Flat-Earthists Darwin shut up after studying finches in the Galapagos Islands." I trembled all over. "I see that now."

"Michelle, would you like to take a break? Maybe have a glass of water?" asked the dude with the square glasses.

"I need more than water, dawg." My voice cracked harder.

"We know that you've been through a terrible experience, Michelle," the blonde lady hand-flapped at me. "Your situation is well known to the committee. The kidnapping. And what you did to save yourself and your friend. We're happy to give you any accommodation that you need today."

"Look, Michelle, all *I* need to know is how fast you think you can run next year," said the black guy in the baseball cap.

"*Weston*," the blonde lady said. "This isn't about the track team. This is about—"

"Litigation, Barbara," he said. "But I don't give a damn about that. Let them sue us. What I need to know is if she's going to spend next year cracking up like this, or if she's going to run."

"Um, ask her the question about the mirror," said the other white-man real quick. He wore a blue cardigan and had a tiny goatee and pale blue eyes.

"Okay." Ms. Peterson lifted up her piece of paper, squinting at it. "When you look in the mirror, Michelle, what do you see?"

"What?"

"It's just a question we ask applicants. It helps us to understand who you *are*."

"You peoples want me to tell you what I see when I look in the mirror?"

"That's right."

"Nothing, lady. I don't see nothing."

"Michelle—I'm sure you see many *wonderful* things that you'd like to tell us a—"

But I wasn't able to disabuse Ms. Peterson of her uncomprehension about me, because that's when all the tears I'd been keeping in my schnoz came blowing out, all over the table. "Oh, what a freak-assed mess!" I stood up. "Goodbye. Thank you, ma'ams and sirs. I appreciate you interviewing me. Nobody in my family ever got this far."

I turned around, walking right back out. More like running out. Jostling through the corridor, I stumbled through the churchlike foyer. "Oh, oh. Jesus Christ in the ghetto, get me the fuck out of here!"

"Michelle," called a voice behind me, just as I reached the door. It was that one guy, Weston. "Michelle, stop."

I slowed, halted.

Walking right up to me, he peered intense-like into my face.

"Michelle, look at me."

"What, sir?"

"It's Mr. Ruiz, and look at me."

I stared up at his coffee-colored peepers, and at his ancient acne scars, even while the tears were still sprinkling down my twitching cheeks.

"You know what *I* see when I look at you?" Mr. Ruiz asked. "*Speed,* Michelle. I saw the tape of you beating Lisa Smithson in Pasadena last January."

"The tape?"

"I'm the new track coach here. I was hired two weeks ago, from Wesleyan."

"Wesleyan."

"It's a college. Anyway, I saw you on that tape, making that record. And more important, I saw the footage of you running on your friend's video—Kiki's video. I *never* saw a child run like that in my entire life. So, when I look at you, I see something, *not* nothing. I see speed. Okay? I see *talent*, Peña."

"It isn't enough, Mr. Ruiz," I said.

"Look, let's talk. Then, maybe, there's another scholarship that you just might—"

"Goodbye, sir, and thank you anyway."

Backing away from him, I pushed through the doors. The light flooded onto my face, and the air, and I saw all the nervous, gifted disadvantaged faces crowding outside the building—black faces, brown faces, and wheelchairs, sign language. I pushed past those hopeful kids. I walked away from Y-Dub and didn't look back.

*

"What *happened*?" King asked me, back in the Range Rover, about ten minutes later. "You look all crucified!"

"Nothing happened."

"What do you mean, nothing?"

"It's over. I'm not getting in. I dropped out of the competition."

"Nuh-uh, you didn't?"

"Yeah, I don't want to talk about it, either. Start the car. Let's go."

King stared at me troublingly with his red weedfreak eyes.

"Chelle," he said, "girl, talk to your bro. I'm here for you, baby."

I pulled my hair, rocking back and forth in the seat. "*Fine!* Tell me, why didn't you just give over that money to the Snakes in the first place? Did you spend it?!"

He swallowed before saying, real careful, "No, I didn't."

"Then why didn't you just pay them what you *owed*? S would have been okay; Frank would be keeping me—Ki would still like me!"

He leaned back on the door. "I—couldn't."

"*Why* you have to hide a hundred thousand dollars from gangsters you know have blood on their mind!?"

"That's *why*, baby."

"Why, what?"

"I couldn't give that money to them because it is *blood* money. Patssi was holding that money when she got killed. Belongs to her, now. I hid it good. It's deep under."

I flopped my head back on the headrest. "Damn you, King!"

"I ain't the only one damned by what went down."

"What are you talking about?" I demanded.

"Silver. After the Burner took out Louie and T-Rock, I knew he was in trouble. You was gone, and he was left surrounded by thuggies who wasn't exactly gonna bring out the best in his personality. I wrote to him: *Man, do like I do. Bury the hatchet. We all suffered, and we all beginning a new life.* But no, he goes out, and he forces four Diegos to get on their knees, and works them over so rough they're barely recognizable to their own mamas now."

I put my hands over my ears. "I don't want to hear about that!"

He pulled my hands off. "A man don't do an act like that unless he has let himself get ate up by the darkness. And I don't *ever* want that to touch you."

"*Why* are you killing me with this if he's really dead?"

"So you don't go through what I did. He *is* dead, and you forget him."

I heard the sound of his rough breathing, and when I slid my eyes over, I saw tears shining on his cheeks. His lips shook.

"Samson, I don't get you."

"I know I hurt you, Chelle." He gripped onto my arm, gentle. "I know even what happened today—just that I fucked it up, somehow. And I'm sorry. I don't know what to do but love you, now. Like we used to. Remember the old days? When we had those parties, by the magnolia tree, and we called you Princess? And we loved you so bad—Chelle, I love you like that, still."

I wiped my face off. "I love you too, Samson."

"You do?"

"Yeah, I do. I love you. You're my bro. But—*hell*, man, just take me home."

King wiped off his face, too, before grabbing on the silver death's head in the ignition. "Home?"

This isn't working, Michelle, I heard Frank tell me, in my head.

I squinted my eyes shut, letting out a big, long breath.

"Just take me to Frank's, King."

Soon we were barreling like thunder down the highway, me empty as a balloon, as we roared through the city, not talking, all the way back to Westchester.

After King drove me back to Frank's house, the first thing I did was go to my room and get on my computer. Opening up my Facebook page, I clicked on my inbox to see the two videos Ki had sent me before my interview.

One was titled KI'S STORY: THE Y-DUB VERSION, 3 MINS 00 SECONDS. The other was called KI'S STORY: PRIVATE, 4 MINS 2 SECONDS.

I scrolled my mouse to the first file, and clicked.

*

Kiki's dark, freckled, hot-eyed face filled up the whole screen.

I'm Kiki Markson, she said. She was sitting in her bedroom in Inglewood, clutching onto her pillow. *And two days ago, I was kidnapped by gangsters, with my friend Michelle Peña. I've never been so scared in my life. Except, it wasn't till it happened that I learned the world is dangerous, but it's really beautiful, too.* She stared at the camera, her eyes bright. *See what I see.*

The image cut from her face to a scene of me, running in that little silver dress. She must have somehow shot this when she'd been driving the Humvee down the highway, away from the Fort.

Aaahhh!!!! I screamed through my teeth like a beast-girl, the veins striking out of my bleeding neck, my muscles ripped like a jaguar's.

The image slow-motioned down. A church music soundtrack started to play.

Aaaahhh, sang a choir, which sounded like it was made up of young nuns, their melody taking up from my hollering. *Ahhhh, sweet angel you are fallen / do you remember when you were innocent / you were loved, then.*

Slowed to dream-speed, I didn't look like a man-eating beast any more, but like a bird, in my silver dress.

The image changed—I melted and reformed, running on the grass while playing soccer with the Snakes. My dark hair flowed down my back, the blood showed through my arm bandage. The screen was filled with gorgeous colors: The ebony of my hair, the copper of my skin, the gold field, the scarlet blood, and the gold-blue sky behind me.

The screen blurred, faded to black. The music faded.

No one's going to hurt you, came my voice. *I'm going to get you home no matter what I do. You're my girl, Ki, you're my girl.*

And then there was the image of Kiki crying under the covers, the night we got nabbed. Her face bulged, quivered. Here came the sound of both our voices, singing, sounding something like the angel-nun voices that had been playing a minute before:

Ki and Mish gonna dom-i-nate
Those li'l girls gone beat your butt
You push them down; they don't hes-i-tate
Cuz they
never
never
never
give up.

The screen cut back to Kiki's face, the way it was at the beginning of the video. A smile played over her mouth.

I think that if you're an artist, you can make the terrible parts of the

THE GOOD GIRL'S GUIDE TO GETTING KIDNAPPED

world beautiful. You can see what I see. You can give yourself hope. She looked worried for a second. *Right?* Swallowing, she stared straight at the lens again. *I'm going to be an artist, someday.*

The screen went black. There were only these words, in white letters:

The End

"Kɪᴋɪ's sᴛᴏʀʏ," ᴡʀɪᴛᴛᴛᴇɴ, ᴅɪʀᴇᴄᴛᴇᴅ, ᴇᴅɪᴛᴇᴅ, ᴀɴᴅ sᴄᴏʀᴇᴅ ʙʏ Kɪᴋɪ Mᴀʀᴋsᴏɴ (2009).

My hand jittered as it moved the mouse over to the second file, marked Kɪᴋɪ's Sᴛᴏʀʏ: Pʀɪᴠᴀᴛᴇ.

I clicked on it.

*

The first thing on the screen, again, was Kiki's shining face. Whereas she'd looked spunky before, now she hunched loose-necked and depressive on her bed.

She looked up at the camera.

I'm Kiki Markson. And this is my real *story.* She shook her head. *Sometimes I worry, Camera, that people are just bad, and there's nothing good or lovely anywhere. I worry that maybe, if I make the world seem beautiful, I'm just lying. Understand? And maybe I should just tell the ugly truth. If you DARE, see what I see.*

On the screen came the image of me running again, but not slow-motioned, and not with any angel music. My legs shredded over the road, and I was screaming at Kiki. My eyes shone red. Sweat dripped down my face. The veins bulging out my forehead made me look beyond brutal.

Aaahhh, I shrieked. *Stop the car, Kiki! Slam the brakes!*

I sounded like a *bruja,* that scary.

Still running, I looked behind my shoulder. The two rhinos and Dragon were coming up behind me on their motorbikes.

The picture shifted to a far-off shot of me running between the motorbikes, and cutting across the road, so that the rhinos crashed in a bone-smashing, bloody mess.

Whup! is how it sounded on the video.

Next came a shot of King wrapping his fingers around Dragon's throat. King looked like a werewolf. His face was terrible, twisted, all teeth.

In my bedroom, my mouth was open—this *never* should have got on film!

You hurt my sister, D, and that is a treason punishable by death.

And Kiki's voice in the background. *Mish! Tell him not to!*

King took his hands off Dragon. *No, no! I ain't going to double my sins with you, you bastard!*

Sssssssss, I hissed. The camera swung, to show Frank holding me in the dark desert. My lips pulled up over my teeth, like a mad badger's. *Samson!*

Can't, Chelle, King said. *Even though you want me to beat him dead, I just can't do it, baby.*

My face twisted. *Damn you!*

The screen blurred, dimmed. Next came an image of me standing over cut-up Book. He was bleeding terrible in Dragon's office at the Fort. Silver and Midget and Biggie stood next to me, freaking out. I looked *cold,* though. I had blood on my chest and my cheek. Peering stern at a passed-out, dead-looking Book, I said, *Yo, Book here can croak like a toad.*

Off camera, Kiki said, *Mish, help him! It's wrong if you let him bleed out like this!*

Wrong's a big word, Ki, with a lot of meanings.

That image faded. She didn't show me sewing Book, the way I had. Instead, here came a scene of me dancing with Silver under the blue lights. Diggy-O rapped wild in the background.

My head was thrown back, and I had a sex-look on my face. Silver thrust his hips toward mine. I looked like a grown woman—no, I looked like a ho.

I started kissing him—and I remember the feeling being so sweet.

Then that image faded, too. The screen flashed to a scene of me in the Vault. It was our first night in the desert, just before I'd picked the lock of the door. I huddled on the floor, peering at Biggie's feet under the door crack. Kiki said, *My mom says that I sort of let myself live in your shadow, and that I just really shouldn't anymore!*

Kiki! I barked. *Do we have to talk about your self-esteem problems now?*

The screen darkened, brightened, and showed Kiki again in her bedroom.

See what I mean, Mish? The world turned you ugly. And I can't tell the truth about that, because it hurts too much. Who are you? And do you even care about me? Because I don't know anymore. She clasped her face, hunching lower over her knees. *I'm going to burn this tape.*

The screen went black.

I stared at the computer for a long time. I felt so dreadful I thought maybe I didn't want to live.

I knew now why Kiki didn't love me anymore.

She didn't love me no more because she didn't think she knew who I was. And I hadn't taken enough trouble to learn about her, neither.

I wasn't the friend she needed.

Ring, ring, ring.

It's Kiki! Leave a message!

"Hi, Ki, it's just me. I've got to talk to you. Call me when you can. See you later."

*

Hey Ki, just saying hey, wazzup? Any chance we can have a little talk?

*

Ki, you got to talk to me someday. You see me say hi in history? It looked like you wanted to say hi back. Xxxxx

*

Ring, ring, ring.
It's Kiki! Leave a message!

*

Ring, ring, ring.
It's Kiki! Leave a message!

*

Ring, ring, ring.
It's Kiki! Leave a message!

It was ten in the morning on a Saturday, about a month after the interview. I sat on my bed and hung up the phone. I looked down at the envelope I was holding. I'd pulled it out of the mail before Frank saw it. It was thin, from Yale-Westview.

I ripped it open.

Dear Michelle Peña,

We regret to inform you that your candidacy for the Martin Luther King Awards scholarship has been unsuccessful. Due to the tremendous number of applicants, we had to turn away many gifted young scholars. . . .

I clutched the letter. I'd known it was coming, but I didn't expect it to hurt so bad.

Oh, I cried, totally silent.

You're not different or special, Michelle, this voice said in my head. *You were just having yourself a fantasy about prep school.*

Of course you didn't get in. Who do you think you are?

I buried my face in my pillow, pressing my hands to my ears.

But the voices didn't stop.

34

Fifteen minutes later, I was still crying so hard it made me kind of scared.

I sat up, *forcing* myself not to bawl anymore. *What the hell am I doing?* I rubbed my face. *Get a hold of yourself! You're Michelle Peña! You're Reina Peña's daughter!* I stared down at the letter. Slowly, I eased my breathing. I crinkled the paper and frowned down at it. *Yeah, fine, no problem. I don't need that place. I walked out of that interview for a good reason. I'm smart, and I've learned my lesson. I don't belong with any of these people.*

I smashed the letter into a little piece of crap, threw it in the garbage. Squiggy wiggled into the room, panting, and started rubbing his back on the floor rug. I looked at him. "Squig, I took a wrong turn, coming here."

He just scratched his little privates.

"My thoughts exactly, homes."

I stood up, scrubbed my nose with a towel, and changed my clothes: jeans, a long-sleeved shirt, Nikes, and a JUDZ jacket. Not the Pendleton, because Frank would sniff that out. I got the replacement backpack Frank had bought me, throwing my Prada heart key fob in it. I snatched my phone, too. I switched off the ringer, so Frank couldn't track me down.

Padding out my bedroom and toward the foyer, I tried to sneak out quiet. But there was Frank in the hall, making a beeline right for me.

"Michelle, good, you're up and at 'em," he said.

"'Sup, Frankie."

"So, how's everything going?" he asked. "Did you have breakfast? I made some fruit smoothies this morning with a lot of bananas for the potassium. And you like blueberries, right? And I put a little protein powder in them, because, you know, it's really important that you get enough folic acid—"

I squinted at him. "Frank, you're kind of jabbering, man."

He tried to smile back, but it looked like he'd just slammed his hand in a door. "Yes, I suppose I am. I *did* want to ask you about something, though."

"I'm listening," I said.

"It's just that I *might* have happened to notice that you are still really depressed. And that you have also completely stopped talking to me. It's just an observation, which some people, if they thought about it, might find troubling. Leading them to get up at two in the morning, make blueberry smoothies, and try to do just about anything else they could think of to make things go back to the way they were."

I patted him on the arm. "Frank, how are things going with that shrink of yours, bro?"

"Dr. Milhaulus was the one who suggested that we talk about emotional . . . *things*. And, maybe that's not exactly my strong suit, but I'll do it if helps you, Michelle."

I said, "Listen, you don't have anything to worry about. You're a good guy. You were *so* nice to take me in."

Frank's mouth went slack. "Wait, hold on a second. I didn't just do it because I'm nice. I *wanted* to, Michelle."

"Sure, Frank. I just turned out to be more trouble than you expected, I get it."

He cleared his throat. "I'm going to give this a try, okay? Here goes: All day long, in my job, I have to deal with people who are really sick, who won't get better. And I accept that." The corner of his eyes sparkled. "But I *have* to know that you're okay, Michelle. It's quite important . . . to me."

He reached down and started patting my head. I felt his nervy, cold fingers on my cheek. Then he gave me a little shoulder squeeze, which I knew qualified as a quarter hug. And *that* almost got me.

But, no, I got a hold of myself. "I've got to go to track practice at school. I'm taking the bus."

"What?"

"Track practice!"

He laced his fingers together, like he didn't know what to do with them. "Okay! We can drop this for now—but, track? You're not dressed for it."

"Uniform's in my locker. I'll call you later; I've got my phone."

He stood back, nodding. "I'm going to make us dinner tonight. And, um, since this went so well—we'll talk some more then?"

"Sure enough, Frankie-pie."

I gave him a big goodbye hug, before walking out, through the front door. The street shone under my feet like a long racing track, gun-black. I dashed down the avenue, fast, just running and running, but not forward anymore.

I was going back, see.

It was time to see my mother again.

35

"**W**ait here," said a woman detention center guard with a wine-colored birthmark on her left cheek. She was nosily supervising a young Latina janitor with a long ponytail, who was scrubbing the hallway where I stood. "Do you have any weapons or metal?"

I tried not step all over the clean parts of the floor. "No, ma'am, and excuse me, but you already asked me that. And I already got frisked, twice."

"Don't mouth me; just park it. Who you here to see?"

"Reina Peña."

The guard blinked. "You mean Queen?"

"Yeah."

She raised her eyebrows, looking at me all over. "That's funny. Carla, check this out. I thought Reina's kids would only be half-human. But this one doesn't have a tail on her, far as I can see."

"Reina's kid?" The janitor girl took a sharp look at me, twitched her nose, then stood up. "I got to go do something." She skittered off, with her bucket and mop.

I eyeballed the guard. "You a comedian, huh? You talk with that funny mouth in front of my mama?"

"What?"

"I said, do you talk with that foul mouth in front of Queen?"

"I'm a guard, and she's a prisoner, child."

"I'll give you one more chance to apologize for calling Reina Peña's only daughter a mongrel, ma'am."

Now the guard didn't look so sure of herself, as I knew she wouldn't. She got a little paler, so her birthmark stuck out even more.

"I'm sorry. Please don't tell her. I was just joking around."

"That's better, lady," I said.

"Just mind yourself. Sit in that room and wait."

I sat. The MDC's visiting was a damn cold gray hall with metal tables where cons slumped and their people pep talked them in cheery voices. Guards stood at every corner. On the walls were signs: *No touching between prisoners and visitors!* As Saturday is the most popular for calling on your felons, the room was full of cons sitting with their tatted boyfriends or their weary mamas holding babies. But despite it being family day, every deuce looked serious depressed, with these terrible pooches under their eyes.

"Oh, oh, oh," cried one of the yardbirds, like twenty-one but blinking out of little pink bunny eyeballs. She sat across from a mama-looking woman wearing a yellow flowered dress.

I went *pfft!* at her disdignified yawping.

"Oh, oh, oh," she continued. "You don't know how bad it is in here, Mom. You don't know who they got in here—what she'll do to you—"

A hefty, red-haired lola bawled, "That monster's got us all paying *protection*—"

"She's got us all slaves!" yallered a skinny deuce with a bloody cut on her cheek.

"Pipe down!" yelled a short lady guard who sounded Haitian.

"You know it's true, Aniyah!"

The front door opened. A woman walked in, and them hustlers suddenly shut up so much it was like they'd instantly croaked from the deadly sight of her.

Reina.

I recognized her right away, though it'd been so long. Long, sleek, shining hair. Clean white teeth. Fresh bronze skin. She was thirty-five years old, twenty when she'd had me. Five foot eight, two inches taller than me. Ropy, good muscles, big breasts underneath the light blue jumpsuit. Powerful legs, snake hips. She would have been a good runner, Reina. But she made an even better mob boss.

Reina flicked her big, whiskey-colored eyes at me before roving them at the silent women. She smiled wide and scary, showing wolf teeth, and tapped on her ear.

"I heard you, Charlene," she said to the yardbird boo-hooing to the yellow dress.

"Oh, I didn't say a word about you; I swear on my mother," she said, pointing to Yellow, who looked like she really wanted to go home.

"After I talk to my kid, I'm going to have to figure out your punishment."

"All right, enough of that, Reina," said the guard called Aniyah.

"Queen, I didn't say nothing," Charlene said.

"Shut up," Mama answered in a nice, light, untroubled voice.

Charlene snapped her mouth tight, and Mama sat opposite me on my bench.

I don't know how long we just sat there looking at each other. Her eyes were shadowy lakes. She drowned me in them. I don't know if what I felt was love. It was something as powerful as that. I didn't feel like crawling into her arms, the way I felt with Frank. She was broad, strong, an Aztec queen. I wanted to worship at her feet. And I was scared of her, even with the tears in her eyes.

She wiped them and said, "I don't got much time. I'm just going to say what I'm going to say."

"Mom, Mama."

"I'm a busy woman, as you can see, *preciosa*. Got my hands full with my underlings, here. And plus Montebello. You seen the books of the 99s?"

"What?"

"The *account books*."

"No—I don't got nothing to do with that—"

"Well, you're gonna. You got to clean up that mess for me. My subsidiary—"

"What?"

"The Snakes. They earned me a damned deficit of one hundred K."

"Mom—"

"Quiet. You know why I told you not to come see me?"

I swallowed, my head hurt. I just cried out, "Ah."

"Do you *know*?"

"Cuz you didn't love me, Mama," I started to bawl. "Even though I'm remembering you all the *time*. I hear you in my head—"

"No. Wipe your face. Don't get weak. That's not why. It's because I had to kick you out of the nest. See if you really wanted normal. You was always sitting on the fence of the Path, not walking on it." She grabbed my face—not too hard. She stared deep into my bones. Her thumb stroked me, just once, over the cheek.

"Queen," the guard called Aniyah warned.

Mama took her hand off me in her own time. "But, nah. You ain't normal. You *me*, ain't you?"

I looked at her, crying.

"Let's hear it, baby," she said.

You're a killer, Chelle! You're a chip off tha block!

"I can't make it nowhere else," I said.

"That ain't no answer."

I nodded. "I'm you. I'm gangster."

"That's right, you *all* me, girl," she said. "What I don't understand is why you didn't kill that pig and take your proper place. What'd I tell you? No *mercy*—"

"I don't—"

"I heard what happened. How you all running away. In the desert. With a black girl—"

"Kiki."

"You blood her yet?"

"She's not a gangster—"

She grinned with half her mouth. "We *all* gangstas, baby. Only question is, what club we in? Or, in your case, which club you ruling? I had one of my boyz coming over there with an Uzi as soon as I'd got word, but you'd already got away. So then I told my rebels to cool it, as I knew you'd be teaching Dragon how much it costs to put a hand on a Peña. But you haven't, yet."

"I was scared—but they couldn't hold me."

"*Course* they couldn't. Listen, Michelle, you ain't gonna get no strokes from me for breaking free of that pipsqueak. Women in our family being stronger and smarter than men is no news. Instead of running from Dragon, you shoulda been *crushing*."

"Mom, King said Silver died!"

She tilted her head. "And why'd you listen to that washed-up?"

"What?"

She snapped her fingers in my face. "Wake up! S ain't dead, Michelle; *Game* is. Poor handicap was shot by the Burner when he was shielding S, and I'll tell you, that was just the beginning of the Diegos taking out interest in what you all owe."

I stared at her. It was like the whole world slowed down, stopped. I blinked; voices got blurry. The relief cracked me *wide* open, and I went frail as water. *He's alive. He survived. But—no—*

"Game? . . ."

"Dead as a stone," Mama said.

"Don't say it's so!" I pressed my hand to my mouth. "But—Silver's not dead?!"

"Not *yet*," she rumbled. "He *will* be if he ever lays another hand on you, though. I'm not saying an ice-blood like him don't have his uses in war. You can utilize him, as long as he keeps his dog collar on. But remember, I *told* you the price of the crown is to keep yaself in ya own command."

I gripped my hands together. "Oh God, oh, thank God!"

She squinted at me. "You still don't get it, do you? Sooner or later that boy's gonna slip your rule and buy it, cuz he got some bad battle madness. And if you show him a woman's weakness—and what I am talking about here is this 'falling in love,' see—then he is sure to become the instrument by which you will fall. He *will* betray you."

I shook my head. "He won't—he wouldn't!"

"He already did. He was the one laying hands on you and bringing you into danger in the first place, wasn't he? Yeah, I see on your face you know I'm right. And that's why I *forbid* you to be with him. That's the law, as I explained when you were younger."

I just sat there, shivering.

Her eyes drilled inside me. "And you are gonna have to follow my law by the letter now. The only way you gonna keep you and your club surviving is to be my knight! You will be knight, now! My *shining* knight. You be my prince! *You* the King now, not Samson, see? He crossed off my list."

"I don't know what you're asking me to do."

"Well, first of all, you are going to find the money Samson hid."

"I don't know where he put it."

"Hell, that doper's simple to read. Just go to the house and *ask* him. He's squatting there, and hiding from the cops, ain't he? That what my boyz say. They've been keeping an eye on him for me. So, you get hold of the cash, and then store it in a safe place." She stood up, looked down at me. "Okay, you got it straight? We done here?"

"I—I'm not sure—I—"

"Only thing you got to remember is that a powerful woman never has got to raise a finger to get business done. That what the men's for. Don't get sticky."

"Sticky?"

"Don't get in the way of a blade, is what I'm schooling you." Snatching out her hand, she took hold of my right arm, with the bullet scar. Even though I was wearing my jacket, she knew where I'd got wounded. She pressed hard on it, and I winced. "See, you already learned that lesson, right?"

"Ow!"

She turned her head. "Okay, Aniyah, I'm ready to go, now."

"Mom! Don't go; I've got to talk to somebody—"

Her eyes were made of black fire. She bent down and kissed me, feather-gentle.

"I love you, Michelle," she whispered. "I love you, baby. I always love you furious. I made you from my body; you are me."

"Oh, Mom!"

"Just do what I tell you, and you'll be all right. You come back next Saturday and give me a report. And I wanna hear you got that money! Cuz you on my payroll after this, baby. I'm gonna make you *work*. Ya got a heavy load of responsibilities, now."

The guard with the birthmark came back into the room. Mama winked at me, then went with her out the door. Reina *paraded* in front of the guard like a royal, not a prisoner. And she didn't look back at me.

All the other jailbirds stared at me sideways. But then their voices started to get louder, as they began to have normal conversations again.

36

Rattle rattle went the bus as I trucked my fanny to Montebello. The travel required a transfer and took about another hour. I had a cracked-up, buzzy-headed feeling inside me, thinking of Game. *Truly dead? And Silver, my boy, is he really doing okay?* Oh, but no, *no*, I couldn't break down. Because I had to protect my soldiers from even more hurt, didn't I? I introspected while the trees and cars flashed outside the window. The billboards grew more Spanish the farther into Eastside I got. In honor of my return to my home country, I took hold of my iPhone, changing my ring tone to Diggy-O's "Uprise! No Blood Like the 99s," though I still kept the ringer off.

Then I was in Montebello.

And then I was standing in front of our old house.

The house my real dad bought us was a one-story, but Mama had added a second. It was a big, dove-white mansion, with large windows. The glass gleamed like it had just been cleaned. To the side stood a garage with a white-painted door.

Outside the house, there were two things that caught my attention. One was the green Range Rover, parked right in the driveway, so I didn't have to be a genius detective to figure who was inside.

The other was the big magnolia tree, on the right side of the lawn. It had a trunk big enough that three girls couldn't wrap their arms around it. Large green and yellow leaves dripped down from the low, curvy branches.

That tree was special to me. We'd all gathered under its branches, laughing, partying. It had wide roots stretching down into the grass, which was mowed, all kept up like the windows. The sunshine dazzled off of the leaves.

Well, that was enough for the tree. I was here for something other than memories.

I walked up to the door.

Knock, knock. "It's me, Samson!" *Knock! Knock!* "Let me in!"

King opened up. He wore a wifebeater and baggy jeans with a rope as a belt. He had rubber gloves on. His hair was a puffy pile. He looked good, though, shiny-cheeked as he smiled at me.

"Chelle, what's going on?"

"Hi, King."

"Everything okay?"

"No, I just saw Mom."

The smile evaporated in a *poof.* "Come in. Tell me what's happening."

I walked inside the hallway, with the blue tiles on the floor, and the pictures of me as a baby on the walls. Pictures of King, too—flexing, posing with guns. Wedding pics with Mama in a white fluffy bridal gown and my daddy in a dark suit, a thick, curling mustache. The front hall opened into the living room, with its beige rug, glass table. A red leather sofa. Framed posters of Frida Kahlo and Diego Rivera paintings. Everything was in perfect condition, just as I remembered it.

"You kept everything up here?" I asked.

He shook his head. "No, Mama's boyz do. They hire a cleaning lady."

"How long you going to squat?"

He shrugged. "Just another couple nights. If Book and Biggie find me here, they'll do their damage. *And* the Burner." King stripped off his rubber gloves. "Here, you want some tea or something?"

"What I want is to know when you turned faithless against me."

"What?!"

"Telling me Silver was dead?"

"Oh, Chelle."

"What you put me through—what I've been feeling and thinking ever since you said that!"

"I didn't lie to you. The boy you knew *is* dead."

"Dammit!" I yelled. "Fine, just for once, tell me the truth. Where's the money, King?"

His eyes turned mournful. "Not that again."

"Please tell me!"

"I did already. That's *blood* money; that's Patssi's money you're asking for. Don't need your blood on it neither. It's deep gone. It's far gone. It's—burned. Just go back to Westchester and forget it."

I looked hard into his eyes. Mama was right, because Samson was easy to read.

"I'm sorry, Sam, but I can't buy the stories you sell any more."

I walked into the kitchen, slow, just looking around while he followed me. White sink with a couple of dishes he'd been washing. White glass lamp, white-painted table.

"What did you say to me, the first time I asked you where the money was?" I asked, as much myself as him. "You were trying to tell me, then, in Chino." I poked in the kitchen drawers, under the sink. Just napkins, detergent.

"What did Mama tell you?" He tailed me as I stalked back to the living room. I spied the shined glass table, the vacuum tracks in the rug. If there were any money hid here, the maid who cleaned the house would have found it, maybe stolen it.

"You didn't hide it in the house, did you?" I asked.

"No, it's gone!" King put his hands on my shoulders. "Whatever she told you, you can't listen! She's the devil!"

My back was to him, and his paws stayed on me. "You going to stop me, King?"

He took his hands off. "No, I told you already—Kenny schooled me, how to live in the right. And even if he hadn't, I'd never tussle you, because you my little girl. I love you, Chelle. I'm telling you this for your *good*. I want you to live in the good and the right. But *she* don't! *She* wants nothing for us but this evilness!"

I started walking toward the master bedroom. That's where first my parents, then just Mama slept. After Dad died, she always slept alone. "In Chino, you were trying to tell me. But Kenny took me away." I made it to my parents' pad. Big red bed, white walls, more baby pictures of me and King on the walls, scattered in with pics of my dad and some soldiers hefting guns. I looked under the bed—nothing. I slammed open the closet. Just Mama's clothes.

I turned, slipped around King, and hurried to the hall.

I replayed the conversation I'd had with him in Chino. I'd gone there just after Tha Force and Lalo tried to snatch me from Rosa Parks. The guard Kenny had led me to the room with the long tables. King had been sitting at the back. His hot eyes burned me from across the room, his big muscley body stretching out his Adidas T-shirt.

Aw, Chelle, they put me in here cuz they know I'm over my adversity, he'd said.

"She say you were just like her?" Samson now asked me. "That's how she does it! She's *seducing* you."

I said, "She told me that finding that money was the only way to keep Silver safe from the Burner—and the rest of the Snakes. I've got to—what's the word? *Depose.* I've got to depose Dragon. Knock him off the throne to get them back under Mama's wing, keep them out of harm. And if I'm the one bringing them the money they owe the Burner, I'll be the one holding the cards, not him—"

"She'd tell you anything to trap you back in her claws!"

Slipping behind him again, I moved to the staircase, ran up it.

. . . *I'm over my adversity,* he'd said. *I've been keeping it peaceful, cuz I've been busy thinking. And reading. Like, about Jesus? And Mohammed? And that Gandhi?*

I skidded into my old room: little blue bed, white wall hung with a painting of me when I was ten. Giant eyes, apple face, blue ribbon, white dress. Innocence. Samson had actually painted that one of me—I'd sat in the kitchen while he did it.

No—shut my mind to that. No time for heart-softening recollections.

I went to my old little bureau, yanked open all the drawers. No cash, just neatly folded tiny girl clothes inside. Same in the closet.

I walked out. Into King's old room. Double bed, old quilt. But where there used to be posters of girls, guns, and cars all over the walls—now there were tacked-up drawings, beautiful. Drawings of me, in charcoal. Drawings of our mama, in pencil. Drawings of Dad, in red chalk. Drawings of a magnolia tree. Drawings of Patssi: lollipop-yellow hair, heavy eyeliner, ruby lipstick, dark shadows under the deer eyes. She was laughing. She'd been a laugher, her.

I studied that last picture. "You drawing again? Kenny said you were doing art."

"You've got to *listen* to me."

"You were in love with her, weren't you?"

He went quiet at that.

"You were in love with Patssi," I said.

"*Yeah,* course. She was my soldier. She was my vice president in the Snakes."

"More than that."

He choked up. "She was my only other family 'sides you and Reina and . . ."

"And Dad."

"Yeah, and Dad."

My eyes shifted from Patssi to the drawings of the tree.

It was our house's big magnolia tree. We'd partied under it. We'd sat in its shade. I'd sat right there on that branch, lit by torchlight, and Mama was in her canary diamond and her blue eyeshadow. Champagne on my skin. *Princess, you the Princess.*

Suddenly, I remembered what King had said to me in Chino.

I'd told him: *Samson, I'm here because Dragon says you owe.*

His eyes had got really big. *They try and take you someplace?*

Samson, I think this might be stimming you a little bit too much, Kenny had said, standing by me. *I'm going to wrap this up.*

Chelle, listen, just go to the tree and—

What do you mean? Tree?

You know what I'm talking about, Princess!

Kenny had dragged me out while King yelled for me. *Chelle! Chelle!* And then the door slammed. I couldn't hear King any more.

"The tree," I said, still looking at the drawing. "The magnolia tree. That's what you talked about in juvie. You wanted me to have money after I ran from the Snakes."

King eyed me warily, stuttering out a lie. But then, he just suddenly looked awful, sad, and old. "No, don't."

I ran down the stairs, and out the front door. He raced after me, hollering.

The magnolia tree in front of the house had long, tough roots, surrounded by clay-colored dirt. I crouched down, searching all around it. Everything about the tree looked normal, in order. *Except*—right behind the magnolia was a patch of earth, a smidge darker than the rest. Fresher dirt, though you could barely tell anymore.

King had stole that money, and been prisoned right after, about a year and half ago. From what he'd fessed to me in prison, I figured he'd buried the money right before he got penned. Almost enough time had passed to wipe away any trace of where he'd buried the cash. But not quite enough.

I was on my knees, in the earth. King stood before me, backlit, so strands of sunlight peeked bright from behind his head.

"Get me a shovel, Samson."

"No."

I ran back in the house. Dashing into the garage from a side door, I stumbled into that dark, cool room. Inside, I could see Mama's old red Mustang, gleaming. Spare tires hung up on the walls, other junk. And a shovel. I grabbed it.

Back in the yard, King sat on the porch, with a hellishly morose look on his mug.

"Like I told you, I would *never* lay a finger on you. But I am protesting you, girl! I am trying to show you by example that you got to live peaceful and honest, without corrupting yaself with tha Life. *And she is using you, Chelle!*"

I went behind the magnolia, stabbed the shovel in the ground.

Dig dig dig, I went. *Dig dig dig.*

With King still watching, I kept shoveling, maybe twenty minutes. When I'd finally burrowed about two feet under the earth, there it was—a white bit of plastic poked through. I chopped the dirt even faster, sweating like crazy. In another ten minutes, I dug up a suitcase-sized square wrapped in Hefty bags.

Breathing hard, I ripped the plastic open. A layer of newspaper was underneath that, then wax paper underneath that, then cloth underneath that.

Then the most gigantic fortune of cold green money I ever saw in my life.

As I tugged back the cotton wrapping, a wad of hundreds spilled out like confetti.

I grabbed it up. Benjamin Franklin peeped out. But ol' Ben didn't look so good. Black gunk stuck to the bills, covering up his pageboy hairdo.

When I rubbed the black gunk on Benjamin's face, I saw it was more black-*red*, and as it warmed on my skin, it felt something like oil.

My hand was stained scarlet. "Oh, God." Sick, I looked up at King on the porch.

"I told you it was blood money, baby girl," my brother said.

"I'm sorry, Samson." I still hunkered over the cash, under the soft yellow leaves on the magnolia. "I'm sorry you lost your Patssi."

"My girl died," he wept. "They killed her—"

"Are they out of hiding?"

"Who, the Snakes? I ain't going to tell you."

"Where's the safe house? Are they still on Orwell Street?"

"Don't do anything; put it back. It won't lead to nothing good. It won't help you if you bring that money to them—"

I put the packet of dough under my armpit and walked away from my brother.

*

I found the Snakes easy enough, on account of the ol' "all-clear" Shakira poster on the front door of 5446 Woolf Street, only two blocks from Orwell. This new safehouse was a shacky dump with peeling gray paint, a busted-looking wood roof, and a crumbling brick chimney. The porch was made of rotting wood, and the door was already foolishly tagged with a Snakes set.

I pushed the handle of the front door, and walked inside.

"*He's dead; he's gone!*" Midget was screaming in the trashed-out living room while the other Snakes maddogged around a now shaved-headed, fear-eyed Dragon.

I stayed in the shadow of the front hall, spying without getting seen myself, yet.

"I don't even know why we took your call today, Cheater," Eager said to D. "We should still be scattered."

"I told you," Dragon hissed. "I got a girlfriend working in women's MDC giving me intelligence that something's up."

"Forget it. I'm going to Alaska or something," Lalo said. "Work in a restaurant. Make Eskimo food."

Eager said, "We gotta *beg* Reina for mercy, man!"

Midget pointed at Dragon, the tears streaming down his face. "We gonna feed you to Queen. We all see you now!"

"What about what I done for Silver?" Dragon yelled. "S, I was the one *dragging* you out from under the Diegos' fucking firestorm! And that's the *second* time!"

I darted my eyes from boy to boy—there, *there* was Silver, standing on the far edge of the room. He'd wrapped his right arm with gauze that extended from his shoulder to his elbow, and his face had whittled down from the work it must have took not to get dead from the Burner's bullet. I nearly cried out at the beautiful, living sight of him—but I clamped my mouth shut, because me howling like a weakling was not going to get me what I wanted—what I *needed*—today.

"It was Game giving up his blood for me," Silver said in a grinding voice. "And Midget's right. *She* told me what you are and what you did. I say it is time to take a vote, men."

"You already elected me!" Dragon hollered.

"My friend, this is not an election," Silver said. "It is a *trial*."

"Leave him alone," Force screamed. "Biggie, Book, back him!"

"I'm still with you, boss," Biggie said, the scar on his face gone snow-pale. "Me and Book feels the same way, right, man?"

Standing next to him, Book was still as huge as a pro wrestler, but I could see he was thinner in the cheeks, I guessed on account of his getting so roughly cut by King. He squinched up his face.

Dragon said, "Book, you owe me the same as S!"

Book shrugged. "Um, let's be practical, homes. Hmmm? Because we all gonna be some *dead* Mexicans unless we get two things. One, that's Reina's protection. Two, it's the fucking money to pay that mothafucka."

"Well, I got what you need, boyz," I called out then.

"Huh?"

"Who said that?"

"You hear something?"

Everybody turned around.

Stepping out of the shadow of the hallway, I held up the plastic-wrapped package.

"*Waahhh!*" Lalo yelled when I popped out. "Oh, man! Give me a heart attack. Thought you was the Burner—"

"I got your money here, babies, so you don't have to worry about that anymore." I shook the package at them. "Here is one hundred K, detected and dug up just this minute by my own hands, and brought to you as a gesture of pure fidelity and love, my brothers!"

"How'd she get in here?" Dragon yelled. "Snatch her and crack her! She's ninety pounds of conniving!"

Silver's eyes opened like moonroses, like moonlight. "Hey, Michelle."

"Hey, baby," I said.

He smiled so gentle at me. "And here I was thinking you made a clean getaway from us."

"Aw, nah, you boyz won't be able to get rid of me after this." I walked into their circle. "Hey, Eag. Hey Midget. Man, I am so so sorry about Game, Midge. But I'm here for you now."

Midget's face collapsed. He put his hands over his eyes and wailed, "P, they took my boy."

"Aw, P!" Eager said.

"Li'l Princess!" Lalo said.

"See if she's bluffing about the money," Dragon said. "Book, get it from her."

Book half-limped over to me, the *Kill Ya Sucka!* shave-job grown in, his skinnier face looking older and even meaner than before.

I looked straight up at him, keeping my hold on the package.

"Hey there, P," he said, not yet reaching for the money.

"You lookin' pretty solid for a kid who got on the wrong end of my bro's knife."

"It's been a trial, but I lived."

I peered down at his belly. "Show me how you doing."

Book lifted his shirt to show the long, scary-looking scar that ran from his side almost to his belly button. It was red and raw, and still had some stitches in it. "They said whoever sewed me up saved my life."

"Well, you know how people exaggerate." I gave him a wink, handing him the package. In the next second, the tied-up wads of hundred-dollar bills spilled out on the ground.

"Oh!"

Eager, Midget, and Lalo scrambled over, grabbing them up.

"It is, it is—it's money," Midget said. "A lot."

"A hundred K," I said.

"It's got something on it." Eager touched the crud on the bills. "Gross! Blood!"

"Well, there's your money, then," Dragon said, the scared coming off him like a stink. "So just take care of her. She's an enemy combatant; she's a—she's *a bitch!*"

When he said that word to me, I began to grin at him dangerous and full of teeth.

"Why you smiling like that?" Dragon foamed.

"Uh-oh," Eager said. "I seen that face somewhere before."

"That's how Reina smiles when she's in battle," Force hissed.

Midget said, "Yeah! Reina smiled like that before she had Carlos Gaitan gut Victor Venezuela, remember?"

D swung his eyes all over the room. "Oh, hell, oh, hell-a-lujah."

I said, "Snake-men, before we go any further today, I got something to ask you."

"What?"

"Do you love me?"

The boyz looked back at me, eyes like question marks.

"That's the one thing I need," I said. "Because you're going to *have* to love me if you're going to have me ruling you."

"Ruling you?" Eager asked. "But Silver, like I was saying before, what about you being the one taking over?"

S shook his head. "I'm a soldier, not a King."

"You not gonna rule nothing!" Dragon hurtled himself across the room at me—just as Book caught him under an arm. "Oh, Christ-a-mighty, Mother Mary! Let me go! S, you my cousin! And Book, I brought you into the Snakes. I got you and Big out of a shelter—"

"Book, quiet him up," I said.

Book snuggled his bicep around Dragon's throat. "Eghh!"

"Time to pay or play," I said. "So let's hear it."

"What you think?" Eager asked, raising his eyebrows. "Ya think she'll be loyal?"

"She did come back with the money," Lalo said. "Could have kept it for herself, especially holding a grudge with us 'napping her."

"She could get us back in with Queen, too," Book said.

"Man, I don't know; this is happening fast," Biggie said, weakening when he saw how Book was decided, and the ugly color of Dragon's face.

"She stitched up Book, and S said at the party she was trying to save me and Game from D's slaving," Midget said.

"Still, she is *young*," Book said.

"And female!" Force said.

"Dummy," I said. "Reina's been ruling menfolk for an age—and Michelle Bachelet got elected prez of Chile in '06, so get with the times!"

"Sure," Lalo said. "P could do it good enough."

Midget said, "It's decided for me, P, just as long as you send me on a mission to cap the Burner."

"We're going to answer what happened to Game," I said.

"Then I love you."

"And the rest of you?"

"Yeah, yeah, why not," Lalo yelped. "Me too, I love you!"

"Okay, sure," Eager said, slowly nodding. "You're smart, and you're *mean*, too. And plus, hell, you know I got love for you, P."

"Good," I said.

"What are you doing?!" Dragon yelled. "You can't be pledging to her!"

Book still had D in a headlock, and he clamped down harder.

"Efff!" Dragon squealed.

"I give my love to anybody who saves my life," Book said.

"And you won't be having no vengeance on Samson?" I asked.

"Ummmmm."

"Answer me!"

"Yeah, sure."

Great.

"And you, Biggie?"

Biggie didn't talk. He just looked at the ground, making a mouth.

"Sure, too. Why not?"

"I'm listening."

"Okay, I love you."

Oh, God, I trust these dudes about as deep as they'd bury me.

I looked at Silver. His Casanova eyes shined at me.

"I love you, Michelle," he said.

His voice sent shock waves through my blood, but I knew this wasn't the time to show it. I only tilted my head at him, as Queenly as I could, and then I bored my eyes into Force's skull. "And what am I going to do with you, Force?"

"Oh, man, you know I never liked you, P." He started crying. "But it looks like you the new Queen, and I don't want to live in no exile!"

I seethed: "After you pulling a blade on me, I've got half a mind to draw and quarter you, boy."

"No, I love you, P," he managed to get out. "Please, don't chastise me, Michelle!"

"Swear it," I said.

He looked at Dragon out of the corner of his eye and wept. "I swear. I love you. You got me, ass and soul."

"It is decided that you are on probation, punk," I spat, after a couple beats of thinking. "I'd rather keep a little rat like you where I can see you, anyway. But if you give me one cause to revoke my devotion, I'm gonna be walking down a red road with you."

"Thank you, ma'am," Force breathed.

I looked at the rest. "All right then, my knights! Now is the time for all you to prove your love. I have given *my* oath." I pointed at the crudded money. "And I have sealed it in blood. Now you must do the same."

"No," Dragon said, sheep-eyed.

"You took everything from me D," I said. "As the Queen of this nation, I find you guilty of cheating and slaving your own kin."

"And I am your retribution, bro," Silver said, an ice-look invading his eyes.

Fast and maddog brutal, S sledge-hammered Dragon with his good left hook. *Slam! Slam!* Even shot-up and arm-damaged, he punched him vicious in the face, and tore at his throat. His face was like a lion's. His teeth showed white and red-stained from D's own blood. D pulled away, twisting, screaming, and too shocked to counter with any real defense. Silver used his advantage by covering him up with his wrestler's body, head-butting him, kicking him, and I heard the crunching sound of ribs. Everybody else was too scared of S's calamity to get in the way. They stood around dumb, and stunned-silent. Biggie turned away. Force started crying.

"What's going on here?!" I suddenly heard behind me.

I turned just as King raced in, heavy-footed and bellowing.

"We're doing what Mama trained me to do, Samson," I said. "Don't you know the ruling hand's got to be made of iron?"

My brother grabbed me, crying, "Don't, Chelle. You were doing so good!" Then to Silver, he yelled, "Stop it! No more violence!"

Silver didn't listen. He punched, kicked, choked, slapped, beat Dragon's blue-red face into the ground. But suddenly Dragon swung his body up, arrowing his eyes into mine, and crying out of a red mouth.

"What she gonna do when she finds out you did this to me, P?"

"I don't hear you, traitor," I said.

"What's Kiki gonna do when she finds out what you are?"

"Shut up," I yelled. "Don't you talk about her!"

But Dragon, he'd pushed the right button on me. I breathed rough, now seeing Ki's horrified face when Samson had started to strangle Dragon in the desert.

Mish! Tell him not to!

"Okay, Silver, stop now!" I screamed. "He's had enough!"

"No, no!" Silver bellowed.

"I said stop it!"

S kept hitting him, kicking him, cutting him.

"Pull him off!"

It took Eager, Midget, Book, and Biggie to yank him from Dragon, who looked like a curled, red hedgehog there on the ground.

"Don't worry, I'll close your eyes soon enough, D," Silver said in a soft, killer's voice, while the others held him.

"S, I said *cool it!*" I barked. "Somebody check Dragon."

But just as Eager bent over him to take his pulse, we all heard: "You bitch!"

"Can you walk?" I asked. "You need a doctor?"

"Fuck off! Fuck you!"

"Okay, then," I said. "Get out. And stay out."

It took a minute, but Dragon tottered up, staring at us like a terrible ghost.

"I'll get you," he shrieked, before half-crawling out the door, past me and Samson.

Now bloody and crazy-haired, the rest of the boyz stared back at me.

"Um," I said. I was shook bad. What had I just done? "Jesus Christ!"

"Michelle," Silver said, gripping his arm. He was sweating, with veins pumping out of his neck, teeth bared. But his eyes said: *Get it together! You've got to lead these boyz now.*

I nodded at him. *Oh, God. Okay, I'm all right!*

"P, what now?" Midget asked.

I pointed at my brother. "Uh, as I said, the money I brought you clears Samson's debt." I was careful not to call Samson "King" because that was me now, and not him.

"Ain't you *human*?!" Samson spat. "Beating on him like he's an animal!"

"You are entitled to your opinion, Sam," I said. "But take it someplace else. Why don't you wait outside, drive me home when I'm done here?"

Samson pulled out the silver death's head key chain from his pocket, tossed it to me. "Drive yourself."

He stalked out. I clasped my fingers tight over that death's head.

"That belongs to you anyway," Silver said. "That's the symbol of our King, and you just got kingmade by law, girl."

"I know it," I said.

"So. What now?" Midget asked.

I loped over to the bag of money on the ground, picked it up, and pulled out a couple of clean bill wads. I threw them at Midget.

"First thing is, all of you get another safehouse, *now*; this is too close to the old one, and Burner could just come busting in here any second. And *don't* tag the new pad."

"Gotcha," Eager said.

I went on: "I'm gonna safehouse the money in Westchester, but next week I'll come back for us formalizing our realliance with Reina—and yes, Midget, for dealing with Freddie. Okay?"

"Okay."

"Let's hug on it."

We had ourselves a merry, sweaty, tearful hug session, there. I kissed every boy on the cheek, sealing the deal.

When that was finished, I kept my hold on Silver and nodded at the other boyz.

"All right, make yourselves scarce," I said.

They scatted to the backyard.

My mother had warned me off him, but right then, *no* one could keep me away from Silver: I hugged onto him, tight. His face was flushed, a glowing dark pearl. The fierce danger still glinted in his eyes, but it softened when he brushed back my hair.

"I thought you were dead!" I began to weep.

"For a minute, I did too."

"Why didn't you tell me you were all right?! You just dropped out of sight!"

He shook his head. "After everything that happened, I thought maybe it would be better if I stayed out of your life, like you wanted in the first place."

"I don't want that anymore."

He laughed, lifted me up, and kissed me, soft and long. Soon he started squeezing me. "Grr! Oh, gawd, girl, I missed you!"

I touched the bandage wrapped over his shoulder. "But Silver, get this—I don't want you to go rogue on me ever again!"

He winked. "I love you, baby, but I don't got a dog collar on me."

"Silver!"

He said, "Look, you are the ruler, and I will follow your command. But I am a man now. And we are coming into a war with the Diegos. So I will do what I have to do to protect you and our boyz."

"Don't think you can scare me," I said, hugging him tighter.

"Oh, no?"

I looked at him brutal serious. "Well, if you do, you won't know it. I won't be running from who I am anymore."

He stroked my cheeks, my neck. "That's my brave girl. Aw, sweet-face, do you think you can love me again? I'm not talking about going back to how it was. I've been through the fire, and I am blooded into tha Life. You've got to love *this*, what I am. But the man I am still loves you, Michelle."

I closed my eyes and put my forehead on his chest.

I forbid you to be with him, Mama had told me. *If you show him a woman's weakness, then he will become the instrument by which you will fall. He will betray you. . . .*

And Samson: *A man don't do an act like that unless he has let himself get ate up by the darkness. . . . The boy you know is dead. . . . Silver's turned into a Stone-Cold.*

Had he?

I remembered again the death-look in his eyes when he went for the Burner in the desert—and smelled the sweat and blood on him now, from beating Dragon and not abiding my order.

I pressed my ear to his chest and heard his heart.

Wha-whump, wha-whump, wha-whump.

I looked up. "There's ice in you now wasn't there before."

"It's a fact."

"I don't care! I *love* you, Silver; I always have! You're the one I came back for."

His lips touched mine again. We kissed gentle. His hands stayed on my shoulders as his mouth brushed over my cheeks and my eyes.

I held him closer, pressing against him. I inhaled the smoky scent of his hair. I put my lips on the scar brightening his neck.

My hands reached up, under his shirt. Smooth muscle and silk skin.

We were breathing hard. Moving faster. His tongue pressed deeper inside my mouth. My lips traveled over his jaw, his throat.

Then I bit his neck, burning my mouth over his beautiful face, loving him as uncontrolled as any battle madness and starving for the hot, sweet taste of him.

An hour or so passed, which I spent in Silver's arms. But after a while I knew I had to go, take care of business, and figure out what I was going to do next. So I finally tore myself away from S. I grabbed up my backpack and stuffed it with the money.

Hefting the bag on my shoulder, I walked away from my new kingdom, my heart going crazy.

The death's head key chain clicked my pocket as I hoofed it four blocks back to my mama's house, and the Range Rover.

When I looked up, I saw Samson in the driver's seat.

"I remembered you're too young to have a license," he sighed.

I walked up to the car, tried to smile. "Maybe I can just live with you. Here, in our old house. What do you say?"

"No. Besides, you've got that nice Frank."

I bit my lips. "That's not working out. He's not going to keep me much longer."

"You set on clubbing with Silver?"

"Yes, Sam."

He sighed. "He's a beast, girl. You think you're gonna pull off a trick by turning an animal back into the boy you remember, but he's the one gonna turn *you* into a Stone-Cold, and for permanent."

"No, he won't."

He eyeballed me. "You're forgetting the lesson both Mama and me learned the rough way. *Rulers can't love, Chelle.* You gonna get burned one way or the other."

I pressed a hand to my eyes. "Let's you and me fight about this later—just tell me I can live with you, man."

He sighed. "My answer's still no."

"Why?"

"Cuz you disappoint me. Just get in the car. Give me the keys."

I stared down at my feet. "Oh. Okay."

King roared the Rover over the highways, until the houses got prettier and the billboards fancier. Soon enough, we were in Westchester. King idled the car in front of Frank's house, with its beautiful lawn and the Lexus in the driveway.

Reaching down, he tugged the keys free of the death's head. He put the death's head in my hands. I got my pack and jumped out the car, looking at him through the open door.

"Samson."

He closed his eyes. "Chelle, I'll always be your brother. But you're not what I hoped you were."

He put the Rover into gear, and then he was gone.

39

As soon as I walked into the house, Frank and Squiggy came running up to me.

"Young lady, where have you *been*?" Frank hollered, his hair all stuck up on his head. He waved an envelope, and his face was a crazy grab bag of super happiness and super madness. "I've been calling you!"

I closed the door behind me, stunned on account of Samson's harsh words. "Huh? I'm sorry about that. I was just—out."

"At track practice, you said—and then what?"

"Just out. Thinking."

He reached down, gripping onto the straps of my backpack. "'Just thinking'?"

"Yeah, Frankie, just trucking around. I'm real sorry if I caused you any worry."

"*You can't do that.* You have to call me and tell me where you are! I told you: I have to know where you are every hour of the day. That's how it works around here now!"

I patted his cheek. "Oh, sugar, you're still all mental about me getting 'napped. I can see how I've worn you down, so I really do understand, Frank: You 'rethinking' foster popping me and all."

"Yes! Jesus!" He pressed his fingers to his eyes. "Okay, but you're okay. Right?"

"I'm fine."

"Ugh! Good!" He growled, but then put his hands over his mouth. Silently, he started laughing.

"What's so funny?

He made himself get serious again. "We'll get to that in a second. Because I am very, very upset. You have to start obeying me! Dr. Milhaulas says I have to set very clear rules with you!"

"Dude, you are flipping."

"Yes, I am, oh my God, oh my total *God!*" Frank flapped the letter all around. "Haven't you checked your phone? Everybody's been calling you! We've both been racking our brains about where you were!"

Squiggy scratched up on me and slobbered on my pants, barking happily.

I pulled my iPhone out of my back pocket, using the hand still holding the skull-and-crossbones key chain. I turned the phone on. I had like thirty messages on it.

Frank gasped: "You can take Latin; you can play lacrosse; they have these fantastic summer abroad programs—when I was at St. Alban's I went to *Florence*. And best of all, you're going to be getting the support you need—they have an entire program for 'sensitive gifteds.'"

"Will you tell me what's happening?"

"I'm sorry I opened your mail. I didn't even look at the address. It came in this huge Fed Ex package with a bunch of registration material, and I thought it was these new racing socks I just bought you. I just ripped it open before I could see—"

Frank stuffed the letter in my face. It was in an envelope addressed to me, and had a sender's address of *Yale-Westview Academy*. I looked hard at it; then I looked at the skull-and-crossbones key chain that was in my other hand.

"But I already got my rejection letter."

"Huh?"

"From the MLK scholarship. I didn't get it."

"What? You didn't show it to me—just, never mind. *Read*."

I looked at that envelope for a long, long, space-and-time-bending moment.

Then I slipped the letter out of the envelope.

40

Dear Michelle Peña,

You are invited to join the Yale-Westview class of 2012 as a recipient of the Chris Evert Athletic scholarship. As we are much impressed with both your scholarly and track and field records, we are prepared to fund half of Yale-Westview's yearly tuition, a contribution valued at $12,500 dollars per annum. . . .

Frank and Squiggy stared at me. I read that letter twice, three times, and four times, but the words all seemed scrambled and floating around the pages.

"I don't get it."

"You are *in*," Frank said. "On half scholarship. You are in!"

"But I didn't apply for an athletic scholarship," I stuttered. "I don't understand."

"This came this morning—when you were out *brooding*," Frank said. "And in it was a letter from a Coach—what was his name?"

"Weston Ruiz?"

"Right, Coach Ruiz. He wrote that Yale-Westview gives out twenty athletic scholarships a year. And you were his first pick. He wrote a personal letter. He thinks you're amazing."

I gripped onto the letter, staring at it. That letter was confounding all gangsta-birthright resolutions I just made with the Snakes. I started shaking so bad that I dropped the envelope, and a little shamrock-shaped, gold-tone charm with the Yale-Westview insignia tinkled out.

I stuffed my death's head in my back jeans pocket and picked up the charm super careful, like it was a two-pound diamond ring that I would get arrested for so much as looking at it. "But Frank, how am I going to pay for it? They didn't give me full scholarship."

He frowned at the same time as he smiled. "Twelve and a half thousand's a little high with my mortgage and Stephen's alimony, but who cares? I already wrote out the first check. I don't care about the money."

"I don't get it—why'd you do that?"

"Huh?"

"You told me this whole foster care business wasn't working, but that I was going to be all 'fine.'" I said. "And I know what that means. That's going to make the fourth time I heard that little speech, and I'm like a pro by now interpreting that lingo what people use before they dump ya butt."

"Wait a second," he blustered. "We had that conversation a month ago—you've been thinking that all this time?"

"Yeah, course! I've been waiting to get kicked out ever since. I just thought you were too chicken to pull the plug quite yet."

He hunched up his shoulders. "Michelle! I didn't mean that I didn't want you. What wasn't working was my *parenting*, because I am such an amateur at this that it's basically malpractice! That's what I was just talking about: I'm seeing a psychiatrist—a *child* psychiatrist—so I can learn how to set these parameters with you."

"W-what's a parameter?"

"*Rules*, that you will *obey*. Like not going off to see your brother when I tell you not to because I don't think it's safe, and then you getting kidnapped and giving me an aneurysm!"

"Oh." I started looking googly-eyed at him. "Oh, okay. Wow, I didn't get that."

He waved his hands in the air. "Oh, no, you're not going to cry, are you? I mean, that is—it's okay if you do. I totally understand." He broke into a smile. "See, I can do this!"

"I just thought . . ." I crumpled the letter a little in my fists. "But Frank, I still can't take this. I can't take your money. I don't want charity, you know?"

"Michelle!"

"Look, Frank, I can't take your money because you don't love me, man."

He crossed his arms and sighed. "Right."

I nodded. "Right."

"No, not 'right.' I'm just saying 'right' because I knew we were going to have to deal with this. Michelle, I know this is hard for you, but I am not a perfect person."

I nodded. "Yeah, that ain't news to me, Frank. You know, I got that part already with the no-touching and the shrinkage. But I never minded about that. It's the *not loving me* that gets me down."

He said, "What I'm trying to tell you is, Stephen did not just break up with me because he didn't want to caretake you."

"What are you talking about?"

"I happen to have this really annoying and kind of life-destroying problem with telling people close to me how I feel about them." Tears filled his eyes. "But just in case you ever wondered, it doesn't mean that I don't have it inside me."

I watched him *so* close, not breathing.

"If you have questions about me, you just have to look in your heart, Michelle," he said. "What does it say?"

My mouth trembled and gave way. "Oh, oh, my heart's for you, Frank," I sobbed.

"O-oh, yes," he stammered. "That's nice. So. And what does your heart say about me?"

"You love me."

The tears started flowing, and he rolled up his eyes. "Uhm, okay. This is all really healthy."

"You're so weird," I laugh-cried.

He said, "Michelle, you have to decide if you want me to be your foster parent, even though I can't give you everything you want."

I started wiping my face. He wiped his, too.

"Oh, well, you know," I gabbled, my shoulders shaking terrible. "Yeah. Sure. It's no big deal."

He patted me with his stiff twiggy fingers. "Okay. That's good. That's good, right? I think we've made some progress here."

"Oh, whatever, Rain Man. I love you and you love me, dawg, okay?"

Montebello Montebello! Uprise Montebello!
We burn you down ya give us trouble!!!

"Agh! What is that *racket*?" He put his hands to his ears.

"It's my phone."

"Perfect, good, just get it. That's got to be her. She said she was heading out—I'm just going to get a really, really big drink, to settle me down a little . . . or maybe a smaller drink, because that would set a better example. So I guess a medium-sized drink." He patted me again. Then he walked off. "No, a big drink."

"Got to be who?" *Click.* "Hello?"

"Mish?"

It was Kiki.

"Mish!"

"Um, is that you, Ki?"

"Mish, I miss you!" she barked out.

I clutched onto that phone. "What?"

"*I miss you*," she said. "I want to be friends again."

My eyes started crossing. "Oh, okay. You do?"

"Didn't you get all my messages?"

I said, "Oh, no, I didn't. I've been kind of—busy."

"Listen, Mish, I'm really sorry—"

"No!" I yammered, doublefast. "*I'm* the one who's sorry. I know now Ki; I figured it out! I didn't listen to you enough—and I tried to rule you, but that wasn't what you were needing—"

"Not seeing you anymore has *so* beyond sucked!" she howled, so loud that I heard an echo. I was in the hall, and it was as if I could hear her voice on the other side of the front door. Sweating all over the phone, I took a step to it. Then another.

"Ki, where are you?"

"Standing on your porch."

"What?" I opened up, and there she was: blue dress, big silver sneaks, bows in her hair, a stack of pink-bead bracelets hiding the rope-scar on her right wrist. Her mouth trembled in her heart-face. "Oh, Kiki!"

I stood there, in this suspended animation. I wanted to hug her but was afraid to.

But then I bawled: "Kiki, we got each other in common. And I'll learn about your movie craziness, and I won't boss you anymore, because I see how almost-tough you are! I really get it, all right? You beat the hell out of me, girl, but I learned—"

"I just bussed over when Frank called at the house because, you know—because, well, I *hate* my mother!" she sobbed, putting the phone down. "Like you have no idea what kind of control freak *hell* I've been living in. And when Frank called here—and told me, I got so happy that I knew I didn't care—about anything that happened— I don't even care about your brother—"

"You don't?" I touched the pink beads covering up her wrist. I lifted them up to see the scar, all mottled and ugly, the color and texture of wadded-up newspaper.

"Well, yeah, I care about that, because it's totally disfigured," she cried, looking down at it, too. "And actually, I do care about a lot of the things that happened. So just never mind that I said that; I was getting carried away. Like, you need to understand that I am now so over being the sidekick! And you can *never* lie to me again; that's a total deal breaker."

"Okay, I get it, and I'll change," I said.

"*Promise me.* Because I am completely serious, Michelle."

"I promise you, Kiki!"

She put her hands on her hips. "You do? Well, good. Okay then. I'm glad we could come to an understanding." Peering down, she spied the gold-toned shamrock Y-Dub charm sticking out my fist, and started fingering a little necklace she had slung around her throat. It was a gold chain with the same shamrock on it. She looked at me from under her lashes. "Because it would be beyond depressing if I had to ignore you . . . at *school.*"

"*You got in?!* And you heard I did from Frank?"

She jostled me so hard she almost judo-flipped me. "*Yes!* I got my letter this morning! *We're both going!* I can't believe it! I can't believe we did it!"

I half-dragged her into the house. Frank ambled out of the kitchen, drinking a tiny Scotch.

"I can't *believe it!*" Kiki kept screaming. She did a little shimmy in the hall, waving her arms. "When I heard, I was like—Oh, *man!*" She kept hollering for a little while like that. She only stopped when she saw Frank. "Hi, Frank! I told you she'd come back from practice, you ulcer monkey!"

"Yeah, sorry about all the calls, I just had this really terrible feeling—but never mind, right?" Frank said. "Are you staying for a celebration dinner? Italian subs."

Kiki wiped her tears. "Oh! Dinner? I can't. My mom hates Michelle so much it's starting to get a little *noir*."

He crunched his eyebrows together. "That's bad. We've got to fix that."

"You've got to convince her, Frank!" Kiki said. "I've got to have dinner here tonight! We've got to talk about Y-Dub and all our plans."

Frank shrugged. "All right, let's go to the phone; I'll do my best."

Kiki ran off after Frank, down the hall, toward the kitchen. I was so bedazzled that I stumbled after them when they scooted away from me, scared to even let those two out of my sight.

But then I realized that all I was doing was staggering around under the heavy weight of my backpack.

I walked into my pink, frilly, girl-bedroom. I was worn out. I teetered around, my letter and shamrock charm clumped in my hand. Slipping off my backpack, I threw myself down on the bed and stared up at the ceiling.

"Wow," I whispered. "Wow, and wow."

I was high as the moon. My soul was full as the ocean.

I couldn't believe it. Just like *that*, I had the good life I wanted.

Both lives that I wanted, I mean.

It's here I remembered why my backpack was so heavy. While I could hear Kiki and Frank smooth-talking Mrs. Markson in the kitchen, I stared at it like it was a bomb. I looked out my doorway with guilty eyes before walking over it and closing the door shut. Slowly, I unzipped the pack and tipped it onto the bed.

The tied-up packets of money spilled out, green and black-red. I touched them, light, with the tips of my fingers. I smelled the earth still staining the white plastic bag that Samson had used to bury them in. I saw Ben Franklin's faces piling up until they covered almost my entire bedspread, so I sat there surrounded by my riches and responsibility.

My hand was still in the bag. It hit something: cold metal, a piece of leather. I brought it up. It was the pink key chain heart fob whatsis, with the silver studs glittering in the light coming through that window. My fingers closed over it. *I promise you, Kiki.* That's what I'd sworn to her, that I'd always tell her the truth.

And what had I just said to my foster pop, out there in the hall?

My heart's for you, Frank.

I knew that the law of the jungle worked just as good in Westchester as it did in Montebello, and that Frank and Ki would make me walk the plank if they *ever* knew I was gangsta.

So was that the end of the road, then? I could give the money back to the Snakes, give up clubbing, and never answer to "P" again.

Or I could go back to Montebello, to my boy and the reign I was born for.

That old question again: Where in the damn world was I headed?

I looked around my room: pink pillows, purple comforter, which my dad bought special for me. I wanted to stay in this house, with Frank and Ki and Squiggy. I wanted to spend my days trying to hug Frank while he bupped me with his frisky little elbows.

But my lips could still remember the feeling of Silver's warm, soft mouth. *I love you. The man I am never stopped loving you.* The truth hit me like a punch: Even if I had wanted to welch on him, I couldn't, because I was back to loving him permanent now. And then I also recalled my boyz pledging me, and the ghostly sound of Game's machine-gun-shotfire stutter. *I pledge my oath to you, and I have sealed it in blood.*

And I could feel my mama's blood beating in my veins, too.

You all me, girl.

Quo vadis, right? Maybe all the time I'd been headed straight *here*, to this harsh minute, when I could finally see with a crazy clarity that I would *never* fit anywhere perfect, no matter what name I used. I was Michelle *and* P, Mish *and* Chelle.

I peered at the cash, the bag, the bed. I tucked the money back into the backpack, sliding it deep under the bed.

I looked down at Kiki's heart key fob in my hand. Reaching around, I slid out the death's head from my back pocket. I took the keys from the heart and slid them onto the death's head's ring.

I hesitated, but I took the heart fob, sliding it on the death's head's ring, too.

I rummaged around the bedspread, until I found the gold-tone Y-Dub shamrock that'd dropped there. On it went, along with the heart and the skull-and-bones.

The three jewels glittered in my hand, strange and unruly looking together.

You've got to make a choice, Silver had told me, out in the desert. Civilian or gangsta, Westside or East.

But I couldn't choose.

I listened to the sounds of giggling from the kitchen, as Kiki and Frank started making subs. I wanted them to stay happy forever. They wouldn't be so cheerful, though, if they ever found out what I knew then.

I was a good, good girl, and that was a fact. I could race; I could love; I could survive. And one night in the desert, I could run quicker than all of mankind. But there, in my bedroom, with my future unfurling beautiful before me, I understood I would *never* stop looking over my shoulder, never stop being chased. All the bad I'd tried to leave behind would catch up and trip me one day: Mama's eyes piercing mine, and her smiling like a wolf because she knew I was like her; Silver's Stone-Cold heart maybe froze to ice forever, but me loving him unchanged. I couldn't race the pure, straightforward line, because I wouldn't heed the warnings, and wanted *everything*— Silver *and* to call Frank dad. Westchester *and* to be a Montebello Queen. And that's why, in my whole life, I would never be free.

The Westside sunlight glinted over the three charms in my hand. Heart. Shamrock. The death's head shone up at me, grinning, like it knew my secrets.

Boom chaka chaka, boom chaka chaka, fast girl, you a fast good girl. Boom chaka chaka, boom chaka chaka, fast girl, oh I'm a fast bad girl—

But not fast enough, I knew.

I was Michelle Peña, the speediest girl you ever saw in your whole life. Still, I couldn't—I wouldn't—outrun my past. I'd always turn back from the civilian world, toward *him*, to S. No, I saw then that I couldn't escape my own double heart. It would always be beating like thunder inside of me, no matter how hard and long I raced.

This book could not have been written without
Andrew Brown,
Ben Schrank,
Anne Heltzel,
Maggie MacMurray,
Fred MacMurray,
Maria and Walter Adastik,
Claudia Ballard,
Anna DeRoy,
Virginia Barber,
Shana Kelly,
Theresa Evangelista,
The faculty and deans of Loyola Law School.

Thank you for everything.
xoxoxoxoxoxoxo